THE MOST PRECIOUS SUBSTANCE ON EARTH

SHASHI BHAT

McClelland & Stewart

Library and Archives Canada Cataloguing in Publication data is
available upon request.

ISBN: 978-0-7710-9496-5
ebook ISBN: 978-0-7710-9497-2

This is a work of fiction. Names, characters, places, and incidents either
are the products of the author's imagination or are used fictitiously.
Creative liberties have been taken in describing locations, high school
grade levels and curricula, and with dates related to book publication,
TV broadcasts, exhibitions, and other real-world events.

This novel contains non-graphic discussion of topics that may be sensitive
for some readers, including sexual abuse, harassment, eating disorders,
drug overdose, and self-harm.

Book design by Kelly Hill
Cover art: J614/Getty Images
Typeset in ITC Galliard Pro by M&S, Toronto
Printed in Canada

McClelland & Stewart,
a division of Penguin Random House Canada Limited,
a Penguin Random House Company
www.penguinrandomhouse.ca

1 2 3 4 5   25 24 23 22 21

For the girls who stay quiet

"Silence is a woman's best garment."
—SOPHOCLES

"[Kids] don't remember what you try to teach them.
They remember what you are."
—JIM HENSON

Contents

PART ONE

Why I Read *Beowulf*

I STARTED READING *Beowulf* about a week ago, not because it was on the syllabus, but because I am in love with my English teacher. I would read anything for him. The book's cover is stark and greyscale, a black background with the title in white block letters. Below the title is the outline of a man, but just his top half—like a passport photo, except the outline is filled with silver chainmail. I keep turning back to this picture on the cover and wondering how they made it look three-dimensional, half expecting the pattern of metal to bulge into discernable features, to turn into a man's face.

Once I finish the book, I will drop casual references to it in class or at English Club meetings. "This reminds me of my favourite epic poem," I will say, pretending I don't know that it's also my English teacher's favourite epic poem, and then I will quote from it brilliantly, lingering on the alliteration. Mr. Mackenzie will pause, turning away from the blackboard to face me, still holding a piece of chalk in his hand. Sometimes, in my most reckless moments of imagination, I see him dropping the piece of chalk in amazement.

I am not sure yet exactly which passages I will quote. I'm only on page four, which I reached a few minutes ago, while sitting in the hallway outside the English office with my best friend, Amy. As per our routine, we arrived exactly forty-five minutes before the morning bell, by the side entrance closest to our lockers. We unloaded textbooks and binders and reloaded with different textbooks and binders, then wandered over to the English office, making ourselves comfortable on the ground beside the door while cackling over inside jokes we've shared since Grade 6. Today, as usual, I'm reading and Amy is peeling the varnish off the floor. The varnish lies in a loose coat over the hardwood, and cracks as we step over it. In the short time I've been attending Sir William Alexander High School, I've already seen so much of the building deteriorate; it seems like every day another part of it breaks off. Back in September, I bicycled by and looked at the school—at its heritage red brick and white trim, its tall, narrow windows, its spacious, dandelion-filled lawn—and I thought, with affection, *That is my high school*, relishing the still-newness of Grade 9. Just at that moment, a piece of one of the window frames freed itself from its hinge and fell to the pavement.

Amy peels the varnish off the floor in patches all over the school. During lunch, she peels the floor of a second-floor alcove, where we eat with our legs crossed in front of us, sandwich bags in our laps, backs against the concrete walls. During fourth-period Phys Ed, she peels the floor in the gymnasium while we stretch, and then leaves the waxy scraps in small piles here and there. Later, when we're made to do push-ups, people's hands and shoes sometimes land on these piles and their limbs go sliding sideways. Eventually, the whole floor will be stripped bare.

Today, she's taking breaks from peeling the floor to peel her breakfast orange, trying to unravel the skin in one long, unbroken strip.

"You're getting floor germs on your orange," I tell her.

"Um, excuse me, it's a tangerine," she says. "And I'm

strengthening my immune system." She wipes her hands on the pockets of her cargo pants. "I had a bowl of dirt instead of cereal this morning. Gravel instead of marshmallows."

To the tune of the Cheerios jingle, I sing, "The one and only Gravel-O-oh-oh-oh-oh . . ."

"What was *that*?" She looks at me askance.

I cringe. Lately, she's been resisting my banter. My word-play and cereal commercial parodies go unappreciated. These days, Amy seems to disagree just to disagree. Already this morning we had a difference of opinion on whether to eat at Tim Hortons or Pizza Corner after school.

Amy: "Sugar beats cheese."

Me: "Dough beats sugar."

Amy: "Tim Hortons has both sugar and dough."

That gave me pause, so we invented a Dough-Sugar-Cheese version of Rock-Paper-Scissors and settled on going to the Halifax Brewery Market, which has all three.

Then we sparred over whether Americans have the right idea about making the drinking age twenty-one.

Amy: "If we were Americans, it'd be seven more years until we could celebrate our accomplishments with champagne."

Me: "That's two additional years for us to accomplish something."

Next, we debated whether a moustache can make some-one handsome.

Me: "Maybe . . . in the right light . . . on the right face . . ."

Amy: "No. Don't be stupid."

I can't tell if it's only in my head that our exchanges have grown pricklier. Did we always fall on opposite sides of an argu-ment? I catch myself conceding, letting her have the power. A month ago, during March Break, Amy got a boyfriend. Now I worry she might drop me, like gym clothes turned pink in the wash, or a hair elastic that's lost its stretch.

Mr. Mackenzie appears at the end of the hallway. As he walks towards the English office, I turn to page five of *Beowulf.* Amy deliberately flicks a big piece of varnish at me with her thumb and middle finger. So I go: "Amy, what's wrong with you? Why do you always have to deface our school?"

Mr. Mackenzie nods down at us, unlocks the office, and shuts the door behind him.

Amy turns to me and says, at full volume, "At least I haven't memorized every article of clothing owned by my English teacher."

"Curse you, Amy," I whisper-shout at her, trying to bury my smile. I cup the shards of floor varnish in my palms and drop them right on her head.

She laughs, shaking out her white-blonde hair so the pieces scatter. Amy likes to joke that I spend so much time gazing at Mr. M that I must have his whole wardrobe memorized by now; except it's not a joke, because I know that he owns six button-downs (three shades of blue, one white pinstriped, one cream, and one grey), and four pairs of beige-ish brown pants, and white athletic socks that show when he sits down. Only once have I seen him wear a pair of jeans, at the English Club fundraiser— a car wash to raise funds and awareness for the literature of the Augustan period. We used the money we made to buy used copies of *Gulliver's Travels* and then we just handed them out to people on the street. Mr. M called it "Spreading the Word." He smiled when he said it, his mouth an open oval, thumbs tucked into his front pockets like he was a cartoon cowboy. It took me the first half of the car wash to adjust to this new, jeans-wearing version of my English teacher, but then his effortlessness charmed me, and I decided that his casual style did not take away in the least from his devotion to our cause.

When the bell rings, Amy gathers her stuff and waits while I write down today's date and make a note underneath:

Cream button-down. One shoelace coming untied. I record these lists of clothing, and other thoughts and observations, in a sleek black pocket notebook like the kind Mr. M says Hemingway used to use.

That afternoon in class, I notice Mr. M's socks slouched around his ankles. I dream of ducking down to the half-peeled floor, crawling under his desk, and pulling them up for him.

Because of all this pent-up sexual frustration, I've cultivated a new hobby: interacting with pedophiles in internet chatrooms. Or not pedophiles, but rather one pedophile in particular. His name is Ronald. We've been talking online for about a month. He asked me to think of him as my boyfriend, though he's really more of a manfriend, because he is forty-one years old. When I told him I was fourteen, he replied, *Your age is my age in reverse*, as though that's a sign we are meant to be. He says I'm exotic because of my Indian background, so I haven't told him I was born in Halifax. Four or five days a week, after I'm done with school and English Club meetings, I go on internet dates with Ronald the Pedophile. We have serious discussions about the pros and cons of Netscape Navigator versus Internet Explorer, and about the proliferation and potential of the World Wide Web. Sometimes I send him neat facts I learned from my dad's Encarta CD-ROM.

While I'm upstairs crafting chat messages to Ronald, my parents are downstairs praying. They have created a god room in the basement, where Hindu gods and goddesses hang in rows on the blue walls, staring out with placid expressions.

You are as beautiful as a goddess, Ronald wrote to me once, after describing himself as agnostic. I had sent him a link to the GeoCities page where Amy and I had posted photos of ourselves that we took with her dad's new, outrageously expensive digital camera. We're posing in our oversized gym uniforms out behind the school, miming model pouts I don't think Ronald realizes are ironic. He studied the photos and told me that I'm infinitely more desirable than she is. I know this isn't true. Amy, with her slight figure and fair hair framing her unsmiling face, looks like the young girl on the cover of a V.C. Andrews novel.

I let Ronald know that I regularly watch *To Catch a Predator* on *Dateline,* and now he's into the show, too. There was one segment where the decoy thirteen-year-old invites the predator into a staged family home. The voice-over: "This is a house on an average street, in an average town. It could be *your* town. But there's something very different about this place . . ." The predator enters wearing a large misshapen baseball cap atop his large shapeless head, unaware of the cameraman hiding behind the decorative curtain. The decoy chirps something about going to change into her bathing suit, and the predator smiles to himself and literally starts rubbing his hands together in anticipation, and I bet he has really dry hands. He has this backpack on that's maybe too small for a grown man, and he takes that off and starts rifling through it. But before we find out what monstrous equipment he has in this backpack, *Dateline* correspondent Chris Hansen emerges from behind the decorative curtain and introduces himself, and the predator removes his cap and uses it to cover his face.

Don't worry, my darling, Ronald said, after I synopsized the show, *I am ten times the man he is*. This made me question if Ronald knew how math works. Ten times a pedophile, I thought, as I examined the photos he'd sent me of himself. They featured no other people. Mostly they were of him leaning against a blank wall, his head distorted in a way that suggested he'd taken the photos himself with one outstretched arm.

||||||||||||

During tonight's conversation with Ronald, he asks for my phone number. I've been trying to read *Beowulf* but am wondering if there might be a movie version I could watch instead, and if so, whether the script uses quotes from the Seamus Heaney translation. So I'm pushing the Ronald conversation window to the side of my screen to look this up on IMDb, when he types, *Are your parents home? Can I call you? What is your phone number?* All three questions in a single message. I picture him sinking back into an ergonomic chair in front of his desktop as he waits for my reply. And, maybe due to daydreaming about Mr. M and all my unrequited emotions, I start imagining what would happen if I fell in love with Ronald the Pedophile. He lives in Dartmouth, so it wouldn't be a long-distance relationship. Instead of internet dates, we could go on actual dates to local hotspots, and events like the Halifax International Busker Festival. We could climb to the top of Citadel Hill and take the historic guided tour—something I have always wanted to do, but Amy refuses to go with me. *Would you visit Citadel Hill with me?* I type, and Ronald replies, *Yes*, followed by an indecipherable emoticon. So I type my phone number in one swoop of momentum, without any spaces or dashes.

He dials the number just as quickly. The glossy red telephone on my desk rings, a screaming pair of lips. I let it ring four times, fanning myself madly with my copy of *Beowulf,* the chain mail face fluttering as I try to decide whether to answer the phone. If I don't answer, the call will go to the answering machine, and Ronald will leave a message accessible to my parents, because this is our landline—for some reason they won't get me a cellphone. Also, my parents are not at work or at the store or at a baseball game or wherever it is parents go when strangers call the house. While a weird man preys on their only child, my parents pray in the basement, singing light religious tunes in their atonal voices and clanging finger cymbals that compete with the ringing phone. At any moment, they might put down their Xeroxed Sanskrit mantras and unfold their piously curled bodies to get up from the floor and answer it. I wonder if Ronald would pretend to be a salesman. I think if my parents pick up the phone, Ronald will probably never speak to me again. So I answer it.

There is no pause at all as I hear a soft, wheedling voice say, "You didn't think I'd call, did you?" And then the door to my bedroom opens.

I see a man standing there, peering around the door frame at me with this slow grin and saying, "What do you want for dinner?" because the man is my father. I immediately hang up the phone and tell my dad rice is fine as always for dinner. He asks what I've been doing for the past hour, and I tell him I've been researching the incarnations of all the various Hindu gods.

"Oh-ho—wonderful, Nina," he says, clicking his tongue in approval and giving me a thumbs-up. "Surely I believe you. After dinner I will have a quiz prepared, so get ready!" He walks out chanting the avatars of Vishnu.

The next day I'm at the school's side entrance by 8:15 a.m., waiting to tell Amy about what happened with Ronald. I've been practising telling her the story in my head, adding and deleting details to entertain her. "And then I gave him my phone number," I'll say, "and he actually called." Amy will ask why I expected anything else, and I'll shrug. She'll ask what I'll say if he phones again, and I'll say I have no idea, and then together we'll come up with a plan.

I wait until 8:45. Amy doesn't show. She isn't in Music either, or in Science. So when I walk into English class, I'm not expecting to see her. She's there, though, just not in her usual desk in the second row, next to mine.

She's sitting with her boyfriend, in the far corner, right below a poster that says, *I before E except after C, except when your weird neighbour seizes a sleigh with eight feisty reindeer.* The boyfriend's name isn't even worth mentioning. He was in my Grade 4 class, but everybody avoided him because he was the only kid in Grade 4 who admitted to masturbating. He would try to join conversations, but people ignored him, so he would just give up and stare at the wall. Then one day, he started talking to the wall, telling it things and asking it questions, like "Why won't they talk to me?" and "All I have is you," and so on. I bet he and Amy have similar conversations now.

Before Amy started dating him, and before I had fully fallen for Mr. M, we used to spend class time laughing fitfully and soundlessly behind our open notebooks. The first book assigned to us was *Washington Square*, which we both hated, so we left Post-it notes throughout the pages of our copies to warn off future readers. Our notes said things like *I hate this book*, and *Don't read any further*, and *Aunt Penniman is a flat character.* Now I feel guilty for writing those Post-its and potentially ruining someone's unbiased experience of Henry James, and I've thought about retrieving my copy from the library and removing them. I won't though, because that would be like erasing our history, when already I can feel Amy slipping away.

It's different from that time in elementary school when she dyed her hair with lime green Kool-Aid and turned cool for a week. That whole week she had her lunch on the long, low, mud-coloured radiator at the front of the school where the cool kids sat in a stylish row—a gallery of spiked mohawks and half-shaved heads—while I ate in the cafeteria with all the other loser Grade 7s. When the Kool-Aid washed out, she came back. But I'm convinced that the romantic relationships of weird teens last forever. Weird teens know that they'll never find better than each other. There's proof of this in yearbooks: if you flip through a four-year set at the school library, there's always that couple huddled by the lockers with their arms around each other—the gangly guy with the turtleneck and middle-parted hair and the girl with the Black Sabbath T-shirt, holding one hand up in a rock-on gesture. The following years they're spotted in the backgrounds of other photos but with tighter or baggier pants and longer or shorter hair and more or less rocking on, and so it goes until you read the drippy messages in their grad profiles, announcing that they'll be attending the same university accounting program. Neither is ever pictured with other friends. It might never be me and Amy sitting together and laughing again.

I sit by myself and spend the class trying to imagine Grendel from *Beowulf* and drawing pictures of him all over my notebook in red pen. I compile monster parts from fairy tales I've read: wide white teardrops instead of eyes; teeth protruding from stretching mouths; heads that nearly aren't there, dissolving into the lines of the page. Their torsos are blocky six-packs, short and disproportionate to long muscular arms, skin like leaves bulging with visible veins; their legs attached to a pair of skeletal feet, leaving bony, blood-filled footprints. They stalk over the page of notes I'm supposed to be taking. I pencil a crowd of mesh-faced men into the bottom right corner, axes and daggers cast uselessly aside, knees curling under them like paperclips.

Mr. Mackenzie writes *Mock heroic* on the board and underlines it twice. In the background I hear someone call him "O Captain! My Captain!" because he is one of those teachers who tears up textbooks and says there shouldn't be a rubric for poetry. Mr. M delivers an impassioned speech about some Alexander Pope poem. He asks me a question, but since I've been drawing monsters instead of paying attention, I only know that the poem has something to do with haircuts. I curse myself for not listening and wonder if this is karma for the time I invented a Hindu holiday as an excuse to skip school.

"Disappointing," says Mr. M, and his head tilts sideways under the weight of his disappointment. "You have to do the reading," he tells me, "or there's no point in coming to class."

I want to tell him that I have done the reading—I've done more reading than any of these fools—but he turns back to the blackboard and makes a joke about how his wife never reads any books either, with the exception of Harlequin romances.

Mr. Mackenzie doesn't seem to notice the romance corner of the room, where Amy and her boyfriend are caressing each other's faces. I imagine them framed in a circle on a red paperback cover. In an article on the web, I read that if a boy touches your face, it means it's true love. I read a lot of these articles and they always have useful advice.

The boyfriend bends his neck to lay his head on Amy's shoulder. With his googly eyes shut, he's almost handsome. It's the one time I've seen him look anything other than stupid. The only person's head I can remember being that close to mine is my mother's. It's painful trying not to yearn for that peculiar, intimate warmth of a human skull pressing against you. Amy sighs her chin into the boyfriend's palm. She pulls at his nose and he embeds his fingertips into her cheeks. I worry that they will gouge each other's eyes out.

I wait for Amy by the side entrance after school as I always do, though I'm doubtful that she'll show up. After ten or so minutes, I give up and duck into the library. Nobody's using the computers, so I sign into my chatroom account. My screenname is Hrothgar14, though in retrospect, I probably didn't need the 14. I search for Ronald.

What a terrible day, I write to Ron1956.

You're early, he replies. *What happened?*

Amy ditched me for her boyfriend, I type, and then, because it's not like I'm in a committed relationship with this internet pedophile, I tell him that I have a crush on my middle-aged English teacher and about my moment of embarrassing inattention in class.

After a pause, Ronald types, *Pretend I'm him.*

I suppose what Ronald wants me to do is to enact a sexual fantasy I have about Mr. M via the internet. It's true that I spend much of class time and my own time fantasizing about my English teacher. I imagine us in a warm fireplaced room with burgundy wallpaper and claw-footed furniture, but we've disdained this furniture to sit on the floor. We read to each other from a copy of *Beowulf*—Mr. M holding the book as I turn its pages. Our heads are pressed together, and my hair is draped over one of his shoulders. In this fantasy I have flaxen hair despite being Indian, and I'm wearing an empire-waist gown and a wreath of flowers on my head. Mr. M is dressed similarly in eighteenth-century garb, like maybe a navy waistcoat and white pantaloons. We sip from glasses of wine . . . no, goblets of wine . . . no, chalices of wine, and we're uttering guttural words to each other in Middle English. The fireplace flashes behind us like an unanswered chat window.

The problem with these fantasies is that I never actually get past the reading part, so I don't know what I'm supposed to describe to Ronald. To diffuse the situation, I type the letters *LOL*.

What's so funny? Ronald asks.

I try to think of something provocative to ask him. I write, *How old were you when you lost your virginity?*

There's a long pause before he responds, *Haven't we had this conversation before?* Which doesn't make sense because Ronald and I have certainly never had this conversation before, or even this *kind* of conversation. Our imaginary dates have remained pretty tame and educational, what with my Encarta facts. It occurs to me that I am not the only teenager Ronald talks to on the internet.

He starts typing long strings of barely legible text filled with a shocking number of typos. It's sort of sickening, and I feel a cloud mushrooming under my ribcage as I realize he's describing all the things he's going to do to me, except I don't understand most of the terms. I open up a separate window to look them up on Urban Dictionary.

He begs for a response. I'm thinking of his pictures and how he could be a guy that works at my dad's office. My dad could be right there in an adjacent cubicle, entering formulas into his computer with the Lord Ganesha desktop wallpaper, working overtime for the money to send his daughter to medical school. I haven't yet told him that I plan to get an English degree and specialize in pre-1800 literature.

Ronald's words grow more garbled. He's employed the F-word at least four times. Then there's a pause. He must be waiting for me to say something. I consider the keyboard and then type the letter *m* repeatedly so it seems as though I'm moaning, and I follow it with exactly seven exclamation points.

You are so beautiful, Ronald types, though he spells *beautiful* wrong. I assume he's looking at my pictures. He says, *Are you still having a terrible day? Let me come over and comfort you.*

Through the library door, I see Amy and her boyfriend in the hallway. They are facing each other, hunched over sideways as they peel the floor together, in a long, unbroken strip. They move slowly, focused on the ribbon of varnish that passes through their collaborating hands and curls and trails behind them.

It's possible that Ronald is talking to four different girls right now, four different fourteen-year-olds typing covertly in their high school libraries before catching the bus home. One by one they must sign off, until he's left with a single girl who . . . does what? Answers the phone and talks to him? Invites him home?

Okay, I type to Ronald, *I can be home in fifteen minutes.* I give him my address to enter into MapQuest.

I can't wait to see you, he types. I don't let myself think about what he means by the word *see*.

As I leave the library, I spot Amy and the boyfriend turning the corner at the end of the hall. I head in the other direction, towards my locker. On the way, I notice the door of the English office is partway open.

When I knock on the door, Mr. Mackenzie tells me to come inside. I shut the door behind me and begin speaking without making eye contact. I count the posters of authors that line the top third of the room's walls.

"I just wanted to apologize for class today," I say to him. He's wearing one of his blue shirts and standing, half resting on the desk. The other English teachers have all left. I realize I've never been alone in a room with Mr. M.

"That's all right," he says in his infinitely understanding way. "You've just got to stop being distracted in class. I know you love this stuff."

My backpack almost drops from my shoulders when I hear him use the word *love*. I walk up to him and say, "I do love this stuff. I love books. I'm even trying to get through *Beowulf*, though I admit it's going a little slowly . . ."

Mr. M has chalk dust on the pocket of his shirt. I reach across the arm's length between us and brush the chalk off the fabric with my fingers. He frowns in a way I haven't seen him do before, the skin of his eyebrows pulling together and downward.

Here is where it's like the CD skips—a glitch in time. He lifts the shoulder straps of my backpack and slides them off my arms. He picks me up as the backpack thumps to the floor, and places me on the edge of the desk. The lights in the room are white rectangles in rows across the ceiling, and I look at them because I'm not sure if I'm supposed to look at Mr. M, whose head I want to hold in my hands, but I have this awful feeling that the second I touch his face, his features will turn to chain mail, the metal cutting the tips of my fingers. He pushes his head close to my neck and when he exhales, he smells like coffee, like cough drops, like an old man. He places my hands on the crotch of his pants, and I realize I am supposed to unbutton them. And so I do, very carefully and very slowly, recognizing the beige-ish fabric of the pants; they're one of the articles of clothing I have memorized and written down in my notebook, where I also keep track of my mom's invented idioms and my better homework grades, and where I record when a day is particularly beautiful. He moves one hand to grab my upper thigh, and the other hand under my shirt to grip my naked spine like it's the spine of a *Norton Anthology*.

I think of five things: Thought number one is of all the times I've seen him pick up a book in class and slam it face down, pages spread open on the table. Thought two is wondering how far around the school hallways Amy and her boyfriend have gotten, hand in hand and laughing. Thought three is Ronald searching my neighbourhood for house number 53, parking in my empty driveway, and pressing the round white doorbell, thinking he's about to rape some stupid little girl. Four, I hope my parents arrive home soon, so when this is over, I can phone them to pick me up. And five, I remember the time I overheard Mr. Mackenzie saying to another male teacher, "What a dog," in reference to a girl, an expression I didn't know people still used. It had taken me a moment to realize what he meant, before I convinced myself that I must have misheard him, before I pictured the head of a dog on a female human body, sad-faced and teeth bared.

The Wave

STUDENT COUNCIL Election Week at Sir William Alexander High School is like Oktoberfest in Munich—total chaos. When I arrive back after a few missed days, the hallways are vivid with neon Bristol board signs boasting slogans like *Vote for Brett. He's a Safe Bet!* There's one that says *Free drinks on Sarah* hanging over the water fountain. Kids are flinging around quarter sheets in every shade from goldenrod to lilac, printed with their campaign platforms. Suspended from the ceiling is a painted banner announcing tomorrow's assembly, where each candidate will have five minutes of stage time. From what I hear, much of this is spent lip-syncing.

I'm later than usual. Everyone is hustling down the hallways because the *Mission: Impossible* theme song has started to play, telling us we have three minutes to get to class. Some shrimp in sweatpants darts in front of me and zigzags down the hallway with his fingers pantomiming a gun; pretending to be a federal agent, I guess.

My first class is Music. I hurry in that direction, past the guidance office and the library, past kids handing out packs of Bazooka bubble gum and homemade buttons with their campaign slogans stamped on them, past Amy and her boyfriend smooching outside the boys' washroom like a couple of perverts. Her mouth breaks away audibly from his as I walk by, and she calls out, "Nina? Where have you been?"

I think about stopping, but then I see him—Mr. Mackenzie—walking towards me. He's striding down the crowded hallway, wearing one of his blue button-downs with a white undershirt, and he's a few metres away and then two metres away and then half a metre and then only centimetres. I could reach up and smooth his collar. I've stopped moving, and kids are pushing at my sides in a zombie horde to get to class. He's a foot or so taller than me and looking directly forward. When it's clear he isn't going to make eye contact, I turn my eyes forward, too. Our gazes are two parallel lines. They don't meet. I remember how his face feels: his stubble at my neck, his cratered acne scars against my skin, my head pushed back—and I want to throw up everything I've ever eaten. I can't stop myself from turning my face just enough so I can see his eyes as he passes by. I'm a pathetic sunflower. A candidate for secretary waves a flyer in his face. Mr. Mackenzie takes it. Smiles. Stares straight ahead to his first classroom. He doesn't stop.

In music class we practise scales and I'm thankful for the tedium, the clear airy notes, the damp reed between my teeth, the methodical click of my fingers on the keys. The oboe's black resin is cool against my palms. As I play, I imagine that Mr. M is watching. I've been imagining this for days. I don't think too much about the details and logistics: something involving a hidden camera and him crouched over the computer in his office or house, adjusting the volume and zoom for a closer view, a more precise sound.

When I set my oboe down to hear our conductor chastise the percussionists, Amy, in the chair next to me, leans over and whispers, "What do you call someone who hangs out with musicians? . . . A drummer!" She waits for me to laugh and so I do, though it comes out sounding like I'm underwater, sucking in liquid as I try to get air. Amy laughs at the weirdness of my laugh, and then I laugh for real. I'm not even thinking about this morning. Mr. M must not have seen me in the hallway. I imagine him watching us laugh, until the conductor throws his baton in our direction.

Second period is Science. The teacher announces that we'll be doing dissections. The Satanists at the back of the room start cheering. "I'm so glad you're excited," Mrs. Oberoi says, wearing her T-shirt with the Periodic Table of the Elements on it and rocking on her heels. "And here's what we'll be dissecting . . ." Suspense as she pulls something out from behind the desk. "A leaf!" Everybody groans. One nerd laughs hysterically, and Mrs. Oberoi dashes over to his row to give him a high five. I'm relieved that for once we're not doing some chemistry experiment where I have to worry about melting my skin off with sodium hydroxide.

Amy's my lab partner—we've managed to be in all the same classes this term. She makes up a song about xylem and phloem to the tune of the theme song from *Sharky & George*, a children's cartoon about two fish detectives who solve crimes in an underwater city called Seacago. It's like *Dick Tracy*, but with fish. The summer after we first met, we watched the whole series together on YTV.

"Xylem and phloeeem . . ." Amy sings, then turns the microphone (a nearby test tube) over to me and waits for me to complete the line.

". . . transports water to stems and leaves . . ."

". . . Xylem and phloeeem . . ."

". . . two of nature's mysteries." We are excellent jazz improvisers. There is no topic we can't adapt to the tune of *Sharky & George*.

"Girls, that glassware is not cheap!" says Mrs. Oberoi.

Amy doesn't know how to use a microscope (unsurprising—she doesn't know how to use a Bunsen burner, either). I imagine Mr. Mackenzie watching me slide my scalpel down the leaf's glossy surface, watching me show Amy how to clip the slide into place. I pose my hands subtly, as though I'm a hand model, feeling the thrill of his approval.

"So I tried calling you all week," says Amy. "Were you sick?"

I carefully turn the knob to raise the microscope stage. "Yeah, basically."

"Oh, that sucks. It was bizarre not hearing from you." She props an elbow up on the lab bench and eyes me, waiting.

I missed three days of school. When you add that to the weekend, that's the longest I've gone without speaking to Amy in almost three years.

"I was calling to check if . . ." She hesitates, watching as I adjust the microscope focus. The lens is all smudgy, so I wipe it with a scrap of lens paper.

I think she might say she was calling to check if I was okay. I have this feeling like my sinuses are full. Like maybe I really was sick.

"If?"

She says it fast: "So Sam wants to put in a last-minute bid for Student Council. I wanted to see if you'd be willing to be his, like, speechwriter?"

So that explains the hesitation. She knows I don't really like Sam.

"Why can't he write his own speech?" I ask. I squint through the eyepiece and start sketching what I see in my notebook.

"He's just shitty at writing, and his speech really matters, because . . . you know he doesn't know that many people."

What she means is that he doesn't have any friends.

"The assembly's tomorrow," I protest.

"Yeah, but I'm worried he might give up on the speech, because he said something about a skit, and you know if he does a skit . . ."

"He'll embarrass himself?" And her, by extension.

"Please, Nina?" She takes the microscope from me, so I have to look at her. She's holding it entirely incorrectly. "Please?"

"You could just, you know, play a role in his skit."

She makes this face, like, *Really? Would* you *be in his skit?*

I imagine Amy in a wig and makeshift costume, parading across the stage. That would never happen.

When I enter our English classroom, I accept that Mr. Mackenzie cannot possibly be watching me right now, because he's there, standing in front of the chalkboard. I choose a seat farther back than usual, a few seats behind and to the right of Amy and Sam.

Sam's lunch is the period before this one, so it's usually just me and Amy eating in the hallway alcove. But today I can't stand the idea of eating on the gritty floor while other people's feet clomp around and past us. I want to go outside. The weather has been warmer than usual for Halifax in spring. Girls at our school are already in spaghetti-strap tank tops.

"Do you want to have lunch at the Wave today?" I call over to Amy.

The Wave is a large sculpture on the Halifax Waterfront in the shape of an ocean wave. You're not supposed to climb it, but everybody does. On summer Saturdays, children crawl across its surface, their parents anxiously watching to make sure they don't fall and crack their heads. Amy and I like to perch on the crest of the wave and joke about pushing kids off.

"Aww, that's a really good idea, but I can't today." She mimes a frown. "I have to meet Mrs. Oberoi. She said she'd let me use the faculty photocopier to make copies of Sam's flyers." Sam beams as Amy links arms with him. "You can come with me?" she adds.

"Yeah, no thanks," I say, before turning back towards the front of the class.

Mr. M starts talking about diction, about how some words are intrinsically more beautiful than others: *gossamer, iridescent, diaphanous.* All these words make me think of dragonflies. I bet he sits at home with his wife on their back porch, a dragonfly flying by as they brainstorm pretty words. She suggests something dumb, like *hakuna matata,* which she thinks is one word but is actually two. I write down my own list in my notebook: *magnolia, quill, peony, lyric, pyrrhic, oboe.*

Do I love Mr. Mackenzie? *Love* is the wrong word in this context. I jot down his positive qualities: he is a very good English teacher; he truly inspires the English Club by reading poems aloud in an expressively modulating voice; he looks like Jason Bateman on *The Hogan Family*; he has the charisma of a cult leader. What was Mr. M like when he was a teenager? I get this flash of me sitting next to him on his back porch, asking him about his youth and him telling me about Woodstock. It's possible that as a boy he had keenly anticipated the moon landing. I don't know exactly how old he is. I do know, from his easy references to places like Polynesia, that he has travelled the world. To be honest, I couldn't even tell you which continent Polynesia is in.

Mr. M is asking us what we know about meter, and whether anybody can tell him what *iambic pentameter* means. "Iambic pentameter is totally my favourite pentameter!"

exclaims this kid Fergus. Mr. M glances at me—he can usually count on me to answer these questions.

I put my pencil down and focus on my lap and remember the weight of his body, this sudden awareness that he had a body at all. He'd closed the blinds on the window of the English office door with a single, smooth yank.

It's been almost a week since I lost my virginity to Mr. Mackenzie. I stayed home on Monday, Tuesday, and Wednesday. My parents didn't know. My mom would drop me off at school, and after she drove away, I'd take the bus home. I'd disappear into my dad's armchair, under a bleach-stained *Mario Bros.* comforter, eating Jos Louis cakes and letting the wrappers pile around me. The TV sang to me and told me stories until I fell asleep with my head on the armrest. On Monday night, when the phone rang and my mom said it was for me, I had thought it might be Mr. M. I imagined his voice, affable, concerned. But when I asked who it was, my mom said, "Amy. Who else?"

As class ends, Mr. M stands at his desk to collect our worksheets and hand back essays. His blue shirt is so crisp. How did he keep it so neat through his first three classes? Last Friday, I'd seen the wrinkles in his shirt as he untucked it. There'd been dampness on his belly and on the cool flesh below his armpits; a vaccination scar on his upper arm that resembled a banana chip. Walking home that afternoon, I thought, *How will I ever hand in an assignment to him again?* You have to look him in the eye when you add yours to the stack.

Amy and Sam get up right away, having packed up their belongings before Mr. M even finished speaking. I don't know if I should try to hide myself in the crowd of students or wait until the end. I place my pencils in my pencil case deliberately, one at a time, as though they might break. I put the pencil case in the middle section of my backpack, and my notebook and binder in the largest section. I zip the whole thing closed. This takes about thirty seconds.

He thanks every single student. "Thank you. Thanks. Great, thanks. Thank you—don't forget your name, Fergus . . ." It creates a little melody over the racket of bags and pencils. I put my backpack on and walk towards him, holding my worksheet. It feels like a prop. I used to hope he would say something extra to me, like "Have a good weekend," or "Nice penmanship," or "Marry me," but it never happened. Today, though, as he hands back my paper and I try to hide behind a lacrosse player, he says: "Not a word today, Nina?"

My name is a feather in his mouth.

For lunch, I wander over to Park Lane Mall. It's a city mall, compact enough to be wedged into Spring Garden Road. Its outside is glass, but its inside is a cavern. The stores are a random selection, as though they popped them out of a bingo machine; there's a place where teenagers can buy cheap jeans, a place where older women can buy expensive cardigans, Things Engraved, an independently owned dollar store, a Famous Players, and a bulk candy store. The candy store employee is packing gift bags behind the counter. I go in and slide my hand into a bin full of foil-wrapped milk chocolates. I buy $6 worth, which is the exact amount of change I have on me.

I take the escalator down to the food court and park myself at a table. As I unwrap a chocolate, I think about Sam's speech and make some preliminary notes. The chocolate melts, releasing the sugar and fat that will power me through Phys Ed, my last class of the day. At least the health unit is over.

I try to emulate Sam's voice in my draft, but it's tough because as far as I know his only interest is Jackie Chan movies.

Over March Break, when he and Amy had just started dating, we all watched *Rumble in the Bronx* in Amy's living room, and the two of them started making out *while I was sitting on the couch next to them.* I doubt they even noticed when I left.

Playing a part in the assembly does give me a flutter of excitement, even if it's behind the scenes, even if my words are coming out of Sam's mouth. This must be how Prime Minister Jean Chrétien's speechwriter feels.

The food court is basically an A&W and a Chinese buffet place with green backlighting. I wonder what Mr. Mackenzie would do if I asked him to meet me here. We could meet tomorrow, when everyone who would recognize us is at school, waiting for the afternoon PA system announcement to call their grade to the gymnasium to watch the Student Council election presentations. I could leave him a note. Tuck it between two worksheets. Write it in all caps, like a ransom note: PARK LANE FOOD COURT 2PM.

My mom loves Park Lane. She's thrilled at the efficiency of having a movie theatre and one-stop shopping destination so close to home. When the mall first opened, she found a family doctor and dentist here, and later my orthodontist, her tailor, and my dad's physiotherapist—pretty much every professional I've encountered in the last ten years. So public. Mr. M would never meet me here.

I imagine it anyway: I'm using my pencil case mirror and lining my eyes with the mermaid green eyeliner I bought at the dollar store, when Mr. Mackenzie shows up. It has a detachable pencil sharpener on the end, and I sharpen the pencil right on the food court table, as though I don't care about anything.

"Good colour." He clears his throat and points to the chair. "May I?"

"Of course," I respond. I hide the eyeliner in my bag, but the cedar shavings remain on the table between us. "I read that during World War Two they banned pencil sharpeners in Britain to keep people from wasting wood and lead." Actually, I learned this by watching *Jeopardy!* I've never been on a first date, but if I ever go on one, I will prepare myself with interesting facts.

"That was on *Jeopardy!* not long ago," he says. We are star-crossed lovers separated by age and circumstance.

He points his thumb in the general direction of the Chinese buffet place, then pulls out his wallet and gestures mine away. We pile egg rolls and orange chicken into Styrofoam containers. We eat, grease dripping from our fingers, mouths so full there's no room for words.

At home I look up statutory rape on AltaVista. I'm supposed to be working on my Music 9 group project—a reed and woodwind arrangement of "Mellon Collie and the Infinite Sadness"—but I keep getting distracted, wondering what happens to fourteen-year-olds who sleep with their English teachers. My internet search yields the recent *Dawson's Creek* storyline where Pacey sleeps with his English teacher. What does Pacey do? He defends her honour in a school board meeting by denying their relationship ever happened. They stare moonily at each other. She leaves town.

I pack my oboe and sheet music away and close the internet browser. In my head, Mr. M is still watching me. I crawl over to my CD collection—it's on the lowest section of my bookshelf—and sit on my bedroom carpet, snapping open an Our Lady Peace CD. Mr. M sees me pull the sleeve from the case to read the liner notes. He judges my musical taste. I put the CD in the player and press Play, turning down the volume. There's a guitar strumming, then Raine Maida's rasping, quavering voice that begins deep and rises into a wail. Mr. Mackenzie listens.

I get up from the floor and walk back over to my desk to open up my English binder. The returned assignment is on top, and Mr. M's comments skitter down the margins like blue spiders. I wonder if he graded this before or after that afternoon. I have read over it three times, searching his language for clues. But all it says is *comma splice, fragment, good use of personification*.

My whole room is painted black, and on one wall I have almost finished drawing a four-foot globe in thick white chalk, Atlas crouching below. I continue working on it now, copying the figure from the cover of *Atlas Shrugged*. It's meditative, the *shoom* of chalk under the pressure of my hand as I swirl an approximation of Africa. Mr. M said reading Ayn Rand would narrow my mind. *How does it feel to have your mind narrowed?* I pictured my head in a vise. This was back during the first few weeks of classes, when he was just another teacher, and I had the book in front of me on my desk. I was only a couple of chapters in but adored it already, all these heroic people accomplishing great things.

"Wouldn't it only narrow my mind if it were the only thing I read?" I replied, and his expression turned remote and wary, though I hadn't intended to be disrespectful.

My mom stops by my room on her way to her own, carrying an armful of items tidied from around the house, as she does every night. She drapes an errant sweatshirt over my chair for me to put away. My hands and carpet are covered in dust. "Waabaah! Very creative!" she says, indicating my drawing with her free hand. *Waabaah* is the sound she makes when she is impressed. "Next time we have guests, this will definitely be on the house tour." I notice she isn't looking directly at it, and I'm pretty sure it's due to Atlas's nudity. I've placed his knee modestly, so either it's the juicy outlines of his thigh muscles that embarrass her or it's his long, knobby feet. "Okay, I'm zonked out like a zomberry," she says, *zomberry* being a word she made up at some point. She heads off to bed.

My dad comes by when he's finished with his nightly prayer ritual. "Still awake, El Niño?" He started calling me that after the abnormal weather patterns of 1997. "Don't go to sleep too late. How are things going, anyway?"

"Oh, things are okay," I say.

"Worried about school?" he asks, stepping inside my room. He's in his pajamas—plaid flannel pants and this white undershirt with a faded bear I drew in fabric marker seven years ago. He looks so vulnerable in a V-neck.

"Something like that. More of an interpersonal issue." I know he thinks I'm stressed about a paper or an exam. He touches my shoulder. I will away the pressure behind my eyes. To him, I must appear exactly the same as I always did.

My dad folds his hands together. "Make sure you repeat *Rama Rama* before you sleep. It will help calm your mind." He believes that saying god's name can cure you of anything.

If my parents found out what happened: My mom would go through the Kübler-Ross stages, minus acceptance. My dad would disappear into scriptures and silence. When he dropped me off at a three-day Girl Guide camp two years ago, he cried and told me to remember my values. If I told him about Mr. M, he would sob into his hands. He would never stop.

The next day, I go to school with a plan. Towards the end of the lunch period, I head to the English office. I have a copy of the speech I wrote for Sam, and my plan is to ask Mr. M for his opinion, though Sam phoned my house late last night to say he'd decided not to accept my speechwriting assistance after all. He had something better in mind.

The door is closed, so I knock. Mr. M opens it almost immediately, startling me. He's standing so close.

"Oh, hi," he says. He doesn't invite me in.

The speech dangles from my hand. An obvious ruse. It occurs to me only now that the assembly is about to start, and there's no way I'd be able to give Sam any feedback in time.

"Did you . . . was there something . . ." He holds the doorknob with one hand while the other presses against the door frame, his body filling the space in between as though to block my entrance.

"Could we . . . is it okay if we talk?" I ask.

He lets go of the door then steps back, crossing his arms and hesitating for a moment before he walks over to his desk and stands behind it. I close the door behind me, though I'm not sure if I'm supposed to.

"Do you want to sit down?" he asks, not looking at me.

"Well, I don't know how long this is going to take . . . ?" I put my hand on the back of the chair and stay standing.

"Good point," he responds, making eye contact for the first time, and it's like my whole body hurts.

The room seems different from how it did a week ago. Brighter. More like an office. I can see the flaws in the drywall application, the bits of tape left behind from posters that used to hang there. I can't believe it's the same place.

"Tell me the best-case scenario, as you see it," Mr. Mackenzie says, glancing away again. He reaches into his pocket to jingle his keys and pushes the fingers of his other hand through his hair. There's something unexpected in his voice—an upspeak, a questioning. I can't tell if he's open to negotiation or if he means, like, how do we maintain a working relationship.

Though he's standing in front of me, I imagine Mr. Mackenzie watching me as I try to come up with the best possible answer, the one that will influence what he says next. But I don't know what I want him to say, exactly.

"I know this . . . thing happened totally unexpectedly, but we could still go . . . backwards? I really . . . I think . . ." My words float out like in that PBS show *Ghostwriter*. Every episode, this ghost helps a group of Brooklyn teens solve mysteries, haltingly spelling out clues in the air. Mr. M would think the show was ridiculous. The teens wear primary colours and backwards caps, jackets tied around their waists. They star in their own music videos. They're nothing like real teenagers, which is maybe why I love the show so much.

"Nina," he says, sighing, his exhale sending my air-words swirling away. He steps an inch or two farther back, though there isn't really anywhere for him to go. "You're a smart girl. It's a shame . . ."

I wait for him to finish his sentence, but he doesn't. *Which part is a shame?*

My period started yesterday. Last night I spent an hour in the bathtub, refilling it with hotter and hotter water to try to numb the cramps. When my mom came up from saying her prayers, she knocked lightly and left a plate of cut fruit outside the bathroom door. I remembered what we'd learned in health class about ovulation, the teacher standing and holding her arms up and curled on either side of her, wrists and elbows bent to mimic fallopian tubes. I could feel the blood leaving my body, and I hoped it would take with it everything that was wrong.

"I won't tell anybody, don't worry."

Mr. Mackenzie pauses as though he might add something else, but all he says is "Okay. Okay. Thank you."

I'm trying to think of how to make the conversation last longer. I shrug and my eyes land on the assignments spilled across his desk. "That's okay." I think of the next two months of sitting in his class, receiving his taciturn grammar corrections on my essays.

Would he have driven me to get an abortion?

After a second, he says, "You better get going. You'll miss the assembly." He uses a teacher voice, like *Hurry along. Get to class.*

"It's not a big deal."

"Yeah," he agrees. "Every year that assembly becomes more of a spectacle. You're too mature for that."

On the other side of the school, in the stunning, ancient gymnasium that smells of varnish and everybody's sweat, the assembly is about to start. If I were there I'd be sitting in the balcony with Amy, in the hush and rustle of waiting. The hallways are quiet, empty of students. Then, in the distance, I think I can hear the band playing the school song.

Amy calls me that night and asks me to meet her at the Wave. I duck out of the house and walk over to the Halifax Waterfront. She's there, waiting in the dark at the bottom of the sculpture. It's an armature of metal covered in thick concrete painted a glossy pale blue. It's like a cold tongue rising out of the ground.

To get to the top, you have to be barefoot, or wearing shoes with good grip. You need the momentum of a running start. We stand back together and run, as we've done countless times before, gasping out laughs as we push against gravity. When we reach the top, we spread our jackets over the concrete and cross our legs to sit, and though I'm still laughing, I think of Mr. M and want to die.

Amy tells me, while shaking her head, that she doesn't want to go out with Sam anymore. For the assembly, in lieu of a speech, Sam performed an improvised martial arts routine. He spent five minutes under the blazing lights of the gymnasium stage, slicing the air with his kicks, screaming *hi-yahs* that echoed through the gym as the audience vibrated in unanimous whooping laughter. "He didn't even notice the whole school was laughing at him," says Amy. "It's like he thought they were applauding."

Mr. Mackenzie will stay on at Sir William Alexander until the end of my Grade 9 year. Over those last two months in his class, I'll read the books I'm supposed to. I'll do fine on the assignments. I won't say a word, though every second of watching him teach is a foghorn blaring a warning. I'll go on to Grade 10. That September, when I walk by the English office, I'll see that one of the French teachers has moved in and taken over Mr. M's desk, replacing his books with VHS tapes and a bust of Napoleon.

On the Wave now with Amy, I think about telling her. Her arms fall loosely around me for warmth. She might be the only friend I'll ever feel comfortable touching. The ocean is across from us. It's rising in my chest. My fingertips bloat and grow heavy. I taste salt. My ears become seashells as the sound of rushing water fills them. When you live so close to the ocean you forget sometimes to listen for that sound, and then suddenly, it's there. You forget sometimes that nobody is watching. That you're just another student. You sit at the top of the fake wave and face the real ocean. Nobody is watching, but if they were, it would look as though you're being carried away.

The Most Precious Substance on Earth

WE ARE ON OUR WAY to BandFest and we are going to win. Everyone can feel it. On the airplane from Halifax to Toronto, the band has a hive mind; we're humming an electric rendition of the First Suite in E-flat, the woodwinds tooting out in forceful staccato as we begin the second movement. Brass players purse their lips to air-trumpets, extend the slides of air-trombones. Bandmates in the adjacent row thrum on their trays; I wet my mouth in preparation for my elegiac solo.

"Stop, stop, stop, guys," says Mr. Rees, the conductor, undoing his seatbelt and standing up in his seat. "You're disturbing the other passengers." The other passengers look down at their in-flight reading material as he says this. He puts his hands on his bony hips and scans the rows for culprits. "Remember, you're representing the band. Musicianship is more than talent." The last bit is a direct quote from Mr. Rees's "Rules of Conduct for Band," hand-printed in marker on chart paper and pinned up at the front of the band room back at school. At the start of the year he handed out typed copies and made us all sign and return them.

Earlier this morning the ratio of parents to band members at the Halifax airport was nearly two to one. My mom befriended and exchanged numbers with the two other Indian moms, while my dad struck up conversations with the teachers, questioning them about the trip's educational objectives and confirming for the second time that boys and girls would be staying in separate areas of the hotel.

Corrine, who usually wears raver pants, was today not wearing raver pants. She was the first of my roommates to arrive.

"Tearaways," I said, gesturing at her athletic wear.

"Jeans," she said, gesturing at my jeans. We don't know each other that well.

It was a revelation to learn that everyone in her family, including a hyperactive younger brother, has the same dark bowl cut; Corrine's hair is the colour of lilacs and assumes a new shape every day—it's currently a triangle, like the hair of that lady from *Dilbert*.

Around us, band members were flapping their boarding passes and imitating the bad French accent of the voice making announcements over the loudspeaker. Mr. Rees shouted over them: "Decorum, folks!" The two other chaperones, female teachers he presumably invited so he didn't have to share a room, herded us out of the way of travellers taking advantage of cheap May flights. Then they exchanged eye contact, as if silently agreeing to never have children of their own.

I wasn't sure if Amy would make it in time to catch the flight, though I knew she had paid the trip fees. Her punctuality had been in constant decline, and she'd missed the last few rehearsals. Just before the teachers guided us to security, Amy rolled in with a crimson suitcase, shiny and hard like it was candy-coated. Her mother waved at me without smiling and then headed over to Clearwater to buy a live packaged lobster.

Eunice, our fourth roommate, wandered in bewildered, eyes staring up at the signs listing departure gates, until she finally saw us. Eunice's parents were the only ones who didn't bother parking. They just dropped her off outside and sped away back to their house in Dartmouth (aka the Darkside), a city that had blighted its waterfront with a power plant and refinery. "I've never been on an airplane before," she said. From her expression, I doubted she'd been to the airport before, either.

When the families left, it was just the forty-three of us in identical green band sweaters with a petite white treble clef embroidered on the right breast: a teenage forest in the airport lobby. When we don our sweaters, it's like on *Captain Planet* when the five teens shoot laser beams out of the magical rings they wear, combining their powers to summon up Captain Planet from wherever he usually hangs out. I never watched that show, so I don't know what happens after that, but with the Platinum Band it's like we morph into an unstoppable force of concert band music.

The Platinum Band was originally called the Gold Band, but then Mr. Rees took over as conductor and explained to us that platinum was the most precious substance on Earth. This is false. A French horn player looked it up. One morning before rehearsal started, he got a percussionist to do a drum roll and then announced to us that platinum is surpassed in value by twelve other substances, including diamonds, rhino horns, and meth. "Why not the Rhino Horn Band?" demanded the French horn player, but Mr. Rees took it as rhetorical.

On the plane, five of us are playing a whispered storytelling game. Each person adds a word to make a story:

"There . . ."

". . . once . . ."

". . . was . . ."

". . . a . . ."

". . . gentleman . . ."

". . . bird . . ."

". . . who . . ."

". . . bled . . ."

". . . Ovaltine."

I'm simultaneously working on an arrangement of the *Jurassic Park* theme music with Eunice and Corrine, who are sitting behind me. Corrine's hair rises above her seat in a glorious froth.

Amy is asleep on my shoulder, her elegant nose letting out the occasional whistle. She's the only one sleeping and I'm wondering why; it's still morning. She and I both play the oboe, which is a disproportionate quantity of oboe for pretty much any ensemble. But Amy has a shitty band-attendance record. The Rules of Conduct state that three missed rehearsals means you're out, but Amy is a favourite of Mr. Rees. He once called her a "true musician" (to the chagrin of the French horn player), and everyone knows Mr. Rees is quietly full of compassion. Eventually, Amy wakes up and yawns, checks her new bangs in a compact mirror, and pulls a magazine out of the seat pocket—last week's issue of *Time*. On the cover, two teenagers smile in their school photos. Framing them are the black-and-white headshots of the thirteen people they killed at Columbine High School. Only the killers are shown in colour.

Eunice passes the half-finished *Jurassic Park* score over to me, and I pencil in a key signature before Amy interrupts with a whisper: "Did you hear Eunice was voted most likely to shoot up the school?"

"Shhhh, she's sitting behind us," I respond.

"Even worse, she's sharing a room with us," says Amy, fanning herself with the magazine before opening the air vent above her head.

She goes on to tell me that when the yearbook staff collected anonymous suggestions for superlatives to list under everyone's photos, they received an overwhelming number indicating that Eunice Lam would most likely "kill us all." The faculty advisor didn't let them print this (obviously), so next to her name in the yearbook it says: *Most likely to build a successful dot-com company.*

"I don't see us surviving until morning," Amy adds. "So much for BandFest."

From every exchange I've had with Eunice, it's clear she'd feel infinitely more comfortable holding a flute than any kind of weapon.

"If we're all dead," Amy continues, "does that mean we forfeit the competition and that Ontario school wins again? Like, how many euphoniums does a band need? Or is it *euphonia*?"

"What's the difference between a euphonium and a baritone?"

"Wait, is this a set-up for a band joke, or are you actually asking?"

"Seriously, though, look at her," I say. We not-so-subtly spy on Eunice through the gap between our seats.

Eunice is in Grade 9 and the youngest member of the band. She's been taking private lessons forever, so was let into the Platinum Band a year early. She's the kind of person a teacher would miss in a headcount. Though she is only maybe five feet tall, she walks with a hunch and would look like a figurine of an old lady except that her face is perfectly round—a child's face. She talks incessantly about her private lessons and sometimes disagrees with Mr. Rees on things like whether the timpani are in tune, which is uncomfortable for everyone. At lunch she sits in the hallway or the band room, writing in a purple journal with a tiny heart-shaped lock on it. She's writing in it now.

"That's the kind of diary your mom's work friend buys for your birthday when you turn seven," I say. If Eunice was more interesting, somebody would have stolen, photocopied, and distributed it by now. I try not to be irritated by Eunice, but it's hard. I don't hate her, though. Amy does.

"Yeah, she's like a child," says Amy, propping herself up with her hands to gaze over the seats ahead of us. She sits back down and checks her watch, distracted. Then she turns to me. "All right, when we're downtown tomorrow, I'll go meet up with my cousin and bring the stuff back for us." She mimes smoking a joint. So this is why she came.

Over the winter holidays, Amy's parents sent her to Vancouver to stay with family, and she came back a stoner. She smuggled some weed back inside a hollowed-out jar of peanut butter, which is apparently what people from Vancouver do all the time. Since then, Amy uses words like *bud* and *roach* and *blaze*, which sound like the names of Uncle Jesse's motorcycle buddies on *Full House*. For the month her supply lasted, every time she phoned me I'd hear OK *Computer* playing in the background while she recalled obscure memories from her childhood, like the time she tried to whittle an anatomical heart out of a bar of her mother's triple-milled French soap. "I remember so much when I'm high, Nina," she says, and then forgets to practise for our group presentation on macrophages in Grade 10 Bio.

When I started playing the oboe back in Grade 6, it was three months before I could make a sound. What came out was just tortured air. I'd soaked the damn reed for hours but I still wasn't entirely sure what *embouchure* meant. The only reason I was playing an oboe at all was because my dad had purchased one on a whim at a thrift store.

"Why an oboe?" I'd asked him, as I opened up the case for the first time to reveal the slightly scuffed instrument, separated into three black-and-silver pieces tucked inside a plush blue lining.

"What's an oboe?" he responded.

That was four years ago. It took me a year to manage a B-flat major scale. After two years, my dad invested in private lessons with this Slovenian woman named Irena or Alena or Galena . . . I'm still not totally sure. She sighed passive-aggressively when I used incorrect fingerings, but the sighs must have been a crucial teaching tool because three years in I was researching how to make my own reeds and growing enraged when people referred to my oboe as a clarinet. This past fall, I auditioned and joined the Sir William Alexander High School Platinum Band. I also signed up for about twelve different school activities at the same time, including the Geography Club, though I had no idea what you would do in a Geography Club—map terrain? This wasn't school spirit; I had just wandered into the Activities Fair, held each September in the gymnasium. Every table had an eager, well-adjusted student behind it with a clipboard and a list you could put your name on, and on each list were a dozen other names. Oh, to be a name among other names. I wasn't in the English Club anymore, so I just wrote my name down wherever. Maybe I needed a reboot. Maybe with the right hobby and social group, I could be well adjusted, too. My parents supported this—they believe in community but not in free time. "Just relax" is something they would never say.

Band is the only activity that stuck. It demands a feverish commitment like no other extracurricular. The Geography Club is irrelevant in comparison. Band members outnumber any four other clubs combined. After the hockey team lost yet another championship, half of the team quit and joined band instead. The Rules of Conduct have a sternness behind them, but also logic and mutual respect. That Mr. Rees took the time to write them out by hand counterintuitively makes them seem more permanent. No other club has any rules at all.

Our hotel room looks clean but stinks of the thousand cigarettes that have been smoked there. When I open the window, noisy air rushes in; another brown building faces our brown building, with streetcars and delivery men grumbling in between. We're a fifteen-minute walk from Roy Thomson Hall, which to the Platinum Band is a mythical place. When instructing the band to be quiet, Mr. Rees often reminds us of the time he heard the Toronto Symphony Orchestra perform there, and how during a long rest in the music it was so silent (and the acoustics so sharp) he could hear the ecstatic sigh of a woman on the other side of the hall.

Amy, Eunice, Corrine, and I are rooming together because we're all girls and first-year band members; i.e. there are no other possible configurations. Amy tried to get a pair of female clarinet players to trade so we wouldn't have to room with Eunice, but they and their roommates had already hatched a scheme involving making out with percussionists.

Amy throws open her suitcase over the garish florals of the bed closest to the window. In one half are PJs, underwear, and a Ziploc of toiletries. The other half is full of candy. "Sugar for everyone!" she shouts, and scatters Pixy Stix over the comforter.

"Dude!" says Corrine, picking one up and biting an end between her front teeth.

"Didn't you pack any clothes?" asks Eunice. Amy ignores her and starts undressing, flinging her flannel shirt over the radiator, where Eunice eyes it, probably worried it will catch fire and the sprinklers will go off, drowning our sheet music and destroying our chances of winning BandFest. Amy goes

to brush her teeth wearing just her flared jeans and a polka
dot La Senza bra. Corrine and I start changing too, but
Eunice waits on her bed, fingers threaded over a bundle in
her lap until Amy is done. Then she excuses herself to the
bathroom, re-emerging fifteen minutes later in cotton pajamas. There's a layer of Vaseline coating her face, and a terry-
cloth cocoon around her hair.

"Should we practise?" she asks.

Amy groans. "Seriously?" She points at Eunice and
mouths the words *school shooter.*

But Eunice has already unpacked her flute and fitted it
together. She's sitting on the very edge of her bed, facing
the wall, and playing without looking at the music. She's trill-
ing away.

This is what we did to get here:

Sixty mornings of our bleary, winter-coated parents shov-
elling out their cars in the blue dark to get us into our seats
four minutes before the 6 a.m. start of rehearsal.

Sixty twice-weekly mornings that began and ended with
the sound of noodling instruments and clacking cases and
Mr. Rees yelling, "Quiet, please!"

Sixty two-hour rehearsals, me sitting in the second row,
and Amy—when she was there—drawing fancy-dressed cats
on my sheet music while the trumpet players behind us raised
their bells and blared, tapped their toes, emptied spit valves
onto the squelchy carpet.

Two semesters of classic high-school concert band rep-
ertoire: Gustav Holst; Ralph Vaughan Williams; a medley of
outdated film music (*Jurassic Park, The Wiz, Wayne's World);*
a medley of Mr. Rees's favourite bands (Chicago, The Beatles,
Night Ranger); an up-tempo seventies hit; plus the required

performance pieces (*Pomp and Circumstance*, the national anthem).

Two fundraising car washes in the parking lot of the funeral home next to the school, one in frigid October, icicles dripping from the rims of our buckets, our wet hands raw as winter.

One gingerbread house the Music Council co-presidents built to raffle off at the Holiday Harmonies concert, intended as a gabled Christmassy Victorian but in truth more crooked mansion, royal icing tubed like toothpaste atop precarious walls.

Fifty or more afternoons of solo practice in a rehearsal room coated with soundproofing the colour of a dried sea sponge. I would feel around those walls for a light switch, then play until my fingers cramped. To leave that room was to face the rest of school life, so empty of music and sometimes so bleak.

Forty-three sets of parents opening their wallets, signing cheques.

I wasn't expecting this fierce, cheesy love for a band that is only mostly in tune, where members share obscure jokes from the humiliating skits they've performed at assemblies or about the time the visiting professional flautist accidentally told the flutes to finger their parts and then blushed straight up to his scalp. Sometimes, when Amy describes the transcendent qualities of marijuana, I think about the rehearsal when I took my mouth away from my oboe to sneeze in the middle of "Ease on Down the Road." I lifted my eyes from my music and saw the entire band's shoulders and heads moving in unison, a controlled wave; eighty-four eyes fixed on the slashes of eighth notes sprinting towards the end of the page, Mr. Rees shouting numbers over us as his baton drew violent figure eights. When I put my teeth back over the reed, my shoulders latched onto the rhythm along with everyone else's. It felt like running suicides in gym class: a mix of endorphins and gasped oxygen, blurring into euphoria.

||||||||||||

In the morning we take the subway from our hotel to touristy destinations. We churn in single file through metal turnstiles, a chaperone handing each of us a transit token as we pass. In yellow walkways under the city, Amy casually greets buskers, rolling her shoulders and clapping, offering them coins from her red vinyl purse. One of our first stops is the Toronto Reference Library, a building with the colour palette from *2001: A Space Odyssey* and the architecture of a dystopian government headquarters. Five storeys of curved, seamless white walls surround orange-red carpeted floors and staircases, all visible from the spacious atrium and lit under grids of ceiling fluorescents. Amy and I follow the library's walkways and eye the university students, half-asleep and puddled in their sweatshirts.

We've been put into groups and assigned a worksheet on Canadian composers and instrumentalists. Corrine has gone in search of a restroom to fix her lipstick, so Eunice trails behind us. At one point, she informs us that the library has one of the world's foremost collections of materials related to the life and works of Sir Arthur Conan Doyle.

"How do we distract her," says Amy, under her breath, as I dump my stuff on an empty study table on the second floor. She's figuring out how to sneak away to meet her cousin without Eunice reporting her to Mr. Rees. At first I thought she was inviting me to go with her, and I was ready to say there's no way the teachers wouldn't notice us both missing, but then I realized she'd always been planning to go alone.

"Maybe with some microfiche," I say. "Or by luring her into the rare books archives."

"Oooh. Or how about a sexy grad student." Amy tips her head down towards me and makes googly eyes.

"Too bad she's un-distractible," I respond. "Have you seen her practise arpeggios?"

"Look, I bet she's writing down everything I do in that creepy diary of hers." Amy points discreetly and I turn to see Eunice leaning against a stair railing and frowning as she writes.

"It probably contains a hand-drawn map of the school with a big red *X* over the band room," I say, and Amy's eyebrows leap up. "And a heart over a rudimentary drawing of Mr. Rees," I add.

"Nina!" exclaims Amy, and suddenly we're both stifling laughter, our fists pressed to our mouths.

I can't help it. There's this satisfaction in mocking Eunice; she's so small, so oblivious. I haven't even spent much time with her, but there are nights at home when, over dinner with my parents, I find myself complaining about her. And my complaints consist only of listing her qualities, not her actions. "Why isn't she more self-aware?" "Why doesn't she see she's a target?" Usually, my parents just listen, though once when I looked up my mom was tight-lipped, as if she was thinking, *What did she ever do to you?*

I glance back over at her. Eunice hasn't done anything to me.

For a second, I almost tell Amy she should just hang out at the library with me and stop making things so complicated. When she catches her breath from laughing, she says, in an exaggerated whisper, "*The lonely man strikes with absolute rage.*" I recognize it as a quote from Dylan Klebold's academic day planner.

A month ago, Eric Harris and Dylan Klebold killed twelve kids and a teacher at their Colorado high school. The crime was so violent and had such cinematic potential that it engulfed all other news. Amy's family only got internet access a few weeks ago, but now their phone line is consistently tied up by her reading the killers' diaries. She has a crush on Eric Harris, though he's dead, and I can't tell if she genuinely finds him charming or if it's part of this edgy new image she's cultivating this semester. Harris is the guy at the back of the class who's always smirking, the guy you avoid eye contact with because if he bullies you, he will feel no remorse. But Dylan Klebold, he was just this goofy big-nosed kid with a *Dawson's Creek* hairdo. If he went to our high school, he'd be the tuba player. Harris was a thin, slouching weasel. I can't picture him playing an instrument or walking our halls. The media portrays them as darkly iconic Batman types: the Trench Coat Mafia. Trench coats billowing behind them like black umbrellas against a ferocious wind. And in the same articles: Kids crouching under the cafeteria tables. The kindly teacher, splayed and bleeding in the science lab.

"Oh, hey." I point. Eunice has left us to ask the librarian a question.

"Awesome, see ya," says Amy, and then she darts back down the stairs, across the red carpet, out the revolving doors.

When Eunice comes to the study table, she doesn't ask where Amy went. "Do you want to check out the Arthur Conan Doyle Collection?" she asks.

I can't figure out how to say no, to avoid pairing up with her, so I end up agreeing to go along. She beams as though this is her opportunity, as though she and I have something in common.

Hours later, when the band is having dinner at the Hard Rock Cafe, and Amy is still gone, Eunice seats herself between me and Corrine, and her legs flail beneath her. At home she probably sits on an encyclopedia to reach the table.

"Amy's just in the gift shop," I lie to Mr. Rees, when he counts only forty-two students instead of forty-three.

He squints at me and my stomach twists. "Well, I'll let it go this time, but she should really get permission before going off on her own."

I don't look at Eunice, who has not left my side since the library, and who must know I'm lying. I tell myself that Amy is with her cousin, and I hang my jacket over the back of an empty chair in case Mr. Rees does another headcount. If Amy is dead on the streets of Toronto, I'll have delayed the police search.

When I get back to my seat, Eunice is ordering. "I'll have the veggie wrap, please," she says to the server, though everyone else has ordered burgers. She talks about Schubert for twenty minutes, though we're surrounded by rock and roll memorabilia.

"Schubert died of syphilis because he was a Romantic," I say.

Corrine laughs out loud. Eunice doesn't get it.

When we return to the hotel, Amy is already in the room, sitting on the bed by the window and flipping through channels to find something other than *Friends*. It's almost 9:30 p.m. Eunice goes to shower without asking us if we need to use the bathroom first. One of the chaperones, a choir teacher with a resonant bird voice, knocks on our door to make sure we're all inside and there are no boys hanging around trying to steal our underpants, or whatever she thinks teenagers do away from home. "Don't stay up all night gossiping, girls! Get a good night's sleep," she sings. "BandFest is tomorrow morning!"

When the choir teacher leaves, I turn to Amy and ask, "Where have you been? I thought you'd be back hours ago."

Amy mutes the TV. "Oh, sorry, Nina. My cousin and I

were just on Queen Street West and lost track of time." She pulls out an array of shopping bags from beside her bed. "But I have something for us!" She digs into one of the bags and retrieves a bulging Ziploc. I go to sit beside her, because I've never seen drugs up close, or really at all, except in movies. They're a dusty olive green, dense bunches clumped on dried stems, the curled leaves woven through with saffron threads. The smell through the bag is pungent but fresh, like the tufts of herbs my mom buys at the Indian grocery.

Corrine peers over us. "Oh, now we're in trouble."

Amy shreds the weed with plum-coloured fingernails. I think of the overplayed anti-drug PSA where a crew of bouncing children sings, "*Drugs, drugs, drugs. Which are good? Which are bad? Drugs, drugs, drugs. Ask your mom or ask your dad.*" I start to hum the tune and the other two join in. We're all giggling when Eunice comes out of the bathroom in her PJs, showered and once again having applied a shiny mask of Vaseline.

"Gosh, your skin must be soft," remarks Amy drily. "Like a baby's bottom."

"Oh, burn," says Corrine.

"What are you guys doing?" asks Eunice. "What is that stuff?"

Is it possible she doesn't know?

"Corrine, put a towel under the door," commands Amy. Then, pointing at the smoke detector on the ceiling: "Nina, cover that up." I grab a shower cap from the still-humid bathroom and, climbing on a chair, use a hair elastic to secure the cap tightly over it. Corrine cracks open the window. Amy carefully dusts bits of plant matter off her fingers and back into the baggie, then pulls open the drawer next to the bed and removes the Bible. She flips to one of the blank pages at the end and tears. Eunice gasps on cue. "I don't have rolling papers," explains Amy (though she was out all day and could have purchased them at any time). "Please apologize to your god," she tells Eunice.

"I . . . I don't believe in god," says Eunice. "Guys, I think this is a bad idea."

"Relax, will you." Amy twists the end of the joint, holds the other end to her mouth, and lights it with a hotel match.

"Corrine, if you get caught, who's going to play your solo?" asks Eunice. By now all four of us are sitting on the bed, drawn closer as though we're cavemen and Amy has just ignited the first fire.

"What, her three-note solo in a movie soundtrack from five years ago?" says Amy. I watch her inhale, memorizing her movements so I can copy them. When she passes me the joint, I put my lips on it and breathe in deeply. I'm thrilled by the ring of orange that glows gradually bright, in sync with my inhale. I cough a cloud of smoke.

Because we're total nerds, we put on a recording of our Holst performance piece, played by some distant, professional orchestra. In minutes, my head is floating. I squeeze my eyes closed and I can feel the movement of each extraocular muscle. Violins come slinking through the allegro, strings vibrating like hummingbirds. Even on Corrine's portable cassette player, the audio has the effect of surround sound. I smell shampoo flowers coming from Eunice's hair.

When the joint comes around to Eunice, she sniffs it first, then takes a shallow puff. She scrunches up her face and thrusts the joint back at Amy. "I don't like it." Still, Eunice stays on the bed with us. It's obvious she wants to be a part of the group. She reminds me of this cat I had that would eat its own vomit. I used to wonder if it was motivated by shame.

"What's the difference between an onion and an oboe?" asks Amy.

"Nobody cries when you chop up an oboe!" answers Corrine, laughing with complete joy before falling back on the bed.

"Okay, okay," says Amy, "you won't know this one. What's the difference between a bull and a band?"

"Nobody cries when you chop up a band!" answers Corrine.

"That's enough out of you," Amy tells her.

"A bull has the horns in front and the ass in back," I say, because I've heard all of Amy's band jokes.

"Nina!" Amy screams, gripping my neck and pretending to strangle me, before her hands loosen and she enfolds me in a hug.

"Shhhhhhh." I lean my head on her shoulder. From the recording, the woodwinds emit the purest sound: no breath, no clicks, only exquisite tones radiating through metal. Every chord is like biting into a stack of twenty crepes. My stoned brain remembers our "taped test" for the Holst piece. We had to record ourselves playing our parts individually at home and bring in the tape for Mr. Rees to grade. I spent six hours on mine even though the section was only a few bars long. When I finished, my lips were chapped white at the edges and my index finger ached from the repeated pressing of Record, Rewind, and Play. The day it was due, my mom had offered to drive Amy and me to school, and as I stood in the entryway of Amy's house, she said, "Hang on a sec." I saw her pick up her oboe from the living room sofa and lithely reach across to her dad's complicated sound system. She played this graceful rendition in a single take, so flawlessly I wanted to tear the ribbon out of my own cassette tape.

"It's really time to sleep, guys," says Eunice.

"That's the only thing you've said in like an hour," says Amy. Behind her on the wall is a mass-produced oil painting, shining and full of rolling hills. The whites of her eyes are disappearing under blood vessels, and she's chugging water from a plastic cup. "Go sleep if you want to so badly. Why are you even here?"

Eunice says nothing. She remains where she is, and gazes down at her hand, which is tracing swoops of thread on the quilted bedspread.

"Taking mental notes for later? Why don't you go write about us in your diary," says Amy. "What do you even write about in there? What could a loser like you possibly have to write about?"

Eunice winces. She doesn't lift her eyes.

"Amy . . ." I begin, trying to decide what else to say. Her face has gone grotesque. Dull and scowling. Distorting like a shadow. I turn to Corrine, expecting her to intervene, but she's just observing, spectating even, as she slowly chews a Fuzzy Peach, and it occurs to me that she and Eunice aren't friends; they've only been thrown together by circumstance.

"Have you ever smoked weed? Ummmm . . . no. Do you have any friends? Ummmm . . . no. Does your family even love you? Why did they just, like, abandon you at the airport? Have you ever stayed up past 11 p.m.? Do you have access to explosives?" Amy pushes her face towards Eunice, and I recoil involuntarily, even as I try to figure out what to say, how to interrupt. "Do you research automatic weapons, Eunice? *Do you*? Do you dream about shooting us all to death?" She blinks, eyes drooping and expression blank.

Eunice's hand has stopped moving on the bedspread. Corrine and I don't look at each other.

"Have you ever been naked with a guy? A girl? Have you? Has somebody else ever run their hands over your body? Have you ever *done it*?" Perversely, Amy's voice has only gotten quieter.

Eunice doesn't say anything. She's shaking her head and closing her eyes, absolutely silent. When her eyes open again, they land on the oil painting and stay there. She's somewhere else.

"Have you ever been *fucked*?"

Eunice's eyes go dark and ancient. I think of how she begs Mr. Rees to leave the band room unlocked so she can stay after school to practise. One night I forgot a textbook in my locker, and when I came back to get it I thought the only people in the building were the janitors, sweeping ragged grey brooms in wide arcs down the empty halls. Then I saw the fluorescent lights of the band room, and when I peeked in, there was Eunice, alone, sitting in her usual chair. Her flute wasn't even out of its case, and as I came up behind her I glimpsed her scribbling in her diary, writing in millimetre-high sentences I couldn't read. Her hand gripped the black felt-tip pen as she scratched fervently, each word an abrasion.

Eunice sobs once and curls her arms around herself. Then, lifting her head and staring Amy in the eye, she says: "Yes, I have. Have *you*?"

I consider the way Eunice hunches and slouches, making her body small. We all realize it at the same time. Even Amy has the decency to look away.

When we wake up at seven the next morning, Eunice isn't in her bed. We change into our band uniforms and venture out to the lobby, where the band has congregated in sleepy groups, draped over leather armchairs or bunched up by the free coffee, greedily splashing cream and opening sugar packets. Eunice is there, standing with a potted palm on one side of her and Mr. Rees on the other, next to the hotel's sliding doors. She's in her uniform, holding her flute case, with her music folder tucked under one arm.

"Should we go say something to her?" asks Corrine.

"Maybe I should say something," says Amy, but she doesn't move.

I know it from the way Eunice avoids looking at us, and from how Mr. Rees and the potted palm surround her like bodyguards. The sliding doors open every time she moves to adjust her folder or case, and then close again. I have this new awareness of her body. It's like a word highlighted by a teacher in a book. I'm trying not to notice her pink skin, her softness, her question-mark shape. I haven't been thinking of her as a girl, only as a child.

"She's already told him," I say.

Mr. Rees approaches us and takes us aside.

By noon, Amy, Corrine, and I are on a flight back to Halifax, sitting in separate rows because those were the only seats available. Absurdly, we're still in our uniforms. Our parents will have to pay the flight change fees. I don't know exactly what my parents will say to me, but I know they will worry and worry and pray, and that their disappointment will coat me like a layer of soot. Behaviour that is detrimental to the effectiveness of the band or to its reputation is grounds for dismissal, Mr. Rees reminded us back at the hotel, though when he said it, he seemed sad. Besides the Rules of Conduct, the school has a zero-tolerance drug policy. We're lucky not to have been expelled.

If I lean into the aisle, I can see the back of Amy's head as she rifles through the seat pocket, a dozen rows away. While flight attendants mime safety procedures, I hook the headphones of my Walkman around my skull and sink into my seat. I'm listening to a recording of us from last month's Spring Serenade; to the part of the First Suite in E-flat where everything coheres, where the notes are as clear and confident as pain. I'm pretending that the Walkman is a time machine and that I have returned to April. I'm not sitting in economy class, next to a businessman I don't know, but next to Amy onstage with the band, turning the clean edges of sheet music. When the concert ends, we click off our stand lights in the dark auditorium, like the swift wink of a city losing electricity. The applause fills the air like static. On Mr. Rees's cue, we exit in disciplined single file. We practised this so many times. I follow the green shoulders of the clarinetist ahead of me, careful not to rattle the rows of music stands as our line of musicians curves out the door.

I want to forget that without the band I'm just me. That nothing will ever again be that good.

Earning Disapproval

AMY AND I HOP OFF Halifax transit at the bus stop by the school, the same as we've been doing for two years, but this time the driver doesn't respond when I say thank you. It's the first day of Grade 11, and we're dressed in fishnet stockings, black dollar-store lipstick, and thrifted boots too hot for September. We rented *The Craft* last week, and ever since, we've been emulating Fairuza Balk. At one point in the movie, a bus driver warns her character and her friends to watch out for weirdos, and she lowers her blood red sunglasses and purrs: "We are the weirdos, Mister."

We split up to search for our homerooms, and people in the hallway stare. Arrive with a new look at the start of the school year, and people speculate about your summer evolution. *Maybe she's dating someone older. Maybe her parents got divorced. Maybe she spent the summer in Toronto.* I reach out one hand, lifting my fingertips, and a string of locker doors opens and recoils, spilling binders and backpacks, lunches and love notes—no, that doesn't happen. I imagine it, though.

I pass by the band room; I have no reason to be there anymore. A trumpet player smirks at me from the doorway, like he knows my fishnets are left over from my Grade 9 Halloween costume.

My mom took a picture of me before I left the house this morning. She started laughing and grabbed her camera as soon as I came down the stairs. She told me she's going to mail this photo, along with my horoscope, to all my prospective husbands. When I protested that I'm only fifteen, she said it's never too early to start looking. One weekend this past summer, she invited an aunty (not an actual relative) with a son my age over to our house. The boy small-talked with me as I watched *Saved by the Bell* reruns, hovering by my shoulder because I was too rude to get up off the couch.

"This is one of my favourite shows," he said.

"Oh, mine too," I responded, eyes still on the TV. "It was totally genius of those studio execs to retool *Good Morning, Miss Bliss*. I can't imagine Zack Morris reaching the height of his powers in Indianapolis. Why set a show anywhere other than California?"

The boy looked at me blankly and then escaped to the kitchen, where my mom was brewing cardamom tea. Boys like him have only a surface awareness of pop culture. A short while later, he and I and our moms gulped the tea from stainless-steel cups in the living room and made insipid conversation about our studies and future plans, while my dad hid in the basement fixing the computer. It was too hot to be drinking tea. And I was annoyed to miss the part of the episode where Zack Morris gives an impassioned speech to the school board after the oil spill in the school duck pond.

After that, my mom set her sights on Nishant as the current candidate for my future husband. His family has known mine for over a decade, and often we're the only teens at our parents' weekly gatherings with the temple gang. (Not an actual gang.) A couple of weeks ago, we killed time at one of these get-togethers by dialling up the internet on the basement computer and making fake Shaadi.com dating profiles. I liked that he went along with this idea, which was mine. His profile was from the point of view of a robot. Mine featured quotes from the Wu-Tang Clan, falsely attributed to Greek philosophers.

When he had crafted his ideal robot introduction, he turned to me and gave a sudden grin, and I liked its lack of symmetry. I can't imagine kissing him, exactly. Honestly, something about the idea feels yucky, but maybe it's just his brotherly energy and the fact that we've never touched. I can imagine dating him, though. His skin tone is perfect. And I think he'd be up for Lego Night at the Library. We'd build a Lego robot together and then leave it behind in the library's Lego bin for a lucky child to discover.

As I was trying to select a photo for my profile, Nishant scrolled through Indian women aged nineteen to twenty-five for ideas.

"So much teeth," I said. The women smiled from Himalayan mountaintops. They smiled from desk jobs. They smiled from yoga poses, literally bent over backwards.

"There are no eligible women in Halifax," he said. "Especially Indian women. And especially women who aren't dressed like sluts."

"I wouldn't say they're dressed like *sluts*," I said. I evaluated how much cleavage was visible, how much panty line. How much was too much? I tried to upload the Cookie Monster as my photo, but the site sent an all-caps message chastising me for misrepresenting my identity, so I deleted the account. Afterwards, it occurred to me I should have "expressed interest" in Nishant's profile, to see if he would have "accepted interest," and then we would be connected in this simulated and tenuous way. It certainly would have made my mom happy.

Nishant and my parents come from the same box of animal crackers. They might even be the same animal. He's fluent in two languages besides English. He volunteers at temple functions, takes the coats of aunties and uncles at dinner parties while greeting each one by name, sprinkles chutney pudi on his toast in the morning, and explains to me why Napster is the doorway to moral decrepitude. One time, there was a Carnatic musical performance scheduled at the temple, but the mridangam player got sick so they called in Nishant as a sub, and temple gossip says he did a better job than the actual mridangam player. He's also a hybrid. He understands references to *The Simpsons*. His family moved to Halifax when he was four, so he's as much of a Haligonian as I am. He puts donair sauce on everything. I once heard him refer to Halifax as "the Big City." I've never seen him tuck in his shirt.

During lunch, Amy and I sign out *The Edge of Evil* from the school library. We read it aloud to each other while perched on a concrete block the size of a shipping container outside the school's east exit. We've mused about the purpose of the concrete block: it contains electrical equipment or exam answer keys or the corpses of retired vice principals. We share the concrete block with a handful of other students, one of whom leans over his guitar, pressing the hard chords of a Green Day song. "*The Rise of Satanism in North America*," reads Amy. The guitar guy shifts his eyes to her and then back to his guitar.

She continues, reading from the intro written by Geraldo Rivera. "*Satanism is more than a hodgepodge of mysticism and fantasy . . . It's a violent impulse that preys on the emotionally vulnerable, especially teenagers, who are often lonely and lost.*"

"Harsh but true," I say. I wonder what teenage Satanists have perused this book before us, and which librarian decided to order this book for the school library.

"*It attracts the angry and the powerless, who often sink into secret lives—possessed by an obsessive fascination with sex, drugs, and heavy metal rock-and-roll.*"

"Heavy metal, specifically?"

The inside cover has a 1-800 number for moms and dads of Satanists. (*Is your son or daughter evidencing signs of ritualistic deviate behavior?*) Nearly every case study in the book features a casual mention of animal mutilation. There's a chart of occult symbols just ahead of the index. We copy them into my notebook after tearing out the first few pages of algebra problems. On the cover, Amy draws an inverted pentagram in thick black Sharpie.

"Shall we skip fifth?" she asks, blinking her augmented lashes at me, so I tell my fifth-period teacher I have a gynecological appointment and Amy tells hers she's volunteered to tidy the school's Japanese rock garden.

We take the bus to Shoppers Drug Mart to pick up snacks. I'm walking behind Amy through the aisles, watching her white-blonde hair. It's like a sheet of ice, spanning the space between her scalp and shoulders. When we met in Grade 6 I wondered if it was bleached, but it wasn't. She descends from Vikings. Amy's mom has the same hair, except she curls it into shapes that remind me of the snow formations that pile up on the eavestroughs of our house. A month or so after her mom left this past summer, Amy found her hair products under the master bathroom sink— sprays and pomades and serums and clips that she'd abandoned. Her mother had taken everything else. Amy tried to give me the hair stuff that was still usable, bringing a box of it over to my house.

"Don't you want to keep it for yourself?" I asked, but that turned out to be the wrong thing to say.

She studied the box in her arms. "I was just trying to help you. Do you even brush your hair?" She took the box back with her.

"If you dyed your hair black, you'd look like an evil queen," I tell her now.

"Let's do it."

She buys the cheapest box of colour, then we smoke a joint behind the building and journey over to Value Village. Amy tackles tops while I browse dresses, evaluating each pre-worn item for price, fit, and shock value. She holds up a soft black T-shirt that says *Don't Touch* across the chest. I give her a thumbs-up and she adds it to the pile I'm carrying. Wearing black all the time is harder and more expensive than I expected. It already feels like too much effort. When the other kids in our grade skip class, they go eat honey crullers and make out in the Tim Hortons parking lot.

Waiting in line, we discuss the case study from *The Edge of Evil* where a woman walks in on her granddaughter slitting her cat's throat. "The beloved family pet," I say. "The Satanist's blade."

Amy nods vigorously. "Efficient and clean. Too bad her grandmother walked in."

We're only having this conversation to scare the woman ahead of us in line. She doesn't react, just empties a tangle of costume jewellery from her basket onto the counter. Our arms overflow with clothes that smell of other people's perfume.

I have this idea that goths should smell like nature. When I mention this to my mother as she's making dinner, she chases me around the house with curry leaves and rubs them into my hair. It is hard to run with your black stockinged feet slipping everywhere, chased by an agile mother who never stops reminding you of the triple jump competitions she used to win at your age while living in a country where competitions had fifty times the number of competitors they do here. Then she tells me she read about track and field tryouts in the school newsletter.

"Triple jumping will not help me to achieve my eventual life goals," I tell her.

"A boy whose name starts with N might be impressed by a champion triple jumper," she says.

"No comment," I answer. But later I picture myself leaping across a sandpit in black athletic wear, a cheering Nishant on the sidelines. Afterwards, he carries my trophy for me. I try to imagine us embracing in the parking lot of Tim Hortons, but it doesn't feel right. I revise the image so we are holding hands instead, sharing a box of Timbits. Then I figure we probably wouldn't hold hands while eating donuts. He eats the ones with the raisins and I eat all the others. This seems like the kind of relationship I could tolerate in the long term.

I have nightmares—or, more accurately, horrifying scenarios that I conjure up when I'm awake—where I'm in an arranged marriage to a man from India who's in need of an immigration visa. He has a medical degree but works nights as a security guard while trying to get a licence to practise in Canada, which is like heaving a rock up a mountain—except instead of a mountain, it's a Slip 'N Slide, and instead of a rock, it's your dreams. When he comes home to our ugly mushroom-coloured high-rise in the city outskirts, I put on the rice cooker and massage his scalp while he drinks whatever the cheapest label of Johnnie Walker is and laments this country's unfairness. Weekends are spent at the temple in futile prayer.

I tell my mom about this as we're sitting on the rug in front of the living room coffee table, folding brochures to hand out at a temple event this weekend. We have *Dilwale Dulhania Le Jayenge* playing on the TV, because my mom insisted it was her turn to choose what we watch. My hilarious Shah Rukh Khan impression is what prompted this whole conversation.

"Nina, that is racist," she says. "You are racist against your own race."

"I don't know if I'd go that far . . ." I press a sheet of paper down on the coffee table and run my thumb over it to get an even crease. I have my technique down. It's the same one I use when we mail out the temple's monthly newsletter, though that also involves envelopes, sponge bottles, and stamps.

My mom stops folding. "Have you ever seen your dad drinking Johnnie Walker?"

(I haven't.)

"Have you ever seen me massage your dad's scalp?"

(I haven't.)

"That's right," she says. She picks up a stack of brochures, stands it on its side, and thumps it on the table twice, then wraps an elastic band around it. "Your dad is the one giving massages around here."

"Ha ha ha," says my dad, who we thought was snoozing on the couch this whole time. "Keep dreaming."

My parents bring me along with them when they visit new immigrant families. They and the temple gang volunteer with Immigrant Services, finding new homes for old couches and acquainting the families with Nova Scotian rituals like eating fiddleheads and apologizing. The last time I went with them, the husband asked my dad where the rest of the Indians in Halifax were. "Oh, they'll be here soon," said my dad.

On Saturday, we bring a couch donated by Nishant's family to an apartment in Dartmouth that has no furniture at all except for three mismatched chairs and an Arborite table like the ones at fifties-style diners. The only thing on the wall is a tacked-up illustration of Ganesha. My dad and the uncle load the sofa—mustard yellow and floral and sagging from the weight of decades' worth of rear ends—into the elevator. They angle it this way and that to get it through the door. By the time they're done, they've scratched half the paint off the door frame.

My mom is in the kitchen heating milk for tea, while the aunty brings out a plate of digestive biscuits. We sit on the sofa and put the plate on one of the chairs, because they don't have a coffee table yet. The men are in the bedroom, filling out government paperwork.

"How is school?" the aunty asks me. When I examine her face more closely I realize that, though I've been told to refer to her as aunty, she must be no more than five years older than me.

"It's okay," I say. I chew my digestive biscuit. "Umm . . . how do you like living in Halifax?"

"It's okay." She chews her digestive biscuit. We digest.

After tea, I excuse myself to wash my hands. When I turn on the washroom light, there are tiny roaches shimmying around the corners of the sink and along the baseboards. One heaves its body into the toothbrush holder.

I turn off the light and walk back out into the living room, where my mother is holding the aunty's thin shoulders. The woman cries, wiping her nose on the edge of the cotton sari she's wearing. In a scatter of sobs, she tells my mother about the home in India she left to come live here, about her parents and sisters and aunts and uncles and cousins who live together in a marble and terracotta house by the sea. She's been trying to learn English by watching *As the World Turns.*

"I want to go back home!" she says, beginning to hyperventilate. "I want to go home! *Please. Please.*"

I wait against the wall. My mom catches my eye, then looks away.

The next day, Nishant and I accompany my parents to a temple event. We're in charge of handing out the newly folded brochures at the door. The event provides networking opportunities for new immigrants from different countries. A handful of guest speakers deliver mortifying tips, like advising people to wear deodorant.

Nishant smells comforting and boyish, like Irish Spring soap, but I don't tell him that. I'm playing the long game, the kind that ends in a wedding attended by six hundred.

He points at my large pentagram necklace, which I found on sale at a booth at the Halifax Shopping Centre. "Why are you dressed like that?" he asks, sounding confused.

"I'm experimenting with the occult," I say, because I find the word *occult* intriguing. It means "secret knowledge," which I wouldn't mind having. He doesn't respond, so I also tell him that dressing this way makes me feel protected—waterproof, if not bulletproof. "I feel brave. I have more ownership of my sexuality." For example, nobody's pantsed me in the hallway since last year.

"Right. Great."

"It's not just that," I begin, but he turns away from me to help a man fill in a registration form. The man has brought his children along, and they grip his legs and cower behind them, peering curiously up at me.

"It's not just that," I say again after the man finishes. "I've also been exploring other religions, like Wicca and Satanism—"

"Hello? You're Hindu. We are at a Hindu temple right now."

"I don't mean that I'm becoming a Satanist, I'm just reading up on it. I'm expanding my knowledge. Did you know *occult* means 'secret knowledge'? And Wicca has numerous similarities to Hinduism, you know, with the polytheism and animism and everything." Whatever animism is.

After the event, the temple provides a lunch buffet, and everybody eats in the building's cafeteria. I see Nishant and this new girl, whose family recently immigrated, pick up their food and sit together. My mother comes over and she sees them too, and I can see her marriage-arranging mind twisting around this new possibility. She thinks that I will never get married and will instead cohabit commitment-free with a white guy who never volunteers at community events and who illegally pirates not only music but movies and software as well.

"Go sit with them," she tells me.

"Mom, I don't want to salt his game."

"What? Just go. They're the only ones here your age. Otherwise you'll be sitting with me and your dad and that uncle." She gestures at a sweaty man gripping my father's shirtsleeve.

I take my food over to Nishant and the girl and ask if it's okay if I join them. The girl says, "Of course, welcome!" and I sit. When she talks—about neutral topics such as her recent visit to Lunenburg—she has a slight accent: Indian but with a European twist. When I ask about it, she says she attended an international school in Delhi and lived in London as a child. Her hair is loosely braided, and she wears this jade cotton salwar kameez with a chiffon shawl draped around her shoulders. I can tell she's the kind of girl who excels at Bharatanatyam lessons and remembers which god does what.

Clearly, Nishant is falling madly in love with her, or rather, sanely and rationally in love with her. She's wonderful. When I rise to throw out my Styrofoam plate, he will ask for her number and then he will phone and they will speak of all the things that are important to them, like their Indian heritage and how great it is to be pious. For their first date, they will share vegetarian pizza and say they wish they were eating idli sambar instead. He will notice her hair smells as fragrant as jasmine flowers. Together, they will watch Bollywood movies on VHS without subtitles, and never feel the impulse to mock Shah Rukh Khan. She'll stand up in the middle of *Kuch Kuch Hota Hai* to dance along with the choreography, eyes downcast and demure, hips swinging in a way that is somehow both sensual and modest. They won't have sex, though. They will wait until they are married.

My life will unfold like a game of Mad Libs—a mix of blanks and absurdities.

She is still talking about Lunenburg.

"But have you been to the Maritime Museum? You definitely must visit the Maritime Museum," Nishant tells her. This is a bizarre recommendation coming from a teenager. The best thing about the Maritime Museum is the talking parrot that for some reason lives in the lobby. It's otherwise mostly boats.

"I hadn't heard about it," she says.

"Well, we'll go there." He doesn't include me in this invitation, not that I care. I have been to the Maritime Museum numerous times on school field trips, and once with Nishant and our families. There's a photo of us in an album at home: I'm four and he's six. We stand with a foot of space between us, unsmiling, in front of a cardboard cut-out of the *Titanic*.

||||||||||||

A few days later, I go over to Amy's house in the South End. Since her mom left, her dad has been renting out the base- ment. There are unfamiliar bicycles by the entrance. We go into the house and hunt for snacks. Her kitchen smells vaguely of fish and there's actual produce in the fridge. They used to seem like more of a takeout family; I was envious of how often they had Swiss Chalet. When we were watching a movie in her basement, her mom would sometimes pop her head in with the cordless phone to one ear, to ask for our orders.

Since the basement is now occupied, we smoke a bowl and eat Dunkaroos on the back porch before her dad gets home. Her cat wanders out and we make him hats out of newspaper and take photos with her dad's digital camera.

". . . and then right in front of me he planned a date with her. To the Maritime Museum." I chip at my black nail polish.

"What the fuck? Your life is straight out of a sitcom."

The cat walks over to me, purring. I hug him and he droops in my hands like Nickelodeon Gak. He yawns onto his back and curls sideways as though he's trying to spell *cat* with his body but there isn't enough of him. Amy lights the pipe and then reaches down to hold the lighter flame up to the cat's nipple.

"Amy!" I blow out the lighter as she cackles. The cat rolls lazily in the other direction.

"Relax," she says, "he likes it. Too bad we have to sacrifice him to Satan."

I roll my eyes at her and she grins. Amy isn't a psychopath. Back in Grade 8 I saw her cry while listening to a Boyz II Men album.

I hear her front door open and close. "Your dad?"

"Yeah, he must be home from work." She goes back in and tucks her weed supplies into her oboe case before returning. She sold the oboe over the summer to buy drugs, but her dad doesn't know.

"Nishant doesn't think I'm a good Hindu."

"Wait, you're Hindu?" Amy pretends to fall over, feigning laughter. The cat darts away. "I thought you were a proud coconut." *Coconut*: brown on the outside and white on the inside. She sits back up and stares at me, contemplating. "You have never had, like, an actual problem, have you?"

"That's not true," I say, startled. I'd thought she'd take my side. "What do you mean?" What actualizes a problem?

Her dad fills the doorway. "Pasta for dinner," he says. It's unclear if I'm invited, but if I am, I will politely decline. Swiss Chalet is one thing, but dinners in white households have a choreography I haven't learned. People pass plates around and then balance a dish in one hand while serving themselves with the other and making conversation at the same time. I never ask anyone to pass me things, in case it seems greedy. And I'm never sure how much I'm supposed to eat. To use the washroom, they must ask to excuse themselves, so I never use the washroom. They use fabric napkins and I feel guilty wiping my mouth. They finish dinner at 6:30 and then by 10:30 my stomach gnaws. In Indian homes, dinner is buffet-style and happens an hour after everybody was supposed to be sleeping already. We don't use utensils. My mom says food is more flavourful when you eat it from your hand. We sit on the living room sofa—or cross-legged on the floor if there are more people than seats—and an aunty makes you eat everything and then sends leftovers home with you in reused yogurt containers.

"Amy, is that makeup?" her father asks. She has on a thin cat eye. "That outfit isn't appropriate."

"It says '*Don't* Touch,'" she responds, puffing out her chest.

"Amy. Sweater," he says, frowning in plaid. She gives me an apologetic dads-are-crazy look but goes to get her sweater from the kitchen.

Her dad starts cooking dinner while we go upstairs to dye her hair in the washroom. We run out of dye, so patches show at the roots and this one place in the back, but she tells me it's fine. She tosses her head and her bangs land crooked, an asterisk on her forehead. She fixes them in the mirror as I rub her hair with a fluffy aubergine towel.

"Remember the *Phantom of the Opera* towel?" She snickers.

On the first day of Grade 6 music class, we'd been seated together because of the extremely unlikely coincidence of us both playing the oboe. Most kids in our class hadn't even selected their instruments yet. When the teacher, Mr. Miller, had us stand up one by one to introduce ourselves, Amy said her family had just moved to Halifax from Vancouver. The word *Vancouver* rang through the room like she'd said New Zealand or Tanzania. The rest of us had all been born within a two-hour driving radius of the school.

Then Mr. Miller gave a bitter speech. Amy does an impression of it now, furrowing her brow and deepening her voice: "The music program will be dead before you graduate elementary school." He said things about funding that we didn't understand, and then played a video biography of John Philip Sousa while glowering behind his desk in the back corner, under a massive *Phantom of the Opera* poster. During the video, Amy passed me a note that said: *The Phantom of the Opera poster is a bath towel.* I looked up at the poster/bath towel and realized it was true, and after class we discussed the possible reasons why Mr. Miller would purchase such a bath towel, and that's how we became friends. Periodically, we add to the list of reasons.

"All his other bath towels were stolen," I say.

"He wanted to perform the musical in his bathroom and needed a waterproof costume," says Amy.

"*Phantom of the Bathtub*." I comb out her hair. The music program was, in fact, cancelled by the time we finished Grade 8, and nobody knows what happened to Mr. Miller. I still remember the day Amy and I went to class raving about having just seen *Mr. Holland's Opus*, and he said, "I hate that movie. Don't you see? The teacher *loses* at the end."

I hear a throat clear before I realize Amy's dad is in the hallway, watching us. "What the hell did you do?" he asks. I flinch as though he yelled. I've never heard him raise his voice, although he always seemed like the type of dad who might yell, unlike my dad, who beseeches. Non-Indian dads are different creatures. You can't call them uncle.

"Jesus Christ, what is the matter with you?" he says. "Tell your friend to go home."

He stands there with his arms crossed, seething with a quiet fury as though he has just caught us naked on a flaming pentagram. I hesitate for only a second before I gather up my belongings, because maybe I should help tidy the washroom, which is covered in claw hair clips and gloves and paper towels, black dye and blonde hair. He steps out of the doorway to let me pass, and I think about how nobody this tall ever comes over to our house. He could pluck the winter clothes from the top of our coat closet without standing on a chair like my dad does.

Though it's dark and getting cooler, I wait outside alone for my mom to pick me up. Usually, Amy would wait with me, but her dad made her stay behind in the washroom to clean. I lean against the brick archway that surrounds their front door. Two kids are playing street hockey just a few metres away, clacking the plastic puck back and forth until they lose it under a car. The house door opens, and I turn, expecting Amy, but it's her dad.

"I need to speak with you." He clears his throat again. "Amy is a good kid. She's going through a difficult time, and I would prefer that the two of you stopped spending time together."

I don't know what to say. I want to tell him the hair dye wasn't my idea. Was it my idea? There's a pounding in my chest. And then my hands are shaking, like when I'm getting up the nerve to speak in a class debate. I tuck them under the hem of my shirt. I watch one of the hockey kids crawl out from beneath the car, triumphant, puck in hand. Has Amy been sacrificing animals for real? Why didn't she tell me her dad wouldn't approve of her dyeing her hair?

His words sound practised and formal. The top of his head is bald, and when the porch light shines on his scalp, it casts a strange halo. "It would be best if you didn't come by our house anymore, and Amy won't be visiting your house either. I will be encouraging her to find other friends."

I don't say anything. I wonder what he might know about me that even Amy doesn't know. Or that even I don't know.

"Hey," he says. "Did you hear me?"

The headlights of my mom's car illuminate his plaid shirt. She parks, walks up, and greets him sweetly, deferentially. "Hi there, how are you?"

Amy's dad repeats what he's just said to me.

"How dare you," my mom says. "You asshole. Your kid is the bad one. Not mine." Amy's dad withers like a dried-up spider and dies at our feet.

No, that doesn't happen.

My mom nods her head. "Of course," she says. "We understand."

The hockey kids pause their game to let us drive away. We drive north, past Dalhousie, past the Hydrostone, to where everything looks less historic, less like it belongs in Halifax.

My mom touches my shoulder. "You can't get so close to people. The same thing happened to me when I first came here. You can only trust other Indians." We drive through residential neighbourhoods. Every person we pass is a stranger. She continues: "Indira Aunty is coming for dinner tonight. She has a son the same age as you. He can be a new friend."

"I'm *busy*," I hiss.

"What does that mean? You're busy? I've already invited them. His mom is bringing pulao."

"Why don't *you* go out with him then?"

"Don't be angry," she says, flipping up the sun visor as the sky turns fully dark.

At home, in my bedroom, I dip a cotton pad in Pond's cream and wipe it across my eyelids until the cotton is black. I rearrange the clothing in my closet so colour—an aqua sweater, a denim jacket, a lavender blouse—is back within reach. In my bed, I read the scene from *The Edge of Evil* where a guy rips out a cow's heart with his bare hands.

"It was just standing there," says Danielle from Kansas City, "and they just ripped—while it was still alive—they just ripped its heart out."

Under Microscope

WE ARE WALKING aimlessly around the school track when Amy tells me I'm a bad friend. It's lunch hour and sunny enough to be outdoors. A runner laps us, polyester cross-country uniform rippling in the strong Halifax wind. Amy blows cigarette smoke at his back as he passes, and the smoke twirls and dissipates. There are no teachers around, so there's nobody to enforce the "no smoking on school property" rule.

We pause at one end of the track and, as I kick at a remnant hunk of snow in the grass, Amy says, "Nina, you know . . ." I turn to look at her. "You're not a very good friend." She blinks once and closes her mouth around her cigarette. Her strong jaw seems to clench as she tucks her hair behind her ear. She's dyed it again recently, to an ashy violet.

I crush the snow with the heel of my boot. "Why would you say that?"

"You just aren't," she says, matter-of-fact. We are quiet for the rest of break, as I search over the conversation to figure out what I missed.

The experiment begins in the spring of Grade 11. We're still getting used to the new millennium. I write down the date every chance I get, because it's so satisfying seeing those zeroes all together: *2000*. But there's something anticlimactic about it, too. All that unnecessary hullabaloo about Y2K compliance. All those canned goods in the basement that we'd now have to eat.

Our biology teacher tells us about this doctor in Japan, Masaru Emoto, who took four containers of water and taped a sign to each one:

> *Thank you*
> *Love and appreciation*
> *You make me sick, I will kill you*
> *Adolf Hitler*

He then froze the water and took microscope photos of the ice crystals. Our teacher, Mr. Abernathy, projects these from transparencies, coating the classroom in a luminous wallpaper. We study the images like inkblots. The "You make me sick" crystals are irregular and pocked, like sunken scars. The "Adolf Hitler" crystal patterns remind me of a blotchy brain. In contrast, the containers that had the positive messages form crystals as symmetrical as Denzel Washington's face.

Mr. Abernathy says it has to do with vibrations, an explanation that might apply to *some* of Emoto's experiments—the ones where they murmured prayers over the open containers—but makes no sense for the ones with only the taped signs. Amy and I decide to recreate Emoto's process with two tomato plants, hoping Mr. A will approve it for our independent study project. We plant the tomatoes in the field behind the school, because we no longer go to each other's houses. Amy tucks three seeds into each of the two divots I make in the soil. I croon sweet poems to one and she rudely demeans the other. Only after our experiment is already in progress do I consider the problems and variables: that the seeds are too close together, so each will overhear messages meant for the other and in two different voices; that it's April in Halifax and might snow at any moment. In its lack of controls—its total ignorance of the scientific method—our project is not unlike Emoto's.

"This is not real science," says my dad, who has a Ph.D. in Chemistry from one of India's top-ranked universities. "I could've given you a better idea." He gives me a handwritten list of seven better ideas. But by then it's too late.

After midterms, Amy is failing nearly every course, so I begin tutoring her in biology. We camp out at a table in the main library on Spring Garden Road and review: *xylem, phloem, translocation, transpiration.* Amy is jittery, unfocused, her leg perpetually shaking, her pen spinning in her hand. She slurps an Iced Capp even though food and drinks aren't allowed in the library, and despite having been asked to throw it away by the anxious-seeming librarian. Amy calls the librarian Marian, though I'm pretty sure her name is Sue. Condensation leaves wet rings on the table's laminate surface. Lately, Amy seems to live on sugar and caffeine. In the morning, she gets off the bus with one long gummy worm inching out of the side of her mouth.

We turn to our independent study project, a multi-part assignment to be completed in stages, involving a proposal and a presentation and graphs and reports—the assignment guidelines alone are seven pages.

I pass her the notes I've been writing. "Does this sound okay?"

"Do you ever think teachers give us these crazy long assignments just to reduce their own workloads?" Amy asks. "Think about it, how many class periods has Mr. A given us

to 'work on our projects' or 'visit the library for research.'"
She mimes air quotes. "And what does he do during that time?
I bet he's jerking off in the equipment room."

"Should we add a flare component to our presentation?"
I continue, though I'd like to snap my fingers in front of her
face. "Like a Bristol board or music? I feel like educational
raps have become unexpectedly popular."

"What professional adult wears tie-dyed T-shirts to work?
He just wears them to *seem* as though he's a nice guy when
he's secretly a fascist asshole."

I haven't formed an opinion on Mr. A. He's the breed of
teacher that minimizes interactions with students outside of
the classroom. I want to tell Amy there is still time for her to
boost her grade enough to pass the course—she just needs to
show up and make an effort—but I don't want to sound like
her dad. Or like our calculus teacher, who advised my parents
that if I wanted to get accepted to a decent university I'd have
to "sweat and bleed" calculus. My dad has since adopted the
expression, though he sometimes uses it in the wrong context
on purpose, like telling my mom to sweat and bleed the onions.

Amy's leg shakes so hard it rattles the table. This is unusual
for her, because she smokes a ton of weed—to the extent that
she keeps a one-hitter in the pocket of her backpack and
smokes it before the morning bell rings. She smokes before
gym because she says it makes her legs feel bionic. She smokes
before Calculus because math gives her a migraine. As a result,
she's developed a persistent dry cough, for which she blames
the yet-to-be-removed asbestos in the school walls.

But I love Amy when she's high. She's serene and huggy,
and because she's always wearing black hoodies, her hugs have
a soothing weight, like an X-ray blanket.

"Nina, I have to get going." She gathers up her things
without waiting for an answer. She reaches across the table for

her pencil case, and when she leans closer I notice her makeup is patchy, unblended, as though she put it on in a hurry with a compact mirror. Her lips look like she's been biting off the skin.

"We have to present this on Monday," I remind her.

"Yeah, but it's just the proposal. You can handle that part, right?" She chews her cuticles and waits for me to agree.

"No way, sit down."

"I really have to go."

"Amy . . . Okay. Take these." I hand her the notes. "They're nearly finished. You do the rest, and we can meet Monday morning to go over them."

She gives me an apologetic glance and stuffs the notes in her backpack. She loops her violet hair into a quick bun, revealing the blonde roots. "I really do have to go."

The shoelace on one of her boots is untied, and I think about stepping on it, as though that could hold her in place.

I don't know where Amy goes when she isn't with me or at her house, but I know she goes somewhere. It's wherever she gets her weed from, wherever she meets the people whose names I don't recognize when she mentions them, barking a laugh about some joke that doesn't seem funny. I'm surprised there are places in Halifax that I don't know about. Wherever it is, she found it in the fall, during the brief period when we took a break from each other. Her dad didn't want us to hang out anymore. The nineties were ending, and I thought maybe our friendship was, too.

"What's he going to do, install cameras in the school?" Amy asked.

But to me, what he had said mattered. It was as if I carried his disapproval inside my body, and it changed my frequency. I couldn't relax.

Before the break, Amy's presence in my life was so over-whelming I never even noticed I had no other friends. And then all of a sudden there was nobody to sit with on the concrete block outside the school during lunch, nobody to go to Tim Hortons with after school. When I sang along to *NSYNC, there was nobody there to mock me. Did people notice that I always had an empty seat beside me? I fantasized about picking up an extracurricular with weekly meetings where I could slip into a pre-existing social group. Choir? Trivia Team? I attended one meeting of the Multicultural Society, the least intimidating of all clubs. But when I showed up, there were only three people, all recent immigrants, and I realized I had been mistaken in my assumption that my skin gave me automatic membership. One guy asked, "Why are you here?" Grade 11 is too late to make new friends.

Almost inevitably, our friendship repaired itself after only a few weeks. We had always arranged our schedules to match. In History, our classmate Fergus said something wildly inac-curate about Caligula, and when I glanced up from my desk, I saw Amy spying me from her end of the row. She passed me a note, and when I opened it up it said, *I bet he learned that from the porno version.* I caught her eye again and, in the same instant, we both started cracking up, on opposite sides of the room.

Before that, though, we had moved through the school like two same-charged magnets. And even when we were together again, some of that charge remained.

On Monday, I go to school early with a bouquet of garish plastic flowers I bought from the dollar store. As a joke, I stick them in the soil all around the tomato seedling that we've been treating kindly, hoping Amy will find this amusing. Some girl walks up and says, "Ooh, those are pretty. Where did they come from?" For a second, I wonder if she believes the flowers are real.

Five minutes into Bio, Amy still hasn't shown up. Up at the chalkboard, Mr. Abernathy is explaining something, probably about science, while the kid in the seat in front of me fidgets with a flint lighter under his desk. It makes a rasping sound, sending out occasional flickers.

"Okay folks, project proposals should take up the first half of class, and then we'll do a lab. Volunteers to go first?"

A pair of girls at the front raise their hands. They alternate speaking parts—one says a sentence, the other says the next sentence—cutesy and synchronized and irritating, like twins on the Disney Channel. A couple goes next, the girl in a slouchy maroon toque and the guy dangling keys from his wide-legged jeans. They've been romantically involved for about two weeks, so I question their decision to work together on a semester-long project. Their presentation is good, though. It features both a skit and a Bristol board display. The third presentation is by the other Indian kid in the class, who has self-segregated with the only Asian kid in the class. Anshu immigrated here with her family about a year ago. When she pronounces *eukaryotic* incorrectly, Mr. Abernathy interrupts from a desk at the side of the room, where he is seated like an adjudicator. "It's *eukaryotic*," he says. "Not *eye-car-otic*."

"*Eye-karyotic*," Anshu tries again.

"*EUkaryotic*," repeats Mr. A with an exasperated sigh. He jots something in his gradebook.

"*Eukaryotic*," Anshu whispers.

"Nina and Amy," calls Mr. A. "You're up."

"Amy isn't here," I tell him.

"What's that?" He peers at me over his glasses, mid-grimace. "Amy isn't here today."

"Well, where is she?"

"I don't know." The class turns to watch me, twitchy and alert as bunnies on a public lawn, waiting to see if I'll get in trouble.

"Okay, well, there are no extensions. You can either give the presentation yourself or take a zero."

"We did the work. It's just that Amy has all our presentation notes," I say.

"No excuses, extensions, or exceptions. I suppose you'll be taking the zero." He opens his gradebook, the room so quiet I can hear his pencil scratching.

Amy's dad calls my house that afternoon to ask if I've seen her. "Where could she have gone?" he asks, with the tone and timbre of a child. I haven't heard his voice in months, though he doesn't seem to realize this.

I'm not afraid yet. In my head I hear the theme song from *Where in the World Is Carmen Sandiego?* and think about the odd choice of naming the character after a city—was that meant to be a clue? I search Amy's usual haunts, and it's as though I'm touring the set of a movie I watched a long time ago: Here is the Value Village where we both bought everything we own. Here is the Tim Hortons parking lot where she drank infinite Iced Capps and flirted mercilessly with strangers from other high schools, as I stood like an art installation next to her, trying to look cool. Here is the stretch of the Halifax Waterfront where we sprinted up the side of the wave sculpture at dusk to sit at the top, legs cold against the concrete, the ocean turning deep blue, then black, as the light disappeared.

Later that evening, her dad comes to our door. "What is this?" he asks, standing on our front porch and shaking an empty lightbulb in my face.

"I don't know," I tell him, stepping back to see what he's holding up.

But he doesn't believe me. "What do you mean you don't know?" He keeps holding the glass object in the air and shaking it, his expression a hurricane, his eyes looking past me, into me.

My dad appears behind me and gently shoos me away. He puts his hands on Amy's dad's shoulders and walks him into our living room. He sits him down.

I listen from the upstairs landing. "I've called the police," her dad says. He has also called her mother's sister in Toronto, since nobody knows where Amy's mother is. He searched Amy's room and found drawers haphazardly emptied. At the back of one drawer he found the lightbulb with the insides removed and the outside glass burned black.

They speak for nearly an hour, her dad's voice lifting in panic and collapsing into sporadic sobs, my dad's patient and calming—I picture a pure sine wave rising from his mouth.

School without Amy is like a sitcom where the actor playing the main character suddenly dies and the writers are forced to rework the show around it: there's a negative space, a subtraction in the universe where Amy should be. In the mornings, I snooze my alarm ten minutes and then another ten minutes. When I wake, my stomach is roiling with dread. I'm afraid now, the fear so deep it tangles through my intestines and spills up like bile. I check my email obsessively, but Amy doesn't contact me. I smoke a joint in the grass by our two tomato plants, invalidating the experiment by saying cruel things to them both. "I hope you both die," I tell them, tapping ash onto their heads and imagining their cells recoiling and withering. I hope I die, too. I go to class high and wonder if this is what it feels like to be Amy, half here and half there. My parents begin to avoid me, unsure of how to handle this sullen animal. At night, when he thinks I'm asleep, my dad prays at my bedroom doorway, at a safe distance. My sadness makes them shy; it pours into them like second-hand smoke.

In Grade 7, between Social Studies and recess, our teacher challenged us to draw a map of Canada from memory. All of our maps were terrible. Some were lazy sets of ovals; others aimed too hard for accuracy and left the coasts half-finished. Mine was tentative, with an upside-down rabbit shape in the middle (Hudson Bay) and some wiggly trapezoids up by Greenland. Afterwards, the teacher tasked me with Scotch-taping the maps to the wall beside the blackboard, around an actual map of Canada. The intent may simply have been to humiliate us.

At the start of recess, the teacher left to find coffee and the rest of the class went outside. I lingered, to finish posting the maps. Under the wall of maps was a cabinet where our teacher kept our class files. There was a manila folder for each of us. I don't know why the cabinet wasn't locked.

My file chronicled my boring pursuits—an English award, a copy of my (rejected) Legislative Page application. It was Amy's file that had pulled me to the cabinet with the force of a first crush. I opened the folder under the shield of the cabinet and found homework assignments and self-evaluations where she'd given herself all Bs. There were notes our teacher had made of her meeting with Amy's father. He'd said that Amy needed to be "taken down a few pegs." The teacher had put the phrase in quotes and underlined it. It was the kind of statement my own parents would never have made. Sometimes, after that, when I looked at Amy, I pictured her hanging from a pegboard like the one her dad had in the garage. It held all the sharpest tools: drill, file, handsaw.

Weeks after Amy disappears, she sends an email to her dad confirming that she has left home for good. She's sixteen, legally able to move out, to drop out; it is impossible to compel her to come back. I've been picturing her either dead or far away: speaking hobbling French in a Montreal youth shelter; under a Toronto overpass, grasping a squeegee; panhandling in some greyer, grittier city. Isn't that where you go when you run away? But it turns out she's less than two hours from here, staying on the couch of a friend in New Glasgow.

"She left school?" asks my mom in disbelief, as though I've told her that Amy left Earth for Mars. "But where will she go?"

"I don't know."

My parents and I are having dinner, but I can't eat. I remember the time Amy came over and my mom made masala dosas. Amy, mid-craving, ate three of them. My mom was so pleased she told all her friends. That was before Amy stopped eating real food. She was healthy, and then she wasn't. I thought it was a fad diet. Nobody I knew used *actual* drugs, but every girl in our school was on an experimental eating plan. At the start of the semester, she was the thinnest girl there.

"Don't you ever do that. Quit school," my mom tells me.

"Obviously."

My dad is quiet, the tines of his fork scraping against the stainless-steel plate.

"What 'obviously'?" says my mom. "I knew she was not a good friend for you. It should have been obvious to her, no? That she just threw her life away?"

My dad sets down his fork. He wipes his mouth, and says, "We don't know what happens in another person's house."

I immerse myself in the independent study—now truly independent—even though I know the experiment is pointless. We're not real scientists. It's not as though the results will have any impact on the world. I keep thinking of the jokes Amy would want to add into the report, and how I would have to remind her that the assignment guidelines state we should adhere to a formal style. I check the spelling. I trim the extra commas. I print out the final version, leaving space between sections to ink in illustrations of plants in various stages of life. My report looks like the castle from *Sleeping Beauty*, grown over during a hundred years of sleep.

Days after I hand in my finished project, Mr. Abernathy asks to speak to me after class. He's wearing a cardigan over his tie-dye. My report is open in front of him. I had it bound at my mom's office, but he's pressed open the plastic cover, leaving a permanent crease.

He clears his throat. "Did you really write this?" It takes me a second to understand that his tone is accusatory. He seems to take my pause as an admission of guilt. "This isn't your work."

"Yes, it is."

He has a small smile on his face but doesn't say anything. I wait.

"Okay." It's evident from his tone that he doesn't believe me, though he hasn't read my writing before. All he's seen are my test answers, mostly formulas, facts, numbers. "Look," he tells me, "I know in other areas of the world, copying is more acceptable. It's part of the culture."

I'm from Halifax, I want to argue. Amy was right about

him being an asshole. Instead I say, "I wrote it." I try not to show my contempt.

"Well, it's clear this isn't your writing. Did your partner write it before she left?"

"No," I insist. "I wrote it myself."

"Okay, all right. Whatever you say. I don't have the *physical* evidence to take this case forward, but consider this a serious warning."

He hands me back the assignment. On the front page he's written a perfect grade and, next to it, a big red question mark.

On the library computer I look up Emoto's experiment to see if there's something out there that resembles my report. The only result is on a Grade 4 science teacher's class webpage. It has, verbatim, the same info Mr. Abernathy gave us back in the first week of class, plus some commentary by the Grade 4 teacher. She points out that the human body is 60 per cent water. I picture extracting water molecules from my body, from Amy's, freezing them and examining them under microscope. In the teacher's highly subjective conclusion, she writes: "Only things originating from a kind heart can survive." Is this true? What counts as survival?

I use the library's paper cutter to shred the assignment into a zillion ribbons, then let them drift into the recycling bin. There's a poster on the wall in front of me that claims *You can do anything*. Another hypothesis that will go unproven.

After walking around the track that lunch hour, Amy and I had stood in the back field for the last few minutes, waiting, as always, for the bell to ring. She leaned against the metal side of a portable classroom, her hands twisting a young dandelion. Brooding. She hadn't eaten anything.

I used to think I was an exceptional friend. I thought I noticed everything. I thought it was enough to notice.

Before she left me at the library, I'd had one final look. The last time I saw her. Clomping boots with the untied lace. Chewed lips and cuticles. The unwashed hair of a girl who smokes cigarettes belonging to other people. And that familiar action: arms reaching behind her and holding the bottom of her backpack to alleviate the weight.

Do you want to talk about it? I could have asked—not just then, but so many other times in the years I knew her.

What else do you want to tell me?

What else have we not told each other?

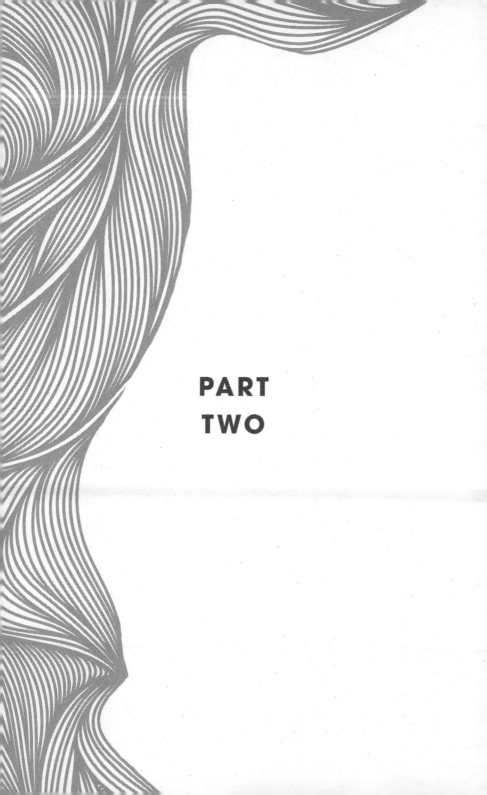

PART TWO

Mute

EVERYONE IS DRUNK. It's like I'm in a John Cheever story—or maybe I only think that because he's all over the syllabus of our Character Development class, where the professor reads stories aloud to us with theatrical enunciation and tells us about the old days when he used to drink with Cheever.

A month and a half ago, I moved to Baltimore to attend a graduate creative writing program. Baltimore is a port city, but not like Halifax, where you always remember you're near the ocean. In Baltimore, you always remember you're in the setting of *The Wire*. My classmates—there are nine of them—seem overwhelmingly American. They're all white and have New York or Southern accents, and their voices boom over my head. Was I this quiet in Canada? I can't remember. In bars, my classmates always know what drinks to order and are decisive about where to sit or stand. When they ask why I decided to apply here, I vaguely mention better funding, though really, I'm not sure: *Why hadn't I just stayed in Halifax?*

We are at a department party at the faculty club. Rooms open into rooms. Each room has a name—The Nobel Room, The Milton Eisenhower Room, etc.—and crown moulding

on high ceilings, and tall windows with pleated brocade cur-
tains. All of the employees are racial minorities, which makes
me question which side of the room I should be on. The
waitstaff carry silver trays covered with bits of puff pastry and
skewered scallops topped with pea sprouts and ginger miso
cream. There's an open bar.

Five of my classmates are discussing their midterm teaching evaluations.

"I read mine after like half a bottle of limoncello," says
Natasha, whose lipstick has left a flawless red half-lip on her
wine glass.

"Mine were excellent overall," says Murphy, who is wearing a bowtie and speaking in a maybe-ironic voice. "I plan to
address the constructive criticism over the next few weeks."

Most of them received comments calling them "inspiring"
and complimenting their clothing or facial features. I can only
remember the two bad ones I received, one of which said,
"Though the course has the word 'creative' in its title, the
instructor does not seem like a creative person." And the
other: "Spoke a lot but said little."

An alum approaches, wearing a suit the colour of but-
tercream, an open collar, and wingtip shoes. He's a former
literary wunderkind who keeps attending department parties
even though he graduated in the nineties. In profile, his hair
is a tilde—a perfect sideways wave. The two older female secretaries fawn over him as he pushes his hair back from his
forehead, and his eyes flit past them for someone more important to talk to. I've developed a guilty, nebulous crush on him
and wish I wasn't clutching a crumpled napkin full of empty
skewers. His critically acclaimed first novel, published a decade
ago, concerns a fictional protagonist who is also a writer and
the same age as him and an eternal bachelor who struggles
with commitment and the meaning of literature while living

and socializing with three friends in New York. It's basically *Sex and the City* with men. Before I fall asleep I sometimes fantasize about lying to him and pretending that I, too, once lived the ennui-filled life of an editorial assistant in New York City, to woo him by way of our commonalities. This is what someone on a WB show would do.

Along with the alum comes Professor Coates, an older, imposing man who is known to scream at people in his office when the door is closed. "A delight to see all of you." He raises his glass. He begins with small talk—"How are you all finding it here?"—and then segues into a discussion of the program's long history and expounds on its notable alumni. "This fellow here," he says, thumping the alum's shoulder, "was on a thirty-under-thirty list not too long ago, as I recall." My guess is that the list came out in 1995. Still, I feel awed to have ascended into this world where writers are real people you know—and I'm ashamed of having not yet published anything. As I'm fretting about this, I sort of lose track of the conversation. And then I'm studying the black cocktail dresses of the other female guests and realizing that I'm dressed quite wrong, in a cotton floral A-line skirt with a hem that lands below my knees. Earlier, when I came out of a washroom stall, one of the secretaries said, "Oh, Nina, I knew it was you from the shoes."

Professor Coates and the alum are discussing a short story, but I can't tell which one. My classmates are all throwing in astute observations about the story's restraint of language and the unmatchable elegance of its ending. The alum makes a pun involving the story's title that causes Professor Coates to laugh so hard he needs to hold his whiskey with both hands. By now, most of the class has gathered around, along with three faculty members. The air is filled with rhetoric.

"You—" says Professor Coates. He's pointing at me. This is the first time he has spoken to me at all. Everyone turns in my direction, smiles fading at his sudden shift in tone. "Why don't you contribute something to the conversation?"

In the background, dishes clink. I say nothing. I've gone mute.

After I was accepted to the program, my peer advisor, a second-year student, sent me a lengthy, stream-of-consciousness email in which he warned me that in Baltimore there were more rats than people. He forwarded a link to an interactive map of health violations at local restaurants, and it was dotted with rodent icons. In one section of the city, he said, a garbage truck had sunken into the street, swarmed by rats that had eaten through the ground below.

Don't live below 25th Street, he advised. *And never take public transit.* I wasn't sure what to make of this—I couldn't afford a car, so how would I get around? *Always lock your doors,* he said. *This is Bodymore, Murderland. The city that bleeds.* This was counter to what I'd read on a tourism website, which had called it "The City That Reads." I suppose this was their equivalent of the Discover Halifax website prominently featuring Celtic fiddlers, when everyone I knew listened to alternative rock.

When I first moved here, following the portentous wisdom of my peer advisor, I read the crime reports and thought about getting a gun. There was a rumour that if you raised your arms above your head on campus at night, sensors would alert campus police. My apartment is beyond the reach of their protection. Each night a man who lives down the street stands on his porch and yells, "Where you going?" at anyone who passes. Once, when I ducked my head without answering, he followed me for several metres. "Hey! Where you going? Will you clean my house?" he shouted at my back, and I could tell from the rising volume that he was getting closer. My right hand clutched my apartment key inside my pocket, ready to use it as a weapon, and when I got to my building I walked past the door and around the block, back in the direction of campus, until I was sure he was gone. After that, I began using my building's rear entrance to avoid walking past his house.

Every day I encounter a new insect in my apartment, each leggier or wilier than the last. The cockroaches travel in packs, like moving rugs. One morning I found a long house centipede curled in the water glass on my nightstand.

To calm myself I read Halifax newspapers online, though the familiar pictures of columnists make my heart ache. I unpack a box and find a rape whistle with my old university's logo on it. I blow into it gently, and the sound is bird-like, unusually clear.

But in some ways, my peer advisor's impressions seem to conflict with what I actually see: A robust set of libraries and museums in stately, sky-lit buildings. Discount shops with chatty owners offering bags of irregularly shaped cleaning sponges for a dollar each. Pies that are far more delicious than any pie I've had in Canada. Laughing people gathering on porches painted lime green or cherry red, seeming so extraordinarily happy that walking past them stirs my sadness.

It turns out my peer advisor's list of safe neighbourhoods is an exact match with the list of gentrified areas I discover on a website describing the city's complicated history of segregated housing. It strikes me that much of what he told me was racism, unadulterated and covert, and from then on, I can't trust what is real about the city and what isn't.

This is Baltimore.

||||||||||||

In undergrad, I stayed in residence even though my parents lived ten minutes from campus. I had a crowd of friends. We met in a first-year orientation meeting, where a team of university employees told us about a girl who left her room door unlocked and woke up to find a man sitting in the chair next to her bed, watching her. Then the orientation leaders handed out the rape whistles and told us to protect ourselves. With the bright objects dangling from our necks, we asked, "When exactly are we supposed to blow the whistle?"

These girls and I shared a bank of showers and ate our meals together, but we did not know one another's origin stories, aside from the basics: Most were from out of province. One had been her high school's valedictorian. Another was a junior golf champion. I had only a vague sense of relative wealth because everyone wore sweatpants, the great equalizer. Besides, there was so much happening in the present—who had time to talk about the past? These were harmless friendships, easy ones, unlike the quicksand friendships of childhood. With this group, I blended in, aside from every now and then, when I would tell a joke and someone would turn to me and say, "You're so funny, Nina!" I would file that moment away to replay to myself later, and then I'd vanish contentedly into the group again. After a while, we said and did things that were funny only to us, like how we referred to our first-year residence assistant, Martin Case, as "Justin Case," or how whenever we saw a long line on campus we would go stand in it and there was always free food at the other end, except for that one time when the line was for a blood drive. We pulled all-nighters and ate donairs and slept through morning classes and still got good grades without Adderall. When we went out, it was to pubs where we knew everyone, and the whole crowd was singing along to "Barrett's Privateers."

||||||||||

On the Friday after the reception, I get a call from a guy in my program. Eli writes fiction but has the expressiveness of a spoken word poet. He says a bunch of people are going to a bar called The Charles. He tells me I should come along and, since we live in the same neighbourhood, we should share a cab.

"Unless you already have plans?" he asks.

I was in the process of spreading Borax on the floor because I'd read that it is abrasive to a cockroach's exoskeleton. "Just a night in reading Faulkner."

"I'll call you when we leave here," he says.

I put heels on first, to stay high above the roaches. I purchased the shoes the day after the department party and now lurch around my closet seeking a dress. A YouTube search yields a makeup tutorial.

Once I'm ready, I start watching one of the *Fraggle Rock* DVDs I rented from Video Americain, a Baltimore institution with a hip French name. The store has 30,000 films crammed into the basement of a Charles Village row house, with sections organized by country and director, and employees who can school you on the early works of John Waters and slip you a bootleg copy of his short film *Hag in a Black Leather Jacket*. There's a Jim Henson exhibit on next week at the Smithsonian, and *Fraggle Rock* was a favourite of mine as a child. I owned a full set of the Happy Meal toys, each with a Fraggle sitting in a car shaped like a vegetable.

The most captivating character on the show is Marjory the Trash Heap, a wise woman literally made out of garbage. Now and then a Fraggle will sneak through the Gorgs' Garden to request her advice. She is a trash oracle. In answer to the Fraggle's question, Marjory and her two nasty rat disciples will sing a nonsensical song, and she'll bop her garbage-pile body around, snapping her banana-peel fingers while one rat accompanies her on the harmonica. How many roaches are in that heap?

I watch an episode, but Eli doesn't call. It's nearing 10:30. How late do people go out in Baltimore? Probably later than in Halifax, I figure, remembering nights I stumbled back to my dorm over cobbled potholes after shared and spilled pitchers of Rickard's Red, an arm thrown over a friend's shoulder, my hair frizzing in the inevitable fog. I watch another two episodes of *Fraggle Rock*. Then it's 11:30. I pace the carpet, and my heels leave a blotchy trail of Borax. I think about texting Eli but don't. Maybe he did this on purpose, I think. Or, more likely—and more embarrassingly—he just forgot.

At midnight I wash off my makeup and go to sleep. In the morning, my phone has one notification: a Facebook message. Anxiety blooms and swirls in my chest, but it's from an older aunty, a friend of the family, who became a social media expert after moving into a home last summer.

> My birthday was lovely with all the loving notes, the little ones and my boys taking me to breakfast and bringing an orchid and carnations. Your mom phoned from Halifax. In short, it really was a nice day except that one of the women I have become friendly with here died suddenly. Hope your day was good, too.

It's like I've been sucked into this Nabokov story we have to teach in our intro classes, where all that happens is that this kid has a really shitty day. He goes to a party at another kid's family's estate and joins in a game of hide-and-seek, but while he is hiding between a wardrobe and a Dutch stove the others forget about him and abandon the game to picnic on bilberry tarts. At the end of the story he imagines faking his own suicide to make everybody else feel bad. I read one of the lines aloud in class—"*One could hear a clock hoarsely ticktocking and that sound reminded one of various dull and sad things*"—and then started laughing insanely. The students laughed along with me in this magical millisecond of connection. I felt so grateful that they got the joke.

The next Saturday I take the Amtrak to D.C. to visit the Smithsonian's Jim Henson exhibit. I join a tour group that stands in a semicircle facing Kermit the Frog in a glass box. His green felt body looks inanimate and small surrounded by all the humans. The woman giving the tour refers to Kermit as "Henson's alter ego."

While she speaks, a scene from *Fraggle Rock* keeps flashing in my head: Boober, who is the Fraggle I most identify with—he's always worried and for some reason doesn't have eyeballs—approaches the trash heap and asks, "Please, Ma'am, can you make me brave and daring and bold?"

After a pause and some banter, Marjory rises from the garbage heap—or rather, the garbage rises and forms Marjory—and she puffs up like an inflatable couch to deliver her pronouncement: "Always wear a hat." She and the rats sing away any follow-up questions.

The tour group rounds a corner into a hall of more Muppets in glass cases. The guide says that, for her, entering this room feels like coming home: "They taught us how to count, how to read . . ."

I hear somebody behind me ask, "So, who's your favourite Muppet?"

When I turn, I see this big, bearded guy grinning down at me. My first thought is that he's so massive he could puppeteer Mr. Snuffleupagus. He's twinkle-eyed and fidgety in a Georgetown sweatshirt, the sleeves pulled down over his hands. I wonder how long he's been standing there, asking women this question.

"Sweetums," I say.

"Which one is that?"

"He's the giant ogre. In his first appearance he tried to eat Kermit, but later he just sang Wagnerian operas." I learned this minutes ago from a placard on the wall.

"Mine is Sam the Eagle, for his integrity." The guy's beard is dense and black with fine wiry hairs; I'm reminded of the Maritimes and the whittled wooden fishermen they sell at Peggy's Cove.

After the tour, we continue to wander together through the exhibit, and he occasionally bumps my elbow with his, pointing out a new Muppet drawing or fact. I like that this physical contact feels uncalculated, just a part of his personality. As we head to the gift shop, I keep repeating in my head the name Charles Etienne de St. Valery Bon, which I memorized for a bizarrely specific weekly quiz on *Absalom, Absalom!* The inner chanting has a calming effect. The big guy, whose name turns out to be James, reads aloud from a children's book about an anthropomorphized stegosaurus, while I peer at turquoise and agate jewellery. We flip through all the art posters in the rack, their plastic frames clacking together one by one.

"I hate to leave you, but I have to get back to work," James says, motioning towards the door with his head because he has a souvenir magnet in each of his hands.

"Oh. It's Saturday." I imagine the next hour: taking the train home, turning the lights on in my apartment, watching the cockroaches scatter.

"I would love to make you baked ziti sometime."

"Okay, sure," I say in an atonal stutter, but inside I am

swooning—*baked ziti.* "I'm a vegetarian, though, and I live in Baltimore."

"No problem. Do you have an eight-inch square baking dish?"

He walks me to Union Station and says goodbye in a Kermit the Frog voice. On the train ride home I start mentally preparing a tiramisu. Out the window, Baltimore is as youthful as a college town. Everywhere, late-afternoon sunlight falling on red brick. I see a rat, but for once it is running in the opposite direction.

In the week before James makes it to Baltimore, we have three euphoric phone conversations—conversations with no allusions to Philip Roth or drunken confessions about our fears of never getting published. He doesn't even want to get published—he wants a Ph.D. in Biochemistry. During our first phone call he tells me that bee venom is acidic. I tell him I've never been stung by a bee, but as a child I was obsessed with the movie *My Girl*, in which Macaulay Culkin's character is stung, has an anaphylactic reaction, and dies. In the funeral scene, his best friend, Vada Sultenfuss, floats past a roomful of grown-ups wearing black, clutches the edge of his casket, and cries, "He can't see without his glasses! Put his glasses on!" Her grief was a sharp object I swallowed. I memorized that scene, trapped in a loop of playing and rewinding my VHS copy in my parents' VCR.

That week, I add a long scene to a story I'm writing about a girl who gets dumped by her boyfriend and then buys ice cream at a convenience store near Point Pleasant Park. As she sits on a bench by the ocean, she becomes so engrossed in the rare sight of a crested caracara alighting on a white birch that she lets the ice cream melt.

We workshop my story promptly that Friday—the same day James is scheduled to come to my place and bake ziti. The professor is a woman who speaks firmly and eloquently, as though her words have an underlying rhythm. She has brown hair cropped an inch below her ears and a clear gaze that looks through you, along with whatever you've written. On the back of your manuscript she'll write a one-sentence critique. Reading it, your mind oscillates and fragments and flowers into a billion ideas. Sometimes, when she speaks in class, she is so brilliant I hold myself still, to keep the enchantment from breaking.

At the other end of the table is a lanky guy named Tom, who says, "There's a real opportunity here in the symbolism, but I don't buy that she'd be distracted by a bird for so long that the ice cream would actually melt."

"I didn't know anything could melt in the Canadian climate," adds Murphy, a charming, affable fellow whose last story was about keeping a woman as a slave.

"What is a South American bird doing on the east coast of Canada?" asks Francis, the fact checker.

"Is it meant as hyperbole, do you think?" wonders Natasha, the only other female student in the class. She wears her scarf looped in ways I try and fail to replicate.

"The whole thing is very lyrical, as your work always is," says Graeme, quiet and serious, nodding at me, "but the sentences are long. Aren't we past long sentences? But beautiful stuff, undoubtedly."

"Can a type of sentence go out of style?" asks the undergraduate next to me, who is auditing the class and evidently hasn't read the story. Nobody has bothered to learn his name. He's been drawing continuously through the discussion, and he has sketched the professor in black felt-tip pen on his copy of the manuscript. It doesn't do her justice.

Our classes are held in a room at the top of a brick tower. It has five tall, hexagonal windows without screens. A bright orange oriole flew in once, whistling and rustling around the top of the table before the caretakers managed to shoo him out again. Now the table has eleven copies of my story on it, dog-eared and scribbled over in various colours of ink. After the discussion my classmates will hand their copies to me, and I'll go to one of those desks in the stacks of the library and read them one by one. I'll highlight each criticism and hold each morsel of praise in my mouth like an everlasting gobstopper.

"Why does this one character have an Indian name?" Francis asks. "Like the characters aren't doing anything Indian . . . Could the story be set in India instead? Or in the dinner scene could they be eating chicken tikka masala?"

"I don't want to be prescriptive," says Tom, his long legs endlessly jiggling under the table, "but you gotta change the names of the twin brothers. One of their names, at least. Who gives twins rhyming names? Why would you do that?"

I can think of two pairs of twins with rhyming names: 1) on the TV show *The Bachelor*, where Bachelor Brad Womack brought on his twin brother Chad to see if the women could tell the difference (they could); and 2) in a comic strip called *Ram and Shyam*, the Indian equivalent of *Goofus and Gallant*. But I don't say this. You aren't allowed to speak while your own story is workshopped, though you have a chance to respond at the end of the discussion. The undergraduate had used this time as an opportunity to explain why everyone's suggestions for his story were incorrect; throughout the workshop you could see he was not fully listening but storing up his responses like acorns in his cheeks.

Out one of the hexagonal windows I can see the grass of the quad and, farther beyond, an apartment building where F. Scott Fitzgerald lived while Zelda convalesced in a nearby sanatorium. Our Character Development professor told us this, gesturing to the building with his copy of *This Side of Paradise*, as I imagined Zelda writhing in a straitjacket worn over a flapper dress.

"The guy's motivations for breaking up with her don't make much sense," says Natasha. "He ends it because she refuses to ask for directions? Is this a gender thing?"

She's referring to a flashback scene in the story, where the couple travels to France and the girl wants to visit the best macaron shop in Paris, so they wander the 6th arrondissement but can't find it. The guy tells the girl that this is the ideal opportunity to practise her French by asking a passerby for directions, but she refuses and won't tell him why.

"Why won't she?" asks Murphy, and they all turn to me, even the professor.

I had the answer figured out when I was writing the story— because the story is partly autobiographical. It has to do with fear, but also with having made fear into a habit for so long that it is now instinctual. I'm trying to think of how to articulate this, but I feel as though I have a cold metal ball rolling in my throat. The professor looks me in the eye for a second before turning back to the page and writing something down.

The truth is I've never been to Paris. I've never even eaten a macaron. I wanted to write about the kinds of relationships that last as briefly as a song. Like the ones I had with my university friends who, after graduation, went off to other parts of Canada and the world, as though they'd never con-sidered staying. We spent four years together, joking in our pajamas and dreaming—and then that time was over. We started an email chain to keep in touch, but it dwindled to nothing halfway through the summer.

After class I walk straight to one of the lower levels of the library (its floors go deep underground, so it is exceptionally quiet). I tuck myself into a study cubicle and read the scribbled comments on each copy of my story, sucking in my breath, saving the professor's for last. When I get to hers, I go through every page, noting each word she has circled and every question mark in the margins. Then I flip to the back to read her final remarks.

You can do better, she's written. And under that: *The best macaron shop in Paris is in the 12th arrondissement.*

James arrives at my door with a backpack full of vegetables and dry noodles. He has a baseball cap on, and it seems like he's changed his beard, trimming it significantly. There's more neck showing, pale and newly shaved. He and the backpack overwhelm my kitchen, which has enough room for a table the size of a bicycle wheel. Onto the table go the ingredients: a lump of mozzarella, a crisp white onion, a can of crushed tomatoes, a container of ricotta, and an assortment of mushrooms in a paper bag. I get out two cutting boards and two knives, and we begin chopping—James on the table and me on the wedge of free counter space.

Prior to his arrival, I swept up the Borax and turned on every lamp to scare the cockroaches into submission. We haven't really spoken yet, except for hellos and a twenty-second tour of my studio apartment: A twin bed that doubles as seating since there's no couch. A desk I found by a dumpster. A shelf that holds only the books I need for my courses—Faulkner, Fitzgerald, Hemingway. ("You must read a lot!" James exclaimed.) He complimented my embroidered Mexican pillows, his positivity so incongruous with the sad nature of my apartment that I wondered if he meant it sincerely, before deciding that he probably did.

Conversation is difficult without the Muppets. When we talked on the phone at night I said silly, flirtatious things—a mistake that was easy to make when the room was dark and the only light was coming from the year-round holiday bulbs dotting the eaves of the house across the street. I could keep my eyes closed, the cool plastic of my phone balanced between my cheek and the pillow. I didn't have to make eye contact.

He chops the mushrooms clumsily. This kind of claustrophobia flows over me—a reaction to his being in my apartment. I want him to go home. I wish that we were finished eating, that he was catching his train and heading back to D.C., so I could comfortably end things by phone tomorrow. This is probably irrational. I try to recall if there's anything about this in my Myers-Briggs profile. I chop the onion with robotic precision. He reaches past me to get the can opener and pauses to rub my back. It feels like the hand of a total stranger.

We eat the pasta on my bed while watching *The Wire* on my laptop.

"They filmed a scene in my grocery store," I tell James.

"I was on the same plane as McNulty once." He leans in and rasps against me with his beard. The ziti is mush in my mouth. The mozzarella has cooled into a skin. I set it on the floor by the bed. James moves closer, wraps his arm around me, and gives me this smooch sort of kiss—all gums and teeth.

"It's bright in here," he says. Then he stands up and turns off all my lamps. It's just us and the neighbour's Christmas lights, and it should feel romantic. Instead, I think of cockroaches rushing through drainpipes and silverfish slipping into electric sockets. I think of the train that will take James back to Washington. Earlier I consulted the schedule in anticipation of his arrival and noticed that the last train left at 11:15. When I take the plates back to the kitchen, I check the oven clock and it's already 10:30. It'll take at least twenty minutes to get to Penn Station. That means he has to leave by 10:50 to be safe.

When the episode ends, he puts on the next one and then
settles back into place beside me. We have time for half of it,
probably.

On *The Wire*, McNulty says, "Fuck this case."

Daniels tells him, "This case is going to move forward
with you or without you."

I keep thinking of the time and trying to guess how much
has passed. James cracks a topical joke, and although I missed
the beginning, I just laugh anyway. He kisses me again, the
brim of his hat joining our foreheads, his hand low on my
back. I turn away, pretending to be invested in what is happening on the show, though I've zoned out of several scenes
and have lost the thread of the story. I try to remember if
James mentioned having a friend in Baltimore that he's planning to stay with. If he doesn't, I can't ask him to stay at a
hotel or take a several-hundred-dollar cab ride back, can I?
And I certainly can't afford to offer to pay for it. Did he check
the schedule? Did he assume he was staying here?

I know I should just ask, so I consider how I might phrase
the question. "Do you know what time your train's leaving?"
Or, more simply: "What time's your train leaving?" But
wouldn't that sound as though I'm trying to get rid of him?
It isn't really that late for a date to end.

When I check the time again, it's 11:00. James will miss
his train. When the show ends, he stretches his long arms
behind him, yawning. "One more?" he asks. "Or is that
enough TV for one night?"

"That might be it for me," I say. "I'm getting sleepy."

He raises his eyebrows. "It's still early, but I guess we
could go to bed. I've got a morning train ride tomorrow."

I go to the washroom and change into my PJs, which I
button austerely to the neck. When I come out, James has
undressed to only his boxers. We get into my bed, and I notice

how small it is for a long man whose knobbed feet angle out from under the blankets. The bed's size forces us close, two spoons pressed coldly together. His beard is against the back of my neck, lips kissing gently. His hand roves over my hip. I make myself stay still. I impersonate taxidermy. James must know I'm not asleep. When his fingers pass my stomach, it's rigid.

Be reasonable, I tell myself. In the morning he'll catch his train and I'll never see him again. I can wait it out, just as I waited out my panic at the edge of Point Pleasant Park last summer, sitting on a bench facing the Atlantic, gripping the weathered seat planks on either side of me, trying to get ahead of my erratic breath. I focused on the caracara poised plumply on a branch, raising the finger-like edges of its wings.

From here it could fly to Portugal and never see a soul.

Hindu Christmas

I'M SITTING IN THE middle of a crowd of people on a huge red-and-gold medallion rug from Canadian Tire and watching a dancer performing solo. She's acting out the Sanskrit lyrics of the song that crackles over the speaker system. Around the temple, statues of goddesses mimic her expressions. Her eyes are kohl-rimmed, giving the whites of her eyes an otherworldly gleam, and when the music turns sorrowful, they widen and brim with tears. Even her chin emotes.

"So expressive," murmurs one of the aunties sitting behind me.

The dancer, whose name is Savithri, is staying at my parents' house. She's visiting from India for a few months to complete a medical technician course, and she also happens to be a professionally trained dancer. My mom says she's related to us, though I doubt anyone could pinpoint how.

Savithri is wearing metal costume jewellery so heavy I can feel its weight on my own neck. Garlands of white flowers hang down her back, attached to a pitch-black braid that flings outwards from her waist as she spins. The performance alternates between quick, elegant leaps and slow poses that require athletic balance. Her movements are angular and fluid, as precise as math. Clusters of bells are strapped to her ankles, producing a tight, rhythmic jingle with each thump of her feet against the concrete floor, which has been painted maroon. The soles of her feet are caked with grey dirt—the temple caretakers seem to paint the floor instead of cleaning it. I imagine the layers of paint accumulating millimetre by millimetre, for centuries, until the floor meets the ceiling and there is no space for us.

An aunty comes to sit beside me. "Nina, how long has it been since I saw you? Do you even remember me?"

"How could you even ask that question, Aunty?" I say, in the cheerful voice I use to communicate with aunties. I have no idea who she is.

"So, how are you liking Boston? Studying journalism, right?"

"Oh, it's, ah, Baltimore." Aunties in Halifax view U.S. cities as interchangeable. Also, nobody can figure out why I would have gone to Baltimore. "It's okay, I guess . . ." I don't tell her I was there to study creative writing, because that would only baffle her, and because correcting her twice seems rude.

"So good to have you here. Heading back after the holidays, I suppose." She squeezes me with one arm, and I'm enveloped in strong synthetic perfume. I let her make her assumptions, while I lean into her warmth.

We clap as the dance ends. Savithri stands with palms pressed together for a second, out of breath, then runs behind the curtain bordering the makeshift stage.

My dad approaches the microphone, followed by my mom. They're part of the temple's organizing committee. They help manage the place, putting up signs that say things like *All Must Wear Modest Clothing Inside Temple*, and making sure the priests aren't siphoning money out of the donation boxes. "Thank you, my friends," says my dad, craning his neck because the mic is set for someone taller. "We are so honoured to see this incredible performance by one of our talented youngsters." Savithri is the same age as me—twenty-two years old. My dad categorizes people as either youngsters or oldies. I'm not sure when you cross the threshold.

"We have only known Savithri a short time, but she is truly a daughter to us." My dad's voice trembles, as my mom nods in solemn agreement beside him.

Savithri appears again from behind the curtain. She runs over to my parents holding a bouquet so humongous I wonder where she's been hiding it. They embrace, and everyone applauds.

"They forgot about you, eh?" asks the aunty, poking me with an elbow.

I shrug.

This is not the first time my parents have adopted a surrogate daughter—a visiting niece or an international student for whom my mom will cook extra rice and also buy a personal-sized rice cooker and deliver both to her dorm room, befriending the girl's three roommates and inviting them all to come to our house to eat more rice. Once it was a French exchange student we were hosting through a program at my high school. I remember my mom ironing her jeans, then holding them up to exclaim over how small her waist was. "Comma sava?" my mom would say to her, the only French she knows.

The exchange student was with us for two weeks. I filled out a form and then she was there, fresh off an airplane, smelling like cigarettes and the Mediterranean, though she had said on her form that she didn't smoke. When we went to McDonald's, I asked her if the French really call it "Le Big Mac." I later overheard her telling her exchange student friend that I didn't speak French very well. A boy in my chem class fell in love with her and stood outside our house serenading her with Savage Garden. One night for dinner, my mom made chapatis, which the girl had never seen before, and, not knowing it was customary to use your hand, she began to eat with a fork and knife. My dad watched the girl, caught my eye, and made a subtle gesture with his head towards my cutlery. Then he picked up his knife and fork, too.

The French girl and I could find no common ground. But Savithri is alternate-reality me. Me if my parents hadn't immigrated to Canada. Me if I'd embraced religion. Me with more expressive eyes. Me if I dedicated myself to something. Me if I could stand on one bent leg with the sole of my other foot tucked into the crook of my knee, arms in a diamond above my head, and never, never lose balance.

I flew back to Halifax late last night. Savithri had been staying in my room, but as soon as I got home, she insisted on moving into the guest room, which has a window so small it could be a porthole. "I'm only in town for a few more weeks," she said, and I realized my parents had told her I'm here indefinitely. I'm not going back to Baltimore.

I feel guilty that she had to stay in my room, still painted black. She seems like someone who'd prefer mauve. She also had to find space in my closet to hang her clothes among my old junk. The shelf at the top dips under the weight of binders and yearbooks. On the floor is a giant Rubbermaid container, a mass grave of stuffed animals.

I pull my Grade 12 yearbook down from the shelf and turn to my grad profile at the back. In Grade 12 you're given space to write personal statements that will sound foolishly outdated only six years later. The yearbook staff provided our class with forms to fill out, with headings like Pet Peeve, Claim to Fame, Favourite Teacher, and Words to Live By. Amy and I had spent four years planning what we would write in ours. *Pet Peeve—Trumpet players. Favourite Teacher—Bill Nye the Science Guy.* We combed through Sloan lyrics for the ones that would make us seem profound. In the end, she didn't graduate, and I left mine blank. Not even a favourite quote.

Next, I flip to the section that features people "Most likely to . . ." These have to be suggested by your peers. I'm not listed. None of my peers cared what I would do after high school. Here's what I did: I got an English degree. After that, overwhelmed by the options outside the snow globe of academia and buoyed by my university friends who had no intention of staying in the city, I stumbled into a creative writing program in the U.S., where they had better funding. One of my professors had advised me not to get an M.F.A. if I had to pay for it. "It's not a job-producing degree," he'd said, wryly. I liked the sound of Baltimore—literally the sound of the word, like rolling gumballs in your mouth. It occurred to me only later that it rhymes with Voldemort. And I didn't know that Edgar Allan Poe had died there, that his last words in the hospital, after they found him slumped in the street, were "Lord help my poor soul."

My first week home, I discover that I got along better with my parents when I was farther away. While I was living in another city, they assumed I was spending my time being productive and achieving life goals, when instead I was caught in a mindless loop of online Boggle.

We fall into a routine. I choreograph ways to avoid them in the small house. This is easy enough, because they rise at dawn. My dad has staked a claim on the bathroom that used to be mine, so there's steam on the mirror when I go to brush my teeth. They're off to work and Savithri is off to her training before I come downstairs. Once they're gone, I emerge to eat Pop-Tarts on the sofa, my laptop on a tray table in front of me. I click through rentals I can't afford, extending the search in a wider and wider radius around downtown Halifax. When my parents are home, I stay in my room, sifting through the papers in my closet and doubting that historians will ever need them for archival purposes.

Before dinner on Friday night, I'm feeling a bit fatalistic, so I wander into the kitchen thinking I'll help my mom—but she and Savithri are already standing there at the counter. My mom is peeling garlic, smashing cloves with the side of a chef's knife and slipping them out of their skins. Beside her, Savithri expertly deseeds a bell pepper. Perhaps they will open a restaurant together. They are humming a song I don't know, lightly tipping their heads from side to side with the fluctuating melody. As I listen, the humming grows into singing. There are no harmonies in Carnatic music—no chords, really, just a single vocal line that they sing at the same pitch. The two of them seem so close, working there calmly and in unison. I don't understand when they formed this connection, and how it happened so quickly, when I have had my whole life.

The next morning, just to get out of the house, I decide I'll visit the main library. "Where are you off to?" my mom asks as I'm leaving. I give only a vague answer, resisting sharing my exact whereabouts to preserve the facade of independence.

My parents need their cars for errands, so I decide to take the bus. I don't think you can really know a city until you've mastered its public transit, until you've coursed through its bloodstream like a virus. Once I'm outside, the early December air wakes me up. Out the bus window, winter in Halifax looks the same as it always does—a white sky, a snowy mountain at each curb, and brown slush filling the road, every parked car transformed into a snow beast. There's enough snow for sledding down the hill in Gorsebrook Park; dots of colour whoosh down the slope and trudge back up again. In their puffy black coats, all the people on the street look like henchmen.

It snowed only once during my time in Baltimore. I walked to campus, and nobody was there except me and a guy from Minnesota. We didn't fall in love. Apparently, the school had called a snow day. In Halifax, a snow day is merely a day, even if you have to excavate a tunnel of ice to reach sunlight.

In Baltimore there were three competing transit systems that didn't properly converge. Halifax transit is more straightforward and familiar, but still my anger brews at the slightest hiccup. On my way back from the library, my tote bag is heavy with magazines. There's a snowbank blocking the bus shelter, and as I try to climb over, my foot sinks into it. Slush comes rushing into a boot that is supposed to be waterproof. I slide forward, my tote bag flying, and as I grab it to keep the magazines from getting wet, I fall over completely. *Come on*, I say in my head, which sounds mild but it's pure rage, and then the bus is late and I want to kick the bus shelter, kick the snow, kick the idiot person standing next to me, who seems to be in no hurry at all. My foot is numb and then it's a sharp icicle. I read that your threshold for pain increases if you swear. You can even hold your hand in ice water for longer. *Fuck fuck fuck damnit*, I chant in my head, but still, nothing feels easier; nothing feels warm enough.

That weekend, my dad calls us to the living room for a brainstorming meeting. He hauls out his stand of chart paper, dragging it in front of the fireplace, then spends ten minutes hunting for a marker, until my mom goes into the kitchen and plucks one from the second drawer. She sits cross-legged on the floor, leaning back against the base of the couch. Savithri peers into the room and then goes to join my mother. They're seated identically, feet tucked under knees as they face me, in the armchair by the TV. Is it preference or martyrdom, I wonder, that neither of them chooses to sit on the couch.

My dad reminds us that there's a holiday talent night coming up at the temple. I can't keep track of the dozens of temple events, including the Bhagavad Gita Recitation Competition (in which children memorize passages and then forget them in front of an audience), the God Drawing Contest (in which children draw gods, with much debate over whether tracing is allowed), Folk Dancing with the Stars (in which there are no stars—they just liked the name), and the newly introduced Top Chef Challenge (in which the temple blows its annual food budget on supplies, the temple chef is infuriated that others are meddling in his kitchen, and aunties pick team leaders, resulting in lingering resentment).

"Okay, now, one question I have," begins my dad, gesturing at his chart paper, where he has written the word *Plagues*, "is what to write on the plaques for participants. Simply their name? Should it say *Participant*? Or the full temple name plus *Holiday Talent Show* . . ." He writes these possibilities down in his shapely print.

"I think you spelled *Plaques* wrong." I point at the paper. "Also, don't engravers charge by the letter?"

"Or would trophies be better?" he inquires, crossing out the *g* in *Plagues* and changing it to a *q*.

"How many plaques do we need?" my mom asks. "There's no more room on the fireplace." It's true, the mantel above the fireplace is three layers deep with plaques and trophies from participation in community events.

"There's room *in* the fireplace," I tell them.

"Ha ha ha." My dad feigns an angry face and shakes his clenched fist in my direction.

"Trophies always end up in the garage sale," says my mom. "Now, who is going to organize the garage sale?"

"Who buys a trophy with someone else's name on it at a garage sale?" I ask.

"You're right," she responds. "Only your dad would do such a thing."

Savithri raises her hand. "Aunty, Uncle, may I make a suggestion? How about magnets?"

"Magnets?" My dad is agape.

"Yes, we did this for a function back home. You can even make them look like small certificates—fancy border and all." She brings up a photo on her phone.

My dad squints at the screen. "Huh, now that's quite practical."

"Waah, what a great idea," my mom concurs, making an appreciative clucking sound.

"Why do we need to give them anything? Shouldn't participation itself be the reward?" I ask.

"Yeah, right." My mom glances at me. "I'll forward the complaint emails on to you."

"I know a printer in India—we can order in bulk," says Savithri.

It's decided: fridge magnets are the best reward for participation. My dad writes *Magnets!* on the chart paper and underlines it twice. Savithri is me if I had bright ideas and contacts at a bulk magnet printer in Bangalore.

Next, we review the dinner menu, decorations, and volunteer assignments that my parents will take to the rest of the temple organizing committee.

"What about the performances?" I ask.

"Oh, that all has been arranged quite a while ago," my mom informs me.

"Your mom and Savithri are planning a collaboration," my dad adds.

My mother rests a hand on Savithri's shoulder. "I will be doing the vocals and Savithri will be dancing."

It turns out they've been practising for weeks. That's probably what I heard them singing in the kitchen the other day, with their Stepford wives unity. I push my jealousy way down, waiting for it to pass like a kidney stone.

My dad thinks for a moment. "There is one spot open. One team had to cancel because that organizing aunty couldn't renew her work visa. But usually the program goes too long anyway, so we don't need—"

"Nina, why don't you put something together?" suggests Savithri.

Though I know this isn't what she means, I see this flash of myself in a Bharatanatyam costume, knees folded in purple silk pleats. I did take lessons for about six sad months as a kid, and classical Carnatic vocal lessons, too, until I faked enough sore throats and menstruation for my parents to realize their money was better spent on home upgrades.

"Umm . . . oh, no, that's okay."

My dad taps his skull thoughtfully with the marker. "We can call that group of kids from the cancelled item—you can organize something for them. How about a Christmas theme?"

"You realize I have no relevant training," I protest, though I know the performers are mostly just interested community members. The same people often appear in three program items, adopting different roles like the cast of SNL, since there still aren't *that* many Indians in Halifax. In fact, one time they performed their own take on the sketch that inspired *A Night at the Roxbury*, though the timing was off and the audience didn't seem to get the reference. Other highlights: couples in a fashion show of Indian historical figures; a ten-year-old doing stand-up; an uncle delivering a monologue from *Hamlet*.

"You'll be great," declares Savithri.

"What are you doing at home anyway?" my mom asks, her tone suddenly sharp. "So far I just see you eating."

Savithri averts her eyes.

Nothing, I think. *I'm doing nothing at all.*

At the start of our first rehearsal, children come screaming through the door all at once, as though simultaneously released from the same minivan. There are eight of them, ages ranging from four to nine. Women are supposed to like children, but honestly I'm indifferent. I can't recall ever interacting with a child. These ones are accompanied by moms carrying babies and/or snacks. My mom helps everyone unpack their winter gear, and they leave uneven rows of slushy boots by the door. There aren't enough coat hangers, so the kids shove their woolly hats and mittens into the sleeves of their coats, and then we pile them on the living room sofa.

I spent the past few days working out a routine to the version of "Jingle Bells" sung by Bing Crosby and The Andrews Sisters. I explain the concept. "So, you folks are reindeer," I tell the kids. "We'll have to choose a Santa . . ." I stand them in a line on our basement carpet and show them one step at a time, a hand on one hip and the other pointing forward and back, then I do a twirl. But this routine is too complicated for the youngest children—the music bops along faster than they do. *Jjjingle bells, jjj jjj jjj jingle bells . . . jingle all the waa-ayyy.* They keep forgetting what comes next and bumping into each other, clumping together at one end when the tiny girl in front pauses to examine her fingernails. With less than three weeks left before the talent show, we'll have to rehearse at least twice a week to figure this out. I have no idea what I'm doing, but the kids don't seem to mind. They're barefoot on the beige carpet, thumping around and waving and linking their arms like a barrel of monkeys. Nobody seems to wonder why we'd perform a Christmas dance skit at the Hindu temple.

When we take a break, I discover the moms have a snack rivalry. One elegant mom has brought a cheese ball, which she places proudly on the ping-pong table for the kids to smush into with Breton vegetable crackers. There's a chocolate sheet cake that the tiniest girl eats with her hands. Another mom has brought spicy roasted chickpeas—"They're very simple to make," she informs us, before going on to describe a two-day, ten-step recipe. A mom with red fake fingernails struggles to open a family-sized bag of Cheezies. These are moms with no food restrictions besides meat. Their kids eat sugar and potato chips and chocolates with alcohol fillings. They drink Pepsi poured from two-litre bottles into Styrofoam cups. Nobody cares about their health or the environment or about making a mess. It's like we're in the eighties again. Some kid has already spilled their Pepsi on the carpet. When I run upstairs to the kitchen to find paper towels, the music from the Bounty commercial pops into my head. What have I become?

The moms sit at the side of the room and watch, which sounds intimidating, but they're buoyant and easygoing, munching on cake and cheese and chickpeas and Cheezies, yapping at their kids to pay attention. I realize it was the parents I was afraid of, and these ones are as forgiving as Pillsbury dough. They seem to trust me. The tiny girl is not accompanied by a mom, but by an older brother who must have recently learned how to drive and so has now been given chauffeur responsibilities. The too-cool teen has claimed a chair among the moms and is eating a malodorous tuna sandwich he brought with him in his pocket, peeling back the plastic wrap a centimetre at a time. I wonder if eating fish is his method of rebelling against his vegetarian upbringing. He's wearing a jersey and slouching in this calculated, casual way.

One creative girl with two tight pigtails invents a new move, so we incorporate it into the routine—the eight reindeer put their hands on their waists and do the twist, and the moms clap in encouragement. We crown the girl "Rudolph."

"Will I get to have a red nose?" she inquires, nose wriggling.

"Obviously," I tell her. "You're Rudolph."

All the other kids congratulate her. Nobody is even jealous. I imagine myself having eight children and living in a shoe.

"Which reindeer am I?" asks a speedy little boy, so I name him Dasher. Then they all want names, so I tap their heads like I'm the queen of Duck, Duck, Goose and list the reindeer names, which I somehow still remember: "Dancer, Prancer, Vixen, Comet, Cupid . . ."

"Vixen?" The mom with the red nails widens her eyes and points one long finger at the imp whose head I've just tapped. The chickpea mom slaps her on the back as the other moms cackle like Statler and Waldorf. Even the tuna sandwich teen cracks a smile.

At our next rehearsal, we're trying to decide who'll play Santa. There are only eight children, whom I've already given reindeer names, and I haven't thought this far ahead. Proportionally it wouldn't make sense—these skinny, long-limbed, brown kids work perfectly as reindeer, but Santa?

"You could be Santa!" suggests Rudolph. The kids cheer.

"Nope, not happening," I tell them.

I review my mental Rolodex of uncles for one who might fit the part. In the meantime, we run through the next section of the routine until the kids are fidgety, and then we break for the mom-provided repast. While they're feasting, I go upstairs to my parents' walk-in closet to hunt for my dad's old Santa outfit. It's there among the costumes and props of shows past: peasant skirts and Yakshagana wigs and an enormous homemade wheel from the time they acted out *Wheel of Fortune*.

I bring the costume back downstairs and gather everyone for the second half of practice. To the tuna sandwich teen, whose name is Anurag, I say, "Anurag, you will have the great honour of playing Santa."

He aims a finger at himself, eyebrows raised in a question.

"Come on, man. You have to be here every week anyway."

He shrugs without protest and puts on the costume over his clothes, stuffing a sofa cushion into the red shirt and tying the black plastic belt around himself. Dasher punches him in the pillow-stomach. Anurag looks at himself in the mirrored door of our prayer room and cracks up. "Yo, this is crazy, man! Ahahaha. Okay, I'll do it."

I'm in the living room watching a recording of the latest *Gilmore Girls* episode because I don't have any friends who still live in Halifax. "Hey, Mom, guess what I'm watching?" She's in the foyer, carrying a laundry basket at her hip.

"Oh, Lorelai and daughter." She puts down the basket and perches on the arm of the couch. I don't think I've ever heard her say the show's real name.

We used to watch *Gilmore Girls* together every Tuesday night, while my dad snoozed in an armchair. This was for the best. When he was awake, he asked a lot of questions and pointed out logical flaws, like the fact that Rory was accepted to both Harvard and Yale even though she was so insipid.

My mom used to tell me we were like Lorelai and Rory— not only had one been in the womb of the other, but they were also best friends. "Yeah, not quite," I'd respond. They were closer than clones. In comparison, my mom and I grew uncomfortable during the romantic scenes, the next-level Jess-and-Rory chemistry burning up the screen as my dad snored away. My mom has always been such a confusing mix of traditional and savvy and witty and prudish. I didn't really value her sense of humour until I was in Baltimore, where I fell into the habit of texting her. Her messages are like Emily Dickinson poems, all dashes and unexpected capitalization. One time I sent her a photo of a Hindu artifact I'd tripped upon at the Walters Museum—a stone sculpture of Nandi, a decorated, watchful bull like the one outside my parents' temple. She texted back: *Where did they Steal Him from.*

"Did you have a childhood crush, Mom?" I ask her now, partly to tease her, but also because I really want to know.

"Oh no," she says. "We didn't have things like that."

"Like what? Human emotions?"

"Ha ha ha." She and my dad have this artificial ha-laugh they do when they don't appreciate my jokes. I don't know which one of them started it. "You know I'm getting old." She's in her mid-forties. "I don't remember from so long ago. What is good for memory? Sudoku? Ginkgo biloba?"

Savithri comes up behind my mother and puts her arm companionably around her. Doesn't she have her own parents? My feet are stretched out on the sofa, but I move them to make room for her. In this episode of *Gilmore Girls*, Lorelai and Christopher are bickering. They have recently gotten married.

"Well, we all knew that was a bad idea," says my mom.

On the screen, Luke and Christopher—Lorelai's recurrent suitors—silently charge towards each other in the Stars Hollow square.

"Why are these men fighting?" asks Savithri.

"They're in a love triangle," I explain.

"Has Lorelai been married before?" my mom wonders. Neither of us knows.

"I'm never getting married," says Savithri.

My mom turns to her in alarm, her mouth beginning to form the question she doesn't ask.

"I have too many things I want to do," Savithri adds firmly, eyes fixed on the TV. For a moment, I love her, if only because she has failed my mother in a way I haven't yet.

"But I sent you that boy's photo." My mom sounds injured.

"I know, Aunty. Thank you so much for thinking of me, really. But I am not interested in finding a husband. Marriage just isn't for me." From the way this comes out—formal and succinct, and perhaps a little tired—I have a feeling this is a statement Savithri has made before.

I see my mom working this out in her mind, preparing to protest, though she can't. Savithri isn't her daughter.

With my mom's sewing machine and a few yards of soft camel-coloured fleece I buy on discount at Fabricville, I sew eight smocks, and eight pairs of reindeer antlers for the kids to wear like headbands. In the collection of old costumes, I find Rudolph a red sponge nose. From the neighbour's yard, I scavenge a cardboard microwave box while it's only slightly damp from the snow, then cut off the top and bottom and shape it into a sleigh. I add a curlicued base using extra pieces of cardboard. The plan is for Anurag to wear the box-sleigh over his costume, so it appears as though he's sitting in it. I paint the whole thing red and gold, then add two long ribbons at the front to tie to the reindeers' wrists, to keep them in formation as they "pull" Santa along.

One night after dinner, I'm trimming the last thread on the eighth pair of antlers while Savithri and my mom rehearse their piece for the show in the living room. I can hear my mom tapping out the rhythm with her palm on her lap and humming a few bars—or whatever bars are called in Carnatic music. Savithri's feet are light on the hardwood. Then they stop and discuss. "I think we should try that part again," suggests Savithri. They repeat the section. Then stop and discuss again. This goes on for hours.

Later, I hear Savithri call out. "Nina? Uncle? Please come join us for one minute?"

My dad comes over from the kitchen where he was secretly eating peanuts straight from the cupboard. When we go into the living room, Savithri is flushed and winded, in tights and a cotton tunic, strands of hair coming loose from her ponytail. She's pulling wrapped gifts out of a tote bag. "I know it isn't Christmas *just* yet, but I have something for you all."

"Oh, no," says my mom. "You shouldn't have."

"Why did you do that?" asks my dad.

Over the past two decades, my family has phased out Christmas. A photo in our 1986 album shows stockings hung on the mantel, and my dad in a Santa costume, holding up an unsuspecting two-year-old me. At some point I got old enough to realize that Santa wasn't an Indian immigrant. It was around the time we decided stockings were nonsense—just whose enormous socks were these supposed to be? And then the tree stopped working. A branch went missing so we had to turn that side to the wall. We had inherited the tree from an uncle, and it was the plastic kind with a base and trunk that you needed an engineering degree to assemble.

Then we ran out of gift ideas. We already had too much stuff. I'd buy my parents tickets to a show at Neptune, but they preferred the lazy home-theatre experience. My mom would go to Bayers Lake and gift me blouses with wide arms and big flower prints and bizarre cut-outs—maybe it was cruise wear? "We don't really need anything . . ." one of us would say, thinking of the trash heap of last year's Christmas.

Savithri presents my mom with a membership to an Indian music streaming site, handing her the log-in info she's printed inside a glittering card. "It's popular in India now," she tells her. For my dad, she produces a wrapped item in an odd shape. He unwraps it shyly, revealing a megaphone. "To grab every-one's attention in the temple."

"Thank you soo soo much, Savithri!" my dad announces into the megaphone.

Then she takes out one last gift from the bag. It's for me.

"Oh, you didn't have to . . ." She passes me a small cream-coloured box. Inside, there's a silver pen, cushioned in black velvet. On the side of the pen, my name is engraved in delicate script.

"I hope it's the right thing. I heard you're a writer."

I examine her voice for sarcasm, but there isn't any. "Oh, that was just . . . I'm not . . ."

My parents look away and fidget with their gifts, while Savithri smiles hopefully at me.

"It's beautiful," I say to her. It's a pen for someone with dreams. I hold it in writing position. It's almost weightless.

With only days until our performance, Anurag comes to rehearsal and hands me a CD. It has *Jingle Bells* Sharpied on it in boyish print. "Try this version," he says. When I press play on the CD player, there's a tearing sound.

"What *is* this?"

"Just shut up and listen for a sec."

It's Bing Crosby's "Jingle Bells," but slower, with new gaps in the music. Spliced in are the background instrumentals from "Ek Ladki Ko Dekha Toh," from *1942: A Love Story*, an iconic Indian song and a favourite among the temple gang. The movie came out in 1994, but the song feels older—it's gentle and bright, innocent and wistful, with humble instrumentation. Anurag's mix never reaches the lyrics, and if you know the original song, this creates an almost unbearable feeling of waiting.

Despite the change, the kids' steps fall easily into the new music, as though Anurag built their delays into it, leaving time for their legs to jiggle into place.

"Holy crap, Anurag! Are you some kind of DJ mixologist?" I don't know what the terminology is.

"I dabble," he says.

"This is *so* good!" I high-five him and he tips his baseball cap at me.

On the night of the show, the results of the God Drawing Contest decorate the temple's entryway. The drawings' proportions are all a little off—a wonky forehead; a goddess eye looking askance—giving the entryway a haunted house effect. It'd be a fun joke to bring a date to the temple at night and then leave him there.

"Jingle Bells" is a hit. "Christmas with Indian spice" is one uncle's glowing review. The kids move slightly out of sync, skipping like a record, in the most hilarious and endearing way. They frolic through propped-up cardboard evergreens, on which I've draped string lights and tinsel I found in storage near our family's defunct Christmas tree. They dance past artificial snow I made out of big billows of cotton harvested from the bodies of my old stuffed animals. Anurag is unrecognizable with a fake white beard. He even made his own fake eyebrows out of white felt. When the kids run off the stage, I give each one a three-pack of Ferrero Rocher, to compensate for the magnets they'll receive at the end when the participants are called up during the meandering Vote of Thanks.

Savithri's dance is last. I sit amidst a gaggle of children still wearing their antlers, uncrinkling the gold foil to inhale their chocolates. My mom sits on a small carpet at the side of the stage next to three musicians playing mridangam, veena, and flute. The temple hall is dark and hushed as she begins to sing into a microphone, keeping time with her hand on her leg. A spotlight follows Savithri as she enters and takes deliberate steps to the centre of the stage. Each of her movements holds distinct clarity and control, and each step matches exactly the pace of my mother's palm. Savithri is poised, flawless, sweating from exertion. Even as her dancing seems effortless, you can see how hard she has worked.

My dad drives Savithri to the airport. She waves at me and my mom from the car window and then she's gone. Christmas Day comes and goes, uncelebrated in our house. I line up some tutoring jobs by emailing a flyer to the parents of my reindeer.

After Christmas, Anurag texts me an invitation to see a band he's in with some college kids. The venue is an unmarked building not far from the Commons, and inside it resembles a murderer's studio apartment, with painted-out windows, next to which the band sets up. There's some seating—a sunken couch in front and a scattering of mismatched chairs. The rest is standing room. It's hot in the small space. I hold my jacket and scarf in my armpit. The room is smoky, like maybe dry ice is hidden somewhere behind an amp.

Anurag stands by the bar, beside stacks of red plastic cups. "Are you old enough to be in here?" I ask him.

"Relax," he says. "Be cool."

The crowd is barely college-age. Blasé youths sport piercings, half-shaved heads, and first tries at facial hair. They wear ill-fitting clothing that fails to hide their attractiveness. There's one set of parents who are so excited to be there they buy me a drink.

Anurag nods at someone across the room and then heads over to the drums.

A guy with scene hair, one of the band members, gives a quirky and philosophical introduction. "We're observers. Pattern-makers." He pays homage to the band's wealth of musical influences, listing names I am not hip enough to recognize. He refers to himself as a "rhythm scientist" and I'm like, hang on, can you just call yourself a scientist?

I visited the band's website earlier, thinking I could acquaint myself with their music to appear less like a neophyte. But the clips I listened to were atonal and arrhythmic. I didn't get it at all. At the start, I thought the band was tuning or warming up, but it turned out that was part of the song. The music begins like this now, a mess of tones, manic and chromatic. You can only tell it's moving forward by the volume, which gets gradually louder.

It's a gentle crowd. Most stand almost still, good-naturedly bobbing their heads. One guy wearing a bike helmet flails his arms with abandon.

Now the music nearly falls together but not quite; it's three time signatures at once, with syncopated rhythms, the string instruments tautly ruminating like the musical equivalent of anxiety. I watch the girl at the xylophone throwing around her mallets in a method that looks random but must be practised, the violinist refusing to release her note, the keyboard player leaning into the sustain pedal like he's urging it forward, and Anurag, drumsticks in hand, paused, waiting for the beat to land.

When it does, it's a cathartic crash. The music picks up speed, while the musicians nod and jerk their heads, eyes pressed shut in trance-like concentration. A drumstick flies out of Anurag's hand and he just grabs another and keeps playing. The sound is overwhelming, the percussion replacing my pulse and knocking me out of joint, the hi-hat shimmering in my chest. I'm not here anymore. I'm plucked out of this room and dropped back into Baltimore.

The night of one of my many panicked phone calls home. House centipedes scrambling across my ceiling. Roaches crawling in my bed. I kept thinking I felt their legs on me. Attending class and then avoiding my apartment by going to the library and trying to read all the Faulkner I'd been assigned—why was there so much Faulkner? The more books I read, the more books there were left to read. When the library closed, I'd go back to my place and then watch three hours of whatever I could find for free online, the room lit like a stadium in Texas. I got into this habit of phoning my parents to occupy my brain. It started out as complaining—about roaches, about how lonely I was. I could hear their impatience, the weary anticipation in their voices—they were at work; they had guests over. These were long phone calls, twice a day, and then three times, and then four, and then in the middle of the night—it was an hour later in Halifax, but sometimes I was too afraid to sleep, and I knew they would always answer the phone. They took shifts. Soon I was crying so hard it turned into screaming. We had the kinds of conversations we never have in person, because it is too much to look into somebody's face and watch them breaking down.

"Be brave," my dad would say, over and over.

"What does that mean—*be brave*," I spat, during that last phone call. "That doesn't *mean* anything."

He booked the flight and paid for it. A week later, I flew home. I cried messily in the airport, in front of strangers, and as the plane lifted off, I already knew I would regret giving up so easily.

After New Year's, my dad comes to my room to talk to me. "I have made a plan," he says. "You will go back to school and finish your degree. You can still go back. The classes haven't started yet, right? You can still go back, no problem. I have made a call to a couple we know there, just an hour outside of Baltimore. You can stay with them, no problem."

"I *can't*," I tell him.

"No, listen to me. I can even come with you. I will take time from work and stay there until you are comfortable."

It's true; it has only been six weeks. I haven't missed much at all aside from end-of-term parties and the winter break. My grades were fine. My partly completed thesis is still right there in my suitcase.

"I can't go back. It's too late. I already told them I was leaving."

Before I left, I'd notified my advisor, submitted a statement of my intent to withdraw, and filled out forms with the registrar. I dropped out in a responsible and official way. And I signed away my funding. I can't get it back.

After I explain this to him, my dad sits down at the edge of my bed, thinking. I imagine his hair turning whiter in front of me as his mind churns for a solution; then I watch his body deflate. In Halifax, the snow is still falling, building its cold, quiet weight, insulating our house from sound.

"It's important to finish what we started. I should have . . ." He can't look me in the eye. "It is my fault," he says. "I wish I had told you to stay there."

You Are Loved by Me

ALWAYS KEEP A DESK between you and your student. Always leave the door open when you're alone with a student. Never hug a student. Never even think about touching a student.

That's about all I remember from teachers college—that and wondering if these rules have always been taught. None of my training seems of any use to me now, as I'm delivering a spiel about plagiarism, at the very start of my first day as a real teacher. To the fresh group of Grade 9s in front of me, I say, "So my friend was telling me about this time he was teaching a class and a student of his turned in a short story." I actually read about this on an internet forum, but I'd like to give the impression of having a rich social life. "The story has some typos, but it's decent writing. The protagonist has a wooden leg—that's an interesting detail, right?"

The students nod. They're sitting at their desks, backpacks slumped like docile dogs at their feet. I've arranged the desks in a U-shape, loosely spaced out, which I read was an optimal classroom configuration. A boy in a camo T-shirt stands and wanders up through the middle of the U, and I'm thrown off. Is he going to ask me a question? No, he walks to the pencil sharpener beneath the whiteboard to sharpen his pencil. There's that familiar rolling and gargling sound and sawmill smell, incongruent with the totally unfamiliar situation I'm in. I feel like I'm facing in the wrong direction, like I should be on the other side of the room, listening instead of talking. Do students not bring sharp pencils on the first day? Do they not use mechanical pencils now? Or pens, for that matter? A girl in a striped hoodie—Renée, I think—has her cellphone in her hand. Her expression is aloof, glancing down at the phone and then back up at me. Am I allowed to confiscate cellphones?

"Then a Bible salesman shows up and steals her wooden leg." I realize I'm telling this story all wrong—they won't recognize the references, and the punchline won't land. "Uhh, and it turns out he had plagiarized a Flannery O'Connor story! He just paraphrased the whole thing!"

A girl raises her hand. Her posture is so excellent she must possess a fence post instead of a spine. "Miss, who is Flannery O'Connor?"

This is the first time anyone has addressed me as "Miss." Just "Miss"—a title where a name should be. As though there's nothing that comes after it.

After I tell them who Flannery O'Connor is and clarify that the point of my story is that they shouldn't plagiarize, I pass around scrap paper and instruct them to write their names at the top and answer a series of questions about themselves. *What's your favourite book? What do you hope to get out of this class?*

There's a boy sitting near the front of the room. He has a reddish nose he hasn't quite grown into yet, and is wearing a collared shirt, as though his mom thought the first day of school might also be picture day. He speaks without being called on. "Miss? I have a question. I don't have a favourite book."

I suggest he write down his favourite TV show instead. I look at the clock. It's 8:15 a.m.

They write their responses, heads angled down over their task like sweatshop workers. At the teacher's desk, I search for each student on Facebook—I hear it's a good way to learn names. I click past each photo, scroll down each wall, keeping the cursor away from any Like buttons. They're so young. Their faces are like unbaked bread. A quarter of the class has braces. The girl with good posture, Colleen, has a photo on her page with the caption *Got my braces off!* Her smile looks ceramic. The comments say: *GORGOUS* and *OMG sooo pretty!* The profile of a boy named Louis contains no photos, only fantasy characters he's drawn: a charcoal dragon; an ink manticore with geometric wings. I look up a girl who told the class she goes by Sue, though on my attendance sheet her name is listed as *Soo-mi.* In her profile photo she wears the hugest, sweetest glasses and hugs a younger brother. In class, her glasses are absent, revealing blue contacts, and her hair is highlighted auburn. Another girl—Madeleine—has a profile full of mod-elling photos. In her most recent post, she's sprawled over a fallen tree while wearing a bikini that reveals her adolescent stomach. I close the browser window.

When class ends, the students file out, and after the second-to-last one leaves, the door shuts behind her. There's one kid left—the boy without a favourite book. *Always leave the door open when you're alone with a student.* He's deliberate in putting away his pencils, closing his laptop, winding the power cord. He has a surprising confidence for a student in Grade 9. Earlier, when I had everyone in class pair up and introduce themselves, most of them muttered at the floor and kept asking, "Wait, what else do I have to say?" But this guy's delivery had the bravado of a circus ringmaster: "Ladies and gentlemen!" The class perked up. "Introducing . . . the beautiful Saaarraaah Davis!" Sarah hid her half-smile in her hand and sunk lower in her chair.

I'm standing on the wrong side of the desk as he approaches me to turn in his answers. *Always keep a desk between you and your student.*

"I'm Caleb," he says. He has a boy-band face, despite the nose and the acne scars that cover both cheeks. "It's nice to meet you. I can tell I'm really going to like this class." He reaches out his hand. When he leans in, his breath smells like a tonsil infection.

I put my own hand out, and he grabs it and gives it three vigorous shakes. *Never even think about touching a student.* "Thank you, Caleb. It's nice to meet you, too." I let go of his hand with what I hope is an air of finality. There are ten minutes until my next class, and I've been daydreaming about the flax seed bar in my lunch bag.

"I read that Flannery O'Connor story you were talking about just now on my phone. What a weird-ass story!"

"You read it just now?"

"Yeah, I finished the work early, so I googled it. Weird-ass story, though! That part where they're like totally about to do it in the barn!" To emphasize his point, he waves his hands around like Regis Philbin. His face gets redder. He doesn't break eye contact.

"I don't think that's—"

"They're like, kissing and stuff, and then he totally steals her leg!"

"That isn't really the—"

"Great story, Nina! Can't wait till next class!"

I look up at him—he's about a foot taller than me—and I'm about to tell him not to use my first name (how does he even know it?) when I notice his eyes moving down. There's a slight smile on his face. I can't believe it at first, but then it's unmistakable: he's staring directly at my chest.

|||||||||||

The first faculty meeting of the year is that afternoon in the windowless staff lunchroom. While I inhale the potent reek of ketchup, the principal hands out an agenda, then introduces himself at length. "Don't hesitate to come to me with your concerns," he says. "We're a family here. My door's always open." He's wearing a suit, and I wonder if he's keeping the jacket on to hide damp armpits, like I am.

This morning I changed a dozen times, discarding the crisp outfit I'd set out on hangers the night before, estimating and re-estimating the time needed to drive to school. In the end I decided on the same outfit I wore to my interview—a grey long-sleeved sheath dress and a blazer. But the sleeves are too constrictive, which I realized only when I reached above my head to write a word-of-the-day on the board (today's word: *scrupulous*). They proved equally challenging when I tried to pull down the classroom projector screen to display info about accessing library resources. (It took four attempts, the screen rolling and flapping back to the ceiling each time, and in the end the visiting librarian did it herself.) I wore my glasses and knotted my hair to look older, but another faculty member still mistook me for a student. This might be because I'm the only person working here who isn't white, besides the cleaning staff. Or maybe my face highlights my inexperience, glowing with "no-makeup makeup" techniques I learned from YouTube tutorials where nineteen-year-olds massage jojoba oil into their pink cheeks and sketch new hairs onto their brows. "This looks super natural," each one assures me, but I keep hearing *supernatural*.

We go around the room in a quasi-icebreaker, sharing summer accomplishments.

"I worked on my tan this summer," says Mr. Jeffers, the gym teacher and only other person here who's new. He is ageless and spotless. I wonder when the sun damage will catch up to him.

"I backpacked in Slovenia, which by the way is the raddest place." This from the geography teacher, who wears the highest, blondest ponytail I've ever seen. "They make the most delicious Riesling—dry though, not sweet like German Riesling."

The German teacher does a half eye-roll before catching herself.

"Taught summer school," glowers the history teacher.

"I published my first poem," says another English teacher. Everyone claps. They smile noncommittally after she offers to distribute copies.

"Nina, you have an M.F.A. Isn't that right?" asks the principal.

"I have an almost-M.F.A.," I answer, and laugh, though it isn't funny. "Dropped out." Two math teachers raise eyebrows, and I realize I probably shouldn't have admitted to dropping out in front of a group of teachers. I should have said, "I found my true calling as an educator."

On the agenda: why the school no longer provides markers, holds barbecues, or has an art program. Everyone is outraged about the barbecues. I wonder where the art teachers are now. Next: presentations from the librarian, the vice principal, the guidance counsellor, and the audiovisual assistant. My back hurts in the orange plastic chair. I remember sitting loose-limbed in a similar chair a decade ago, in a high school not far from here.

The principal adjourns the meeting with two announcements: there's a Grade 9 Welcome Dance at the end of the month, and a lockdown drill in October.

"We need two teachers to staff the dance," he tells us. "Parent volunteers will make up the rest." Suddenly every teacher in the room is holding an index finger to their nose. All except me and Jeffers. "Ahhh, we forgot to let the newbies in on our game," booms the principal. "Well, that's all right. You folks don't mind chaperoning, do you?"

I suspect this is only the first game I haven't been let in on.

Two weeks later, I'm teaching a lesson on passive voice. On the board, I write:

The little girl was eaten by the monster.
The monster ate the little girl.

The classroom windows face east, and the students melt into sweat. The pencil-sharpening boy from the first day, Dean, wipes his neck with the back of his T-shirt. When I was in high school, Amy would have written me a note at this point. Folding, passing. The crackle of the page unfolding:

This class is hated by me.
I hate this class.

Do kids still exchange notes?

"In the pair of sentences, the first is passive and the second is active. The second is direct and uses fewer words. *The monster ate the little girl* sounds more intense and threatening than *The little girl was eaten by the monster.*" I deliver that last sentence in a ho-hum voice to get the point across.

Caleb looks riveted. He has two modes: riveted or distracted. In the latter, he'll blab at full volume to whoever's near him, or he'll frown and chew his pencil, drop it on the floor, screech from his chair to pick it up, and place it back between his teeth. But now he's focused—his pencil held at forty-five degrees to the page, his eyes an unblinking blue.

I write:

Mistakes were made.
I made mistakes.

"Imagine a politician saying these lines," I say. Polite laughter. "The second is more specific, and in this case, more honest. Which do you think makes a better apology? Which would you rather hear from someone who had really wronged you? Okay, last one . . ."

I write:

You are loved by me.

I love you.

When I turn, they're alert, activated by the word *love* inscribed on the board. "There's a reason we don't tell someone, 'You are loved by me.'"

"'Cause it sounds like a robot," says Sarah Davis.

"Exactly."

"Far less romantic," adds Sarah McIntosh, who has a heart-shaped face and pulled-back hair. She's one of four Sarahs in her grade. I imagine the hospital nursery fourteen years ago, with rows of cribs marked *Sarah.*

"And creepy as fuck," Madeleine remarks at a low volume to Renée.

"Yeah, no way you'll get laid saying that!" shouts Caleb.

Colleen, sitting next to him, rolls her eyes. "Caleb, that's not appropriate."

"But she said—"

I cut him off and hand out grammar worksheets. A few minutes later, I'm pacing around the desks and supervising, peering over their shoulders to give advice or tell them to put away their phones, when I overhear the conversation between Madeleine and Renée.

"He's so hot I can't even concentrate," says Madeleine. She's wearing a jersey top that skims her midriff, defying the school's sexist dress code.

"Gross." Renée rattles a dozen bangles on one wrist, as she does every five minutes throughout every class period.

As I approach their desks, they quickly fall silent, eyes back on their papers. I wonder which boy they're discussing, and whether a relationship will flower over the course of the semester. In my head a montage flickers: Madeleine and the boy in question sit in adjacent seats, trade coy glances, hold hands under the table. They share a cafeteria cookie, her snapping off an edge and feeding it to him as the rest of the class pretends not to notice. She leans her head on his shoulder as he defends her point in discussion. They nod in unison through my lectures and cheat off each other's tests. Their writing journals become love letters, on which I struggle to write neutral comments. *Try to be more concise. Careful of purple prose.* Then one day they're sitting on opposite sides of the room. Their journals turn caustic. Their essays go unwritten.

After class, Caleb is again the last one left—this has been the case for nearly every class so far. He always has a question. Once he asked where the library was, though it's right by the school's front entrance.

"So . . . that passive voice," he says. "I'm not sure I get it."

"Which part are you having trouble with?" I'm half resting my bum on the front of my desk, to relieve the weight from my feet in their tight shoes. Caleb comes closer to stand in front of me. I edge out sideways and move from the front of the desk to behind it. He follows.

"Like, just the whole idea of it."

Standing between the desk and my chair, I begin to pack up my materials. He's very close now, within touching distance as he blocks my path. The desk sits in a corner of the room, so on my other side is the wall. My shoulders rise a little, like a barrier. "Okay, well, why don't you try finishing the worksheet at home and distill it down to one or two specific questions. Then we can schedule an appointment to—"

"No, but like, just the whole idea of it," he says again, gesturing vaguely with his hands. He leans over me, and too-strong cologne wafts down. I think about reminding him of the school's scent-free policy as I take a small step towards the wall. I hoist my tote bag onto my shoulder, between us. "That looks heavy. I can carry it for you, Miss."

"That isn't necessary." Should I have thanked him for the offer? "Excuse me, please," I say, wheeling my chair out just enough so he's forced to step back and I can get past him. As I head to the door, he falls into step beside me.

"Which way are you headed?" he asks.

"I'm off to my next class." I should have said I was going to the ladies' room.

He accompanies me down the hall, up the main stairwell, down another hall, and around the corner, to the other side of the building, where I disappear into my next classroom with a curt wave.

The next day, as usual, I enter my first class before the students, picking up the occasional crumpled paper or empty plastic cup and tucking in chairs left pushed out by the Anime Club that morning. I pause, noticing a flaw in the side of a student's desk. When I peer down to look, I see the words scratched in all caps into the dark wood: YOU ARE LOVED BY ME.

The class's reaction to Caleb is a study in teenage socialization. At first, they laugh at his trite humour, his nonsensical quips. But when he steps up the buffoonery—he jumps up squawking and grabs his throat when I reference *To Kill a Mockingbird*—they begin to distance themselves. The students on either side of him edge their chairs away. I envy this action, though I know I should model more generous behaviour. I'm the teacher, after all.

After class, Caleb follows me down the hallway, a looming sidekick. He hounds me with questions: What's the homework? (It's written on the board.) How do you write a works cited page? (Consult the handout we just spent twenty minutes discussing.) How do you define irony? (The expression of one's meaning by using language that normally signifies the opposite, typically for humorous or emphatic effect, according to the OED.) What part of India am I from? (I'm from Halifax.) How old am I? (That's a personal question. Grinning, he says I don't look old enough to be a teacher.) What fabric is my shirt made of? (He puts his hand on my upper arm and I jerk my arm away.)

At first I vary my route after each class, stopping by places he can't follow—the washroom, the staff room, the office I share with Jeffers and the geography teacher—but there isn't enough time between classes for this. So instead I simply walk faster, or rush out as soon as class ends, but I can't outpace his longer legs. How do I tell him to stop following me? It's my job to answer his questions. I try saying goodbye to end the conversation, but he doesn't seem to pick up on the cue.

"Caleb, what's your next class? Aren't you going to be late?"

He has a free period. He has nowhere to be.

I consult Google. I type *creeper student what to do*. Most of the articles are about students harassing other students, but I find one about teachers being bullied. It lists a few "proactive measures" to take:

* Don't show favouritism.
* Speak to the student privately after class. Don't confront students in front of their peers.
* Be open to student feedback.
* Model positive behaviour.

- Reward student success rather than pointing out failures.
- Choose your battles.

I poll others for advice: my parents, friends, other teachers, my therapist.

"Can't you have him transferred to a different class?" asks my mom.

"What are you doing for self-care?" asks my therapist.

"Is the student a white male?" asks the school's learning specialist, before giving me a printout of the same article I already read online.

I visit the principal's office, with its always open door. He sits me down in a leather chair normally reserved for parents.

"The key is classroom management. Try to be firm." He makes a fist to indicate firmness. "And have you tried deflecting with humour? A little humour can go a long way," he advises.

"When I have a difficult student, I just shower him with compassion," says the other English teacher, with concerned eyebrows. I've seen her ratemyteachers.com profile, where anonymous students have evaluated the size of her ass, the quality of her breasts.

We read a story in class about a woman who has a double mastectomy, a term Caleb doesn't know. After Sarah McIntosh explains it to him, Caleb asks, "So she had her boobs chopped off?"

"She had cancer," says Sarah McIntosh. "My—"

But Caleb doesn't let her finish.

"Caleb, Sarah was talking," I interject.

Sarah tries again: "My aunt—"

But it's too late. Caleb forcibly takes the floor and holds

it. One by one, the girls in the class begin to say something, but he interrupts them all. I shut him down repeatedly and request that he give someone else a chance to speak. He refers to the character only as "the girl with the chopped-off boobs."

"This is a real thing that happens to people," Colleen tells him.

Sarah McIntosh crosses her arms and doesn't try to speak again.

I ask Caleb to stay after class. As he approaches my desk, I realize I've again made the error of standing behind it, allowing him to block my exit. I make a mental note to move the desk tomorrow, to create more exit routes.

"Caleb," I say, directly but calmly, as the internet has advised. "It's great that you're so engaged in class discussion, but I need you to work on your professionalism—"

"How much more professional can I be?" he asks, his voice rising as his eyes dart wildly. "I participate, like, *all the time*. I'm not failing this class, am I? My participation grade must be really good, right?"

I roll the chair to position it between us, grasping the back of it with both my hands. "It's important that we share the space and give others a chance to participate, too. Part of participation is listening—"

"I listen! Are you saying I don't listen?" He starts pacing a short path back and forth beside my desk, his shoulder bag swinging with him each time he turns. I have to get around him to reach the door.

"Not all language is appropriate for every setting. I'm just asking you to pause and think before you make a comment in class. It's okay if you don't express an opinion on every—"

"Am I, like, in trouble? I have a lot of opinions."

"As I said, I appreciate that you're so engaged. But there are some people in the class we rarely get to hear from—"

"I can't help it if I have a lot of opinions." He places his hands flat on the side of my desk and pushes down so hard it slides forward under his red knuckles, almost hitting the wall.

I stuff my papers into my bag, not hiding my haste. "I have to get to my next class." He doesn't move. To get to the door, I must walk out from behind the desk and pass him. I count to three. I count to three again. Then I hold my breath and go. My arm brushes his as I pass, and I recoil but keep going. I know he's behind me, but I don't stop. I'm dreading and anticipating a large hand reaching for me, grabbing at my shoulder, at my waist. I hear the classroom door slam. I work up my nerve and turn around: "Caleb, please stop following me."

"I'm not *following* you—"

"If you want to discuss this further, we can meet with the guidance counsellor, or you can bring in your parents and we'll have a chat about—"

"My parents?"

"I have to leave now," I say. Then I turn and walk as fast as I can down the hallway, my shoes scraping blisters across the backs of my heels. I walk past the door of my next class and keep walking until I'm at the school's front doors. I go straight to my car, almost running, though it's morning and I have a class starting momentarily.

He's behind me.

"Are you going to call my parents?" he asks. "Miss, where are you going?"

I get in the car, shut the door, lock it.

He's right by the driver's-side window. "Are you going to call my parents?" he says again, louder, through the glass.

I pull out of the parking spot as his palm lands hard against the glass. I drive around the block. I'm ten minutes late to second period.

|||||||||||

The Grade 9 dance is like every high school dance. Fourteen-year-olds gyrate to music I can't quite identify, as its insistent bass radiates up through my feet. The gymnasium lights are off, and a spotlight scans the room as though seeking criminals. It flashes on the handful of kids standing in a loose line against the wall, holding their elbows or making halfhearted conversation, pretending they don't want to dance. Dress code compromises abound. Black bicycle shorts peek out from a girl's rising hemline as she hops to the beat. A boy takes his shirt off and his skinny chest undulates like a snake. A large standing fan—typically used to air out the gym after basketball practice—spins across the crowd, circulating sweaty air. I'm not sure what I'm supposed to do— do teachers dance? Only popular and well-liked teachers dance. I am not going to dance. My job here is just to stand and watch the spectacle, confiscate alcohol if necessary. Jeffers does a dance-walk through the gym that fades as he arrives at the soda and chips. He's surrounded by a group of girls, including two from my first-period class—Madeleine and Renée. Four weeks in, I've finally learned the names of my eighty students. I wander over and put some potato chips in a napkin and hold it in my cupped hand. I eat a chip to have something to do.

"Mr. Jeffers, did you ever go to the Lobster Trap?" asks Madeleine, who is standing beside him.

"The Lobster Trap?" says Renée. "Seriously?"

"That might've been before my time," says Jeffers.

"And then there's Ralph's, of course." Madeleine tips her head to one side, exposing her neck.

These are the names of Halifax strip clubs.

"Sooo gross," says Renée. "Who would want to take their clothes off in a place called the Lobster Trap? Like, which is the lobster and which is the trap?"

I move a little closer to them, so I'm between Madeleine and Renée. "Interesting choice of topic," I tell them. I eat another chip.

Jeffers shrugs. He's attractive, I realize—at least, the kind of attractive that teenage girls have crushes on. His hair is a soft brown; his face is radiant and dimpled. I wonder if he exfoliates.

"So, Mr. Jeffers, have you been to a strip club before?" asks Madeleine. She turns her body towards Jeffers, so they're in a cocoon of space.

"No comment," he says, to a burst of laughter.

How many teachers are lechers? One in a hundred? One in ten? In teachers college, after we were told to keep a desk between us and our students, a guy behind me said, in an artificial whisper, "The desk is to hide your erection," and the whole class erupted in laughter. Every television show I've seen set in a high school also features a teacher prowling the hallways for nubile flesh. Even *Buffy* toyed with that trope, though the teacher turned out to be a paranormal praying mantis.

When a slow song comes on, Dean comes over to ask Renée to dance. I see Caleb across the room. He has replaced his usual T-shirt with a dark purple button-down, not unlike the one Walter White wears after he turns to a life of crime. He strides purposefully towards an unsuspecting girl, opens his mouth, says maybe five words. In response, the girl scrunches her face into a question, and then into disbelief. He moves right into her personal space as she tries to escape into the concrete wall. Caleb scowls in dejection—or anger?—and hunches his shoulders, ape-like. He pivots, sees me, and starts heading in my direction, arms swinging.

I crush my napkin in my palm. Jeffers's face grows curious as I turn abruptly away from the group. Ignoring him, I rush towards the door farthest away from Caleb, and out and down the hallway to the washroom. Inside a stall, I breathe rhythmically for five minutes, then ten. They will wonder where I've gone. When some girls enter the washroom, chattering and giggling, I press the flush and exit the stall. I wash my hands and dry them with a paper towel. I walk back down the hallway. It's empty, yet I walk faster, imagining him waiting by a locker for me.

I stand through two more hours of fourteen-year-olds dancing. Because of his height, I can watch Caleb's head bobbing above the others as he dances alone at the periphery. During slow dances, he weaves over to the wall, then stands there twitching with an energy he can't seem to contain. Other kids wind their arms around each other's necks and waists and I wonder which ones are falling in love. I eat two squares of Sobeys sheet cake from a flimsy paper plate. I shift my weight from foot to foot to keep the blood flowing, purposely staying offbeat so that this isn't mistaken for dancing.

The dance finally ends at eleven. When I search for Jeffers, the group of girls around him has dispersed, except for Madeleine. In the dim gymnasium, her face sparkles with makeup. She gazes up at him, and I don't think she realizes he's a solar eclipse. She's wearing a white bodycon dress she must have bought for the occasion, with sleeves like orchid petals. I picture her at the Halifax Shopping Centre, popping into a Le Château dressing room as her mom stands outside shaking her head. There's something sweet about kids who dress up for school dances. This dress, chosen to make her seem older, does the opposite. Her collarbones stick out at the base of her reedy throat.

Kids start to leave. The back of Caleb's purple shirt disappears out the gym doors. I want to see who comes to pick him up, but I stay inside the gym, scrunching up the plastic tablecloths now dotted with tortilla chip crumbs, stuffing them into garbage bins. I fold the metal chairs scattered around the room's perimeter and stack them on a rolling cart. I kill time. Jeffers and Madeleine stand under a brown paper banner painted with *Grade 9 Welcome Dance* in the wobbling hands of budding artists. The parent volunteers head out, and the last scatter of students exits. I walk out with them to the hallway and help the caretakers clean up, though they try to wave me away.

I wait until I see Jeffers say goodbye and turn in the direction of our office—Madeleine's smile falters but recovers quickly. Then I wait in the dark of my car, until I see a mom in a minivan drive up. Madeleine gets in. They drive away.

I wait another minute. Then I drive away, too.

On Monday, we review procedures for the lockdown drill that will happen on Tuesday morning. "When we hear the announcement, we'll turn off the lights and shut off all our devices. That means phones off." I look pointedly at a student who's checking his hair in his phone screen. He puts it away.

"In a real emergency, wouldn't we keep our phones on to communicate with our parents?"

"Yeah, or the police."

"The protocol says devices off," I tell them. "We'll close the blinds and barricade the door. Then we'll all go under our desks and wait while security clears the building. It shouldn't take more than fifteen minutes, and then we'll get back to the lesson."

I spend the rest of the class grading short stories as the students complete a quiz. I brush eraser grits off the page with the side of my hand, and begin to read Caleb's story:

"She always graded in pencil because she was too nice for red pen." *Good characterization*, I scribble, in pencil. "She was barely older than he was. He couldn't even believe she was the teacher." I know who this story is about. How could I not? In the story, the narrator is the teacher's favourite. "She always answered questions after class." In the story, the narrator is the smartest kid in the room, dazzling the teacher with his insights. I write, *Point of view: How does he know she is dazzled?*

In the story, the narrator and the teacher exchange eye contact as other students say idiotic things. "The girls in the class were superfissial. They wore way too much makeup. But not her." In the story, the teacher gives the narrator a ride home after school. In the car, they discover they have everything in common. She parks in front of his house. She reaches over and undoes his seatbelt. I put down my pencil. He brings the teacher inside his house, upstairs to his bedroom. Nobody is home. "She was eager," the story says. They undress. "She was experienced. She knew exactly what she was doing. He realized she was a whore like the rest of them." The scene continues for a page. "Her nipples," the story says, "were the colour of shit."

I shove the pages away from me. My pencil clatters to the ground, and the students all look up to see what's happening. The room is silent, and my hands are shaking; my stomach is a centrifuge. I need to get to my office. I need to vomit. I get up, grab my keys but leave my things. "How much more time do we have, Miss?" I hear someone call after me.

In the hallway, I hear the clomping of his shoes. The halls are empty; everyone else is in class. I pass by other classrooms and think of banging on the doors for help, twenty-two student faces turning my way. My office isn't far. If I can make

it there, I can shut the door and lock it and call somebody
and ask them what to do. I turn into the area where my office
is. The key is already in my hand, between my fingers, ready.

I unlock the door, open it, enter, and Caleb is behind me.

He grabs the edge of the door so I can't close it. "Miss,
I have a question."

"Caleb, please leave." I step backwards, holding my key
out in front of me. The office is cramped, and my back is
already up against Jeffers's desk. I try to remember self-defence
moves from a class I took years ago. Poke his eyes in with two
fingers. Knee him in the groin. Shove the base of your palm
up into his chin. Stomp your heel down on the bridge of his
foot. Use your strongest body parts against his weakest. I
won't freeze. I won't hesitate.

He pushes his way inside, closes the door, and stands in
front of it.

"No!" I shout. "Get the hell out of here! Please." At
please, my voice cracks.

Poke his eyes. Knee his groin. Stomp on his foot.

"I just want to ask a question!" His eyes bulge down at
me. Only now does he seem to realize how scared I am. "Miss?
Why are you crying? . . . I'm not . . ."

"Please just *go*."

The door opens.

"Hey, sorry to interrupt, but I heard . . ." It's Jeffers. He's
holding a clipboard and wearing a lanyard. "What's happening here?" He looks quizzically at Caleb, and then at my wet
face, and down to the key I'm grasping like a knife. He assesses
the situation in an instant, grabs Caleb by the shoulder, and
hoists him back into the hallway. I fall into my chair. Jeffers
hauls him away.

Alone, I wipe my face with a Starbucks napkin I find in
my desk drawer. I breathe in to a count of four, hold it for seven

seconds, breathe out to a count of eight, eyes on the world map
the geography teacher has taped to the wall. She's used a rain-
bow of pushpins to impale the cities she's been to—there seem
to be hundreds of them, spanning at least forty countries.
There's even a pin in Mongolia. I wonder if she took these trips
alone. She's the kind of woman who would—the brave kind.

Several minutes later, Jeffers returns, knocking gently
before entering.

"Thank you," I say. I'm embarrassed. Suddenly the situation seems much smaller.

"Don't worry about it," he tells me, gently. "I took him
to the guidance office." He sits at his desk. He clasps his hand
over the clip of his lanyard, unclasps it. "Anyway, I owed you
for the other night." I lift my face. "At the Grade 9 dance. That
girl, Madeleine. I . . . I didn't know how to handle it. Thanks
for sticking around. These girls"—he shakes his head—"one
of them makes up a story and it can destroy your life."

I've arranged the shelves above my desk with books I've
brought in from home. They're almost full. It occurs to me that
the books and I could be in this office for another forty years.

"I was looking out for *her*," I say, matching his gentle tone.

Jeffers pauses. Then he nods, meeting my eyes.

We crouch under the desks. We turn off the lights, the classroom computer, the overhead projector, our phones. We barricade the door. I don't mention that I've noticed the door
opens outward, and barricading it is a meaningless exercise.
When a student mutters, "Why do we need a school shooting
drill in Halifax?" I don't tell him that drills are a school's
insurance policy, that nowhere is safe. Caleb is under his desk,
too. He makes eye contact with me from across the room. I
look away.

His story is with the principal. His parents have been called. A meeting has been scheduled.

We close the blinds. Some slats are missing—a person could see us if they wanted to, our faces peering up, targets. The PA system blares, "This is an emergency lockdown alert. Remain calm. Do not leave your place of shelter unless advised to do so. This is an emergency lockdown alert." We crouch under desks in the dark and wait for instructions. So much time passes I wonder if instructions will come at all, or if we'll just stay here forever, in this unprotected space. Nobody makes a sound.

Good Enough Never Is

IN THE PHOTOS ON the Toastmasters website, everybody wears a blazer and smiles. They run international conferences and give emotionally devastating wedding toasts. They deliver eulogies and everybody cheers, "Encore! Encore!" Their charisma is electric. Their handshakes are earthquakes. Confidence makes their skin shine. They've mastered the most daunting challenge of all: speaking while being judged by others. According to the stats I looked up before my first meeting, if you offer the average person the choice between giving a five-minute speech to their peers or sitting in a dark, confined space full of Lovecraftian arachnids, they'll choose the arachnids. Public speaking is scarier than monsters. It's scarier than death.

At the Toastmasters meeting, everybody is dressed like a slob and I feel dumb for wearing a blazer, even though I'm only wearing it because I've come straight from work. I hang the blazer over the back of my chair. We're in a rented, over-airconditioned classroom at Dalhousie. Out the window, university students are hunchbacks with backpacks against a red sunset, gripping double-doubles, hurrying away. As people file into the classroom, they smile at me, help themselves to Styrofoam cups of water and store-bought oatmeal cookies, then sit around the horseshoe of tables. The regulars exchange pleasantries, some in thick accents. A cloud of earnestness puffs up above the group like cigarette smoke.

"First time here?" asks a guy as he slides into the chair next to me. I nod. "Don't be nervous," he says, patting my bare shoulder with a damp hand. He introduces himself as Dave. He's maybe ten years older than me, in his late thirties or early forties, with small, close-set eyes. His strong jaw and grey buzz cut, combined with his paunch, give him the look of an ageing football coach. His muscular legs are spread so wide apart that one of them takes up the space where my legs should go, so I keep mine tucked under my chair.

"You've been doing this for a while then?" I ask.

"Oh, ages and ages. Public speaking has always been something I'm good at."

"Then why did you join Toastmasters?"

"Well, I'm very competitive." He tilts his chair back and balances on its two back legs. "Planning to take this to the next level—you know, the competition circuit."

"Of course," I say, though I can't imagine him pictured on the Toastmasters website.

"So, how nervous are you?" he asks. He leans in as though he's telling me a secret, his breath acrid.

"I'm a teacher, so I'm used to speaking in front of a group. I'd like to get better at it, though—cut down on the *ums* and *ahs*, figure out what my weaknesses are."

Most of the people gathered are seated now. A woman approaches the classroom door. Her walk is a shuffle, tennis shoes quiet on the linoleum. She's slight, in a billowy, aubergine caftan over black tights, and her loose black ponytail swings behind her. Her eyes are steely. She grasps the doorjamb.

"See that girl there?" Dave lowers his voice only slightly, pointing at the door with zero subtlety. "I know her. She's a regular, too, but she never comes inside. Every week she comes right up to the door but doesn't have the balls to come in!"

"So she just watches, you mean?"

"Well, we close the door before the meeting starts. One day she'll make it inside!" He laughs, like he's certain she'll never make it.

I think for a moment. "On Reddit I read about a guy whose stage fright was so intense he had his doctor prescribe Valium just so he could attend the Toastmasters meetings. It must have worked." I make my face earnest. "He attended for years and years and ended up placing third in the international contest. Now he's a stand-up comic."

"Interesting," says Dave.

". . . and that man's name is Conan O'Brien."

"Wow, really?" asks Dave.

"No," I say. "Not really."

I signed up for Toastmasters because, even after six years of teaching, I'm afraid that when I speak in class, my students hear the droning voice of the teacher from Charlie Brown. That when I ask, "What does *Lord of the Flies* tell us about humanity?" all they hear is *wohwohwohwohwohwoh*. At a teaching skills seminar the teachers union offered at the start of the semester, they instructed us to record ourselves during class and watch the footage back to evaluate our posture, gestures, volume, tone, eye contact, nervous tics, etc. So I borrowed a camera from the library and set it up at the back of my class-room, and then I gave my Grade 10s a fifteen-minute lecture. Later, at home, I played back the recording on my laptop. Or I started to, but as soon as I saw my ogre face, and my Humpty Dumpty body, and the stretch marks on my upper arms, and my shoulders rounded like those of a cartoon vulture, I turned

the video off. That was twenty seconds in. After self-medicat-
ing with two glasses of wine, I tried again. "Okay, guys," I
heard myself say, in my warbly pigeon voice. "Ummm . . . we're
going to get started . . ." Upspeak turns all my sentences into
rhetorical questions. "I guess we'll start with . . . ummm . . ."
I clicked the Pause button. Smoked a bowl and watched an old
episode of *Parks and Rec* for a boost of positive feelings before
I pressed Play again. In a loopy haze of wine and weed I
watched the whole damn recording. I felt like I was standing
naked in a sorority house, having my flab circled with the
blackest available marker. Watching yourself public speaking is
something nobody should ever have to do.

In the recording, I talk about the symbolism of the conch.
"It represents order," I say to the rows of zoned-out faces.
Ageing fluorescents flicker over us in the yellow room like in
a scene from one of the *Hostel* films. A student yawns.
"Respect, power, ummm . . . civilization." Another student
extracts his phone from his pocket.

I pull a conch shell from my desk drawer. I borrowed it
from my dad. Every night before he prays, he purses his lips
and blows air into the conch. As a kid, I imagined it was the
sound of an amicable goose announcing his approach before
tucking his beak into my palm. Later, I learned that, according to Hindu scripture, the shell radiates a primordial
music—the sound of the universe vibrating. I've been an
atheist for years, but still, this belief feels exquisite and real.
My dad handles the conch so lightly, like a musical instrument; I always understood it was sacred.

In the video, I hold up the conch with one hand. With
my other hand, I open my creased copy of the novel and read,
"*The conch was silent, a gleaming tusk; Ralph's face was dark
with breathlessness and the air over the island was full of bird-
clamour and echoes ringing.*" When I lean on the front edge

of my teacher's desk, one of my legs shakes incessantly under my rumpled skirt. I instruct the students to pass the conch around. "Whoever holds this has the power. They command attention. They control the silence." A boy in the second row whispers to his smirking friend next to him. When the conch reaches him, he blows into it to make a loud honking noise, and the whole class laughs. I chuckle obligatorily and motion for him to pass it on. I've set the novel down on the desk, so my hands are empty through the rest of the lecture. I hold them in front of me, flopping down from the wrists at breast level, limp and curled—dinosaur hands. I'm a useless, feeble T-Rex, destined for extinction.

After I tell the Toastmasters group I'm an English teacher, I'm given the role of Grammarian. I try to decline but there are only nine people, not enough to take on all the roles, which include Toastmaster, Topicsmaster, Jokemaster, Timer, Ah-Counter, and Vote Counter, among others—there's even a Sergeant at Arms. The roles rotate, but this branch has chosen to keep one guy fixed as the Toastmaster, the genial host. The only other person in work attire, he has the slick appearance of a company president, with thick salt-and-pepper hair swooshing back from his forehead, and a pressed shirt with one button undone at the neck. He ushers us smoothly into each segment of the meeting. With the exception of me and an Asian woman named Annie, the others are all men, in varying shapes, sizes, and colours.

"All right, everybody! Time for Table Topics!" The Toastmaster rolls up his sleeves to indicate we're getting to work. "Remember the goal here is to keep your thoughts organized. Be clear and be brief." Table Topics is a key element of Toastmasters, during which each person gives an impromptu one-to-two-minute speech on a provided topic. Sample topics: Arbour Day, Your Favourite Food, The Difference Between Living and Existing, Bad Movies, How to Get Away with Murder.

Two people take their turns. Their mouths move and they gesticulate and everyone claps, but I don't hear any of it. My body shudders with mild panic—as though panic could ever be mild. The feeling is not so much butterflies but insidious plant growth in my chest, roots finding purchase in my gut, a vine winding its way up my windpipe. And then it's my turn. I stand up.

"Nina, please answer the following question," instructs the Topicsmaster. "How do you split a subatomic particle?"

"Um, what?"

"Just run with it," the Toastmaster encourages. "Follow your instincts."

"Your time starts . . . now," says the Timer.

"Uhhh, subatomic particles." I spend five hours a day speaking in front of people, yet this is my opening statement. "Subatomic particles are . . . well, to begin with, they're very small." The Toastmaster and Annie nod and smile. Dave crosses his arms and leans back in his chair. He clears his throat. The Toastmaster eyes him. "They're tiny. Subatomic. That's like, smaller than an atom." I laugh. "Sorry, I'm terrible at this." Nobody says anything. They've been instructed not to interrupt. A few more seconds pass. I glance down and my hands are curled in front of me. I press them down to my sides. I try to remember high school Physics. I try to remember if I even took high school Physics. "I'm trying to remember high school Physics. But all I remember is failing." This was intended as a joke, but everyone is silent. Annie looks embarrassed for me. The Jokemaster is unamused.

"Thirty-five seconds," says the Timer, with finality.

"I'm sorry, I think that's it for me." I sit back down.

"Good first attempt," the Toastmaster tells me. "Next time you'll make it the full minute. The trick is to segue into a topic you *do* know about—move from the foreign to the familiar. For example, you could've talked a bit more about your physics class and what you learned."

The truth is I did okay in high school Physics. I drew plans for a hotel to be suspended over the Northwest Arm, the narrow inlet separating the Halifax Peninsula from the mainland. I built a prototype out of a Lucite jewellery box and some old VCR cables. There was a flaw in my calculations though, and my teacher pointed out that the hotel would likely go the way of the first Tacoma Narrows Bridge, undulating in a calm breeze then collapsing due to aeroelastic flutter. Hotel guests drowning inside a prism, scraping their fingers against the glass as they tried to escape. After the semester ended, defeated, I removed the VCR wires and gave my mom back her jewellery box. I stopped taking Physics after that.

Dave clears his throat. "What I might suggest—"

"You'll get a chance in the next round, Dave," says the Toastmaster. With his natural authority he's skilled at managing the room, and I get why he's the permanent Toastmaster. He'd make a good teacher.

Annie is up next. She removes her watch before she starts and sets it down on the table where she can see it. "My favourite food is . . . oh gosh that's a hard one. I love eggs. They're so versatile! You can scramble them, bake them, fry them, poach them, boil them." She's killing time. Her eyes swim to the ceiling and I can see her processing, churning up the next thing to say. Every few seconds she straightens up, resetting her posture, as though there's a thread coming out of her scalp that somebody keeps tugging. She's wearing a loose floral dress, and as she moves about it swishes around her knees.

"And omelettes . . ." she sighs. "Growing up I used to go on errands with my mom, and we would stop at the street vendors on our way home—in Bangkok, that's where I'm from, as some of you know. We would stop for kai jeow, Thai omelette. They mix egg with a little fish sauce, sugar, and ground pork, and pour it into hot oil"—she illustrates mixing and pouring with her quick hands—"and then sizzle! And then scoop!" She mimes a chef scooping and sliding the omelette across a wok. She's transported. She's Proust. She's the critic in the penultimate scene of *Ratatouille*, who takes a scrumptious bite of a humble vegetable dish and flashes back to the French countryside of his youth. "It was like a brown cloud. Does that sound tasty? Maybe not." Everyone laughs. "But it was. Yummy and crispy and soft. We ate it right there on the street. I had mine plain, but my mom had hers on top of rice with a sprinkle of soy sauce. When I smell eggs cooking, I think about my mom. I haven't seen her in years, except on Skype."

"Beep beep," says the Timer.

The Evaluator for her speech is Dave. He has thirty seconds to give his feedback. He pushes back his chair. "To start with, you need to speak at a louder volume." He flattens his hand and raises it to indicate volume. He slows down when pronouncing the word *louder*, as though he thinks she won't understand.

"Start with the positives, Dave," the Toastmaster reminds him.

"Right, right, can we start the thirty seconds over?" asks Dave.

"Just this one time," says the Toastmaster.

"Your speech wasn't too bad," Dave continues. "You need to speak louder so everyone can hear you. The thoughts seemed scattered, just all over the place. Like I didn't think you needed the parts about your mom. It was a bit off-topic. I'm not sure I learned anything from that."

Annie nods vigorously and takes notes as Dave speaks, though it's the worst critique I've ever heard. When Dave finishes, the Toastmaster adds, "Great work avoiding the *ums*. I can tell you've been working on replacing them with thoughtful pauses." Annie beams.

During the break, I go visit the washroom, which is down the hallway, around a corner, past a study area with comfy chairs. Sitting cross-legged on one of these chairs is the woman I saw earlier, who left before the meeting started. The Shy Woman. Her eyes are closed, and she's breathing deeply. In that posture, she looks like she might levitate.

The rest of the meeting consists of three prepared speeches, one by Dave. When it's his turn, he stands up by the white-board, marker in hand. His nipples assert themselves through his faded maroon T-shirt. So far, everyone else has simply stood behind their chair. Dave has decided to speak about the difference between male and female thinking. He tries the marker but it doesn't work, so he wipes the board with the heel of his hand and picks up a second marker. When he takes the cap off, the room turns pungent. On the board, he draws a straight line. "This is the way a man thinks," he says. Next to it he draws a mess of loops and spirals, taking up half the board space. "This is the way a woman thinks." I survey the room. The men laugh and nod. The Toastmaster checks his watch. Next, Dave holds up a photo that shows washroom doors at what must be a bar or restaurant. On the door for the men's room are four simple letters smack in the middle, spelling *blah*. On the women's, *blah* BLAH blah *blah* BLAH is written all over the door, in a mess of fonts and sizes and directions, from top to bottom.

His Evaluator, one of the seven men, suggests a snazzier intro and more eye contact, while praising Dave's ideas and humour. "Reminds me of the book *Men Are from Mars, Women Are from Venus.*"

I raise my hand.

"You don't need to raise your hand, Nina," says the Toastmaster.

"Umm, how important are research and facts?" I'm trying to be diplomatic. "Like, you know women don't actually think in squiggly lines. I'm pretty sure I read that men's and women's brains are basically the same."

"It's *satire*," explains Dave, glaring. "You're meant to observe. This is your first time here. You don't have the necessary experience to offer criticism."

I shut up.

We conclude by determining who will prepare a speech for next week. "Nina, can I add your name to the list?" the Toastmaster asks me.

"Umm, I guess so. How long does it have to be exactly?"

Dave jumps in. "About the length of a miniskirt: short enough to be interesting, but long enough to cover the essentials."

"Four to six minutes," says the Toastmaster.

When I was a teenager, I used to imagine somebody was constantly watching me, having set up a surveillance system that followed my every action. If I did something wrong, like being rude to my parents or spilling Gatorade on myself or farting or crying un-beautifully, I'd imagine my viewer missing the imperfect moment, because they suddenly had to go get a snack. Or I'd think, *Take 2*, *Take 3*, and imagine a director's clapperboard slapping closed, erasing my mistakes. I do almost the same thing while practising my Toastmasters speeches over the next few weeks—I stand in front of the mirror or my cellphone camera, and as soon as I fudge a line I start over. As a result, the intros of my speeches are flawless; the rest is a word-blur.

Practising for the first speech, I can't get my failed Table Topic about subatomic particles out of my head. My idiocy is a brain chorus: "Uhhhh . . . like . . . sorry . . ." *Stupid idiot failure loser I hate myself.* I rewrite the speech in my head. But if you could rewrite it, it wouldn't be a Table Topic. After my first prepared speech, a short introduction to myself, the easiest possible topic, the Ah-Counter tells me I said *um* forty-three times. For the next week, every time I hear myself say *um* in regular conversation I want to scream.

I sign up for my second prepared speech, determined to squash the *ums*. After I deliver the speech, the Ah-Counter tells me I said *um* forty-seven times, and I go home and actually do scream, dropping my face to the floor and muffling my mouth with the carpet. Thankfully, I live in a building with a concrete frame.

"You're like a log in a river, trying to float downstream," the Toastmaster tells me. "But you're stuck behind a pile of rocks."

After that, I wear an elastic band around my wrist during speech practice, and I snap it at every verbal tic. "Ummm." *Snap.* "I think." *Snap.* "Uhhh." *Snap.* The elastic leaves matching dents in my skin. I leave it on by mistake one night when I'm out to dinner with a friend, and catch myself snapping it out of habit. I take it off, but when I reach for my wine glass there are red lines marking my wrist. By week five, the lines have become welts. Eventually, the skin breaks. I put on some Polysporin and move the elastic a centimetre lower.

There are always open slots in the prepared speech schedule, due to four or five members who show up every week but make polite excuses when the Toastmaster encourages them to volunteer. Instead, they are spectators, leaning back in their chairs, eating their free oatmeal cookies. I suppose they're there to make friends. How do I protest this unfairness? "Find a Meetup group," I'd like to tell them.

I sign up for one of the empty slots almost every meeting, so eight weeks in I'm already preparing for Speech 6 (Objective: Vocal Variety), though I don't seem to be getting any better. According to the Toastmasters newsletter, audiences and Evaluators will let go of minor mistakes if the overall speech is engaging. But I can't help it. Practising for Speech 6, I get so angry at myself that I smack the right side of my head hard with my palm, sending my head flying sideways. It's like a giant has picked me up and shaken me. I google *Can you injure your brain hitting yourself in the head*, and I'm relieved to learn you'd have to hit yourself damn hard to injure your brain. Brains are cushioned with skulls and membranes and cerebrospinal fluid. Perhaps hitting myself in the head could be a safe method of managing self-loathing. Because it isn't just the *ums* and *ahs*. I could quit Toastmasters tomorrow and it would still be there—the lizard swimming through my cerebrospinal fluid and taking small bites of self-esteem. *Perfection*, he urges, in the language of snakes.

The Shy Woman comes to every session of Toastmasters. On my way into that week's meeting, I find her hovering at the doorway, hands holding the sides of the door frame that seems to carry her whole weight. Her knuckles are tight. Evening light from the hallway's courtyard-facing windows turns her into a seraph. I stand behind her at a distance, waiting, telepathically urging her forward. *Go inside*, I think. Today, her hair is two side French braids wound around her head and into a bun at the back. It's a hairstyle I've attempted and failed at before. How much time did that take her? Did she, too, follow a Pinterest tutorial? She's still in the doorway. *Go inside*, I think again.

One of the men who never participates approaches. "Excuse me," he says, tapping her shoulder. She lets go of the door frame, startled, and steps back. Then she walks, face down but unhurried, away towards the study area.

Table Topics whooshes by. My leg jitters through the whole thing, while Speech 6 plays like an anthem in my head. Vocal Variety is the toughest speech so far, because you have to pay attention to the Four Ps: Pitch, Pace, Power, and Pauses. On my notes I've used red pen to signal intonation, and highlighter to mark pauses. The Toastmasters newsletter suggested exaggerating syllables. My delivery sounds as though I'm reading a book aloud to a child, turning the pages and exclaiming, "*Where's* the caterpillar? *There* he is!"

Perhaps this is okay, because my speech is about a children's book—my own childhood favourite, *The Monster at the End of This Book*. On the cover, Grover waves a furry-armed hello, posed like a salsa dancer while standing next to a green lamppost and a trash can. His eyes are inscrutable—two eggs sunny side up with black yolks. "Please do not turn the page," says Grover, in some variation, on every page. "There is a Monster at the end of this book." The word *Monster* is capitalized, its letters hand-drawn in bold magenta. Has there ever been a reader who followed Grover's instructions and simply closed the book?

My dad used to read it aloud to me when I was five or six years old. "*Oh, I am so scared of Monsters,*" he would say, in a pitiable, frightened voice that smoothed out his Indian accent. He feigned physical effort with each page turn, as Grover used rope and wood planks and nails and brick to build barriers that were invariably destroyed.

"But Grover, you *are* the monster!" I would announce. By then, I knew the story's ending. I lost the book some time later, when we moved houses.

I had planned to conclude my speech by telling the group about how my dad had bought me a new copy for Christmas once. It was the year after I'd dropped out of graduate school and moved back home. He'd left it, unwrapped, for me on my nightstand while I was still asleep. On the inside cover, in the space for an inscription under *This Little Golden Book belongs to*, he'd written: *Dearest Nina—Just to remember those good old days.* I don't know if he'd intended the gift as a symbolic gesture or if it was just something he'd come across at the bookstore, but I'd taken it as my dad trying to convince me that there were no monsters. That I could still be a reader, even if I wasn't anything else.

When the Toastmaster reads my name off the sign-up sheet, I look down at my colour-coded notes. And it dawns on me that the speech I've written is too intimate to share. There is something awful about the idea of performing it in a scripted, stagey voice, then serving it up for evaluation. I don't want to tell this story to these people, whom after eight weeks I still barely know.

"Pass," I say.

The Toastmaster raises his eyebrow in a question. "Are you sure? We have lots of time."

"Umm . . . I'm sure." I snap the elastic out of habit.

At the end of the meeting, Dave makes an announcement. "Annie and I are having some people over for her thirty-fifth birthday this weekend. You're all invited to join us." It has somehow escaped me that these two are together, though they sit next to each other every week. Nobody else seems surprised.

In search of a birthday card, I visit every greeting card store at the Halifax Shopping Centre. But the cards are too froufrou or sentimental or not funny enough or cost eight dollars. And Annie is a graphic designer, so the card should be well designed. I visit a letterpress studio downtown but the cards, with embossed phrases in vintage fonts, seem too irreverent, too hip, saying *Sorry you're so old*.

The party is a snack potluck, so I decide to bring home-made chocolate chip cookies. Mrs. Fields was a Toastmaster. She was a housewife and then her cookie business began to flourish. Her company grew from one store in Palo Alto to hundreds of stores in over thirty countries. Because she kept getting invited to give talks, she joined Toastmasters. Now she's a master of both cookies and toasts. Her motto: *Good enough never is.*

When I google recipes, I always use the word *best*, as in *best chocolate chip cookies*, or *best chicken pot pie*. Then I read all the recipe reviews and make notes on the suggested adaptations. I chill the dough for thirty-six hours as per advice from the *New York Times*. The recipe requires both bread and cake flours, chocolate that's at least 60 per cent cocoa, and sea salt. It takes five batches until my cookies look like the photos. On the third batch, I forget my oven mitts and burn the pads of my fingers when I grab the pan with my bare hands.

On the way to the party, out of time, I stop at Shoppers and spend fifteen minutes reading through birthday cards I've already read. I choose one, but by then it doesn't even matter which.

Dave and Annie live in a low-rise building on South Street. It's spacious and has thin-plank oak floors with an ancient, pleasing creak. The furnishings are sparse IKEA. This new IKEA store only just opened, and already the area is descending rapidly into fibreboard. A mix of Toastmasters folks and Dave's work friends cram together on a sinking sofa and a couple of floor poufs; the rest stand around a dining table, picking at the assortment of mismatched potluck snacks— translucent salad rolls with slivers of red pepper, a tray of cured meats, a plump loaf of banana bread with a burned crust. I add my tin of cookies to the table and stand there, observing the room, figuring out who to talk to. There's a pashmina draped above the window as decor. Dave's weights are stacked on the floor in a corner. A wall shelf holds assorted self-help books: *Awaken the Giant Within; Eat This, Not That!* A silver picture frame holds a photo of Annie and Dave, his arm around her shoulders like a yoke.

"So you guys meet every week and listen to each other give speeches?" asks one of Dave's friends, a smaller version of Dave. He's sunburned and wearing shorts and a polo shirt, revealing thick blond hair on his arms and legs. He's the kind of man who wears summer clothing throughout the fall, even in Nova Scotia.

"Why would you sign up for that?" asks Dave #3, who has kept his shoes on despite the pile of footwear by the door. This Dave is the tallest one. It turns out he's Dave's actual brother.

"The best part about Toastmasters is that it works," says the Toastmaster. He sips wine he brought himself, from a glass with the name of a bank on it. He sits between the two Dave clones, legs extending from deep within the sofa. He balances the base of the wine glass on his protruding knee.

"Toastmasters is about more than public speaking," adds an older gentleman named Hasim, who has deep-set eyes and is rumoured to have lost a child. He's been attending the meetings for three years. I've only heard him speak of fastidious hobbies, like cultivating roses and making origami frogs.

"You guys should join," Dave tells his fellow Daves. "You might learn some new skills."

The Toastmaster looks worried at the prospect of them joining.

"I've got all the skills I need," says Summer Dave.

"Dave joined to meet women," says Brother Dave.

"Another reason *you* should join," says Original Dave. "How long have you been single now?"

"Oh, so did you guys meet each other through Toastmasters?" I ask, turning to Annie, who is adding a stack of balloon-dotted napkins to the table.

"No, we met on—" she begins, but Dave interrupts her.

"I'm the one who convinced Annie to join," he says. "To improve her English. I'd already been giving speeches for ages at that point."

"Dave has no game at all," Brother Dave tells us, "despite having read all those pickup artist books. Memorized them— haven't you, Dave?" He bites into a thin slice of meat, then puts the rest of it into his mouth and licks his fingers.

The doorbell chimes and Annie goes to answer it.

"Oh man," says Summer Dave, "in high school he had a crush on a teacher for four years and at graduation he asked her out." He pauses. "She turned him down."

"And she was old, too," says Brother Dave, guffawing.

Dave is standing next to the window, drinking a beer. "Not true. None of that is true." He waves his free hand, pretends dismissiveness. "Liars."

"But then he went to Toastmasters," says Brother Dave.

"And everything changed," adds Summer Dave.

"Too bad you don't give the speeches while on treadmills," says Brother Dave, stretching out to pat Dave's stomach.

"Or while getting personality transplants," says Summer Dave.

I wait to see if they'll high-five. Something has shifted in Original Dave. His eyes have narrowed. He's sucking in his stomach.

"Cookies?" I offer, passing around the tin I brought. Nobody takes one.

"What was the name of that girl Dave dated . . ."

"Wait, Dave dated a girl?" The Dave clones laugh together.

The Toastmaster shifts his legs and finishes his wine. I wait for him to defuse the situation, to tell us some anecdote about the time he took a trip to Boston and fell in love with a venture capitalist, guiding us effortlessly into a new subject, but he doesn't.

Original Dave is twitching. "Well, obviously I dated a girl. I married Annie, didn't I?"

"Oh yeah, what site was that you met her on again, Dave?" says Brother Dave. "Thaibrides.com?"

Annie is standing by the entryway, holding a plate of banana bread with the burnt parts cut off. Her eyebrows lift as she registers the words. Then her face crumples. She puts down the plate, turns, and leaves the room. She passes by the Shy Woman, who has just arrived and is kneeling by the pile of shoes, untying her shoelaces. She's watching everything, her eyes black.

"Assholes!" the Shy Woman says loudly, standing, laces still tied. Her whole body is trembling. She glares directly at Dave. "Are you going to let them talk about her like that?" The Toastmasters are silent. The other Daves look at each other and then around the room at the rest of us, wide-eyed and smiling close-lipped in fake contrition.

"Assholes," echoes Dave, but he's waited too long. His vulnerabilities are showing. The words bounce off the other Daves like they're rubber; stick to Dave like he's glue.

The Shy Woman has dressed up for the party, in a black silk blouse and a tea-length skirt the colour of frost-covered leaves.

"Hi," I say quietly, forgetting we don't know each other. We've taken the Daves' seats on the couch while they've claimed the space by the table. Some of the guests have left, and the Daves fill their plates, except for Original Dave, who has gone to see if Annie will come back to the party. There's an ice cream cake in a sweating box on the counter.

"So you know, she's not actually a mail-order bride or whatever," the Shy Woman informs me.

"Oh, I know that," I say, though I'd wondered for a second if it was true.

"She has a degree from NSCAD. And she might be from Thailand, but her English is way better than Dave's—she's just not a braggadocious fuck about it like he is. I've known Dave since grade school. I literally once heard him say, 'She and I's.' He thinks I'm Thai, too, but I'm Chinese. And by Chinese, I mean I grew up in Sackville, Nova Scotia. Those two met on a dating site like everybody else."

"I thought you were . . . shy," I say, foolishly. "Why don't you ever come join the meetings?"

"That's me, a Shy Asian," says the Shy Woman, whose name is Jules. When she sees my face, she gives an easy laugh. "Don't worry, just messing with you. I have awful glosso-phobia. That's fear of public speaking. See?" She holds out her hands and they are still trembling. "One word to these assholes, and this happens. I'm glad the word was *assholes* this time. But seriously, I get panic attacks. I get stuck there in the doorway. It's like this force field I can't walk through."

I usually avoid touching people, but impulsively I reach out and take both her hands in mine, holding them firmly, willing them to stop shaking. "Have you ever heard of Zeno's paradoxes?" I ask. I tell her about the one called the dichot-omy paradox. "Imagine you want to walk from Point A to Point B, at the other end of a field. To get there, you first must reach the halfway point. But to get to the halfway point, you must get halfway to the halfway point. And before that, halfway to the halfway point of the halfway point. Halfway and halfway and halfway. But if this is true, you have infinite distances to cross." When I let go of her hands, they're not shaking anymore. "Aristotle said, 'That which is in locomotion must arrive at the halfway stage before it arrives at the goal.' How will you ever get there? It's theoretically impossible," I say to Jules. "But we do it every single day."

A few days later, Jules crosses the threshold into the meeting. She and I arrive early, as we planned, because I thought it might make it easier. "Yet another boring classroom," I say, entering first and flicking on the light switch.

"Zap." Jules shoots starburst motions with her hands towards the doorway, like she's casting a spell. Her hands imitate falling debris. "That was the force field," she explains to me. I can tell she'll do well on Speech 5: Your Body Speaks. After several minutes of working up her nerve, Jules takes a deliberate step through the doorway as though there's a crack in the floor she might fall into.

"Table Topics is first, right?" she asks, sitting next to me at the end of the horseshoe closest to the door. She's been reading the newsletters, too.

The Toastmaster is absent, vacationing in Maine. Dave, the next to arrive, has volunteered for the role. When he enters, he sees Jules sitting there and scowls, but says nothing. He sits on the opposite end of the horseshoe, right across from us. Annie comes in just as the meeting is about to begin, then sits in the middle of the horseshoe, a few seats away from Dave.

From the start of the meeting, Dave has an angry energy, pacing at the front of the room, clapping his hands together to punctuate his statements. He has ideas for how to liven up the session, opening with vocal warm-ups. We sing in monotone, *"The lips the teeth the tip of the tongue the lips the teeth the tip of the tongue . . .*" Dave's voice is like a loudspeaker, and he sings between gritted teeth, clutching every word with his mouth. Next, he leads a massage train, insisting we all stand up and then steering us to the centre of the room to form a circle. We turn clockwise to place our hands on the shoulders of the person in front of us. My hands are on a stranger's shoulders, bony and tense. I massage half-heartedly while Dave buries his hot thumbs too deep into my spine. He corrects my posture with his hands, adjusting, pressing my upper back. "Stand up straight, that's right," he says. "No slouching."

We're back in our seats for Table Topics. With no pre-amble, Dave points at Jules with one finger. "Why don't you start?"

I'm about to protest. I'm sitting at the very end of the horseshoe—I should be the one going first. But Jules stands. She clasps her hands together in front of her and waits. There's a sympathetic whirring in my gut. At the end of the party, I offered to give Jules a ride home. Before we left, we stood by the dwindling shoe pile and said goodbye to Annie, who had washed her face and returned with a bright, fixed grin to serve her own birthday cake. Dave lingered in the kitchen. He didn't say goodbye to either of us. Wouldn't even look Jules in the eye.

He's looking at her now, as he announces that we'll each give an impromptu one-to-two-minute speech on an object we have with us today. Jules retrieves her purse from the back of her chair where it was hanging, and fumbles through it with one long arm. I can see her holding each item and considering it—*wallet, pen, lip gloss*. She pulls out her keychain and holds it up for us to see. Dangling from her set of keys is a miniature stainless-steel piano.

"I've played the piano since I was three," she says. "I think it's the most fascinating and lovely instrument. Ivory keys attached to tiny hammers, tapping on strings. All inside a hollow block of wood that stands on thin legs. Who came up with that? Bartolomeo Cristofori, I guess." She laughs and the sound is musical, delicate and falling. "I bought this keychain at a market in London a few months ago, to remind me of this exhibit I saw at the British Library. They had one of Chopin's handwritten manuscripts just right there in front of me." The keychain jingles in her grip. She silences it, clasping her hands back together around the keys. She tells us she started composing a few years ago, but that it doesn't come easily. She had stared at Chopin's manuscript, moving her face close to the display case, deciphering words in his cramped script.

"I've always been quiet. But at the piano it's like I have permission to be loud. Soft-loud, *pianoforte*—that's where the word *piano* comes from."

When Jules finishes, there's brief applause. She returns to her chair and fixes her eyes on the table, waiting.

"That was brilliant—" I begin, but Dave interrupts.

"You need to speak louder," he booms. "I doubt the people at the other end of the room could hear you."

At this point, the Toastmaster would usually intervene, but today Dave is the Toastmaster.

"Dave, I'm evaluating this one," I say.

"I'm helping her out here," he says. "Volume is key."

"Did you not listen to her speech at all?" I ask. "I don't really think it'd be better if she had yelled it."

"Nobody said anything about yelling," yells Dave.

My eyes land on Annie, who slumps in her seat, exhausted. When I turn back to Jules, she's trembling again, gazing down at the little piano.

"You have to play to win. Don't play to avoid losing," Dave says to Jules. Her eyes are wet, but she doesn't get up. She doesn't leave.

"I'll go next," I announce, standing. I reach into the tote bag I've brought. I had class right before this, and I'm prepared—in my bag is a binder of lesson plans, a pencil case, miscellaneous personal items, and the conch.

I hold up the shell, iridescent and otherworldly, heavy and cold, ridges pressing against my hand. The open end is frilled pink like a girl's dress. Whoever holds the conch has the power. I don't say *um* once. I am perfect.

A Human Shape

I'M AT MY DESK, eating a sandwich with one hand and marking assignments with the other, when Jessica comes into class early. We're workshopping her poem today.

"Hey there," I say stupidly, as she tucks her lean body neatly into her front-row seat.

The poem is about her eating disorder, the draft written in loopy handwriting and purple pen. She's not the first. In the seven years I've been teaching, there's been one nearly every semester. There *is* something poetic about self-starvation—in its hunger and yearning. When I hear the word *fasting*, I always picture a waning moon. And though Jessica's poem includes a tired metaphor about a broken ballerina, she also surprised me by describing hipbones as shark fins jutting from ocean water. It's clear this poem is about *her*, which made it hard to give feedback. *Try to experiment more with enjambment*, I wrote. *Too many similes?* I queried. I considered writing: *This poem makes me want to be sick.*

Grade 10 English is the period after lunch, but I spent my lunch hour visiting my father at the QEII, where he is recovering from a heart attack. I'm hoping I have enough time to finish eating and marking before class. It's a sad sandwich, the kind an Indian bachelor might make if he were living alone for the first time—potato curry on Dempster's multigrain, and one slice is the loaf end, because that was all I had left. And now Jessica is sitting in front of me, so I have to eat with restraint. I chew more slowly. I dab the corners of my mouth carefully with a napkin. For the next ten minutes, she watches me eat my lunch, which, I realize, too late, is composed entirely of carbohydrates.

While examining him after his stent surgery, the doctor told my dad, "Oh, you're Indian. You've been eating too much butter chicken!"

"I told him real Indians don't eat such things," my dad said to me. He was sitting up in his hospital bed, the powder blue bedsheet folded beneath his elbows, and the back of his hand thick with medical tape, as he gingerly unwrapped an orange popsicle. "And our South Indian diet is very different than what you see in restaurants here. In fact, it is the utmost healthy cuisine." After sniffing the popsicle, he set it aside. My dad eats nothing but rice and vegetables. He doesn't eat butter, salt, cream, or fried foods. I've never seen him eat a dessert, though he once claimed to have a weakness for maraschino cherries. He's been a vegetarian his entire seventy-two years, except for one single bite of a hot dog he took at my tenth birthday party. He still regrets that hot dog: "All of you were eating them," he said, "you and those friends of yours, eating hot dogs with such relish"—he laughed at his intentional pun—"and I thought, this is a real North American item I must try . . ."

"Don't blame the hot dog," I told him. "My doctor friend said Indian men have notoriously small arteries." I was sorry as soon as I said it, because my mother, who I had forgotten was in the room with us, started to cry. She was wearing the same shade of blue as the plastic chair she was sitting on, and it looked as though she'd grown four metal limbs.

One by one, the rest of the students arrive. Some days my class appears particularly hostile—there's the sullen boy who always crosses his arms, and the girl with the false lashes who rolls her eyes when I use *Pretty Little Liars* as a hip pop-culture reference (I can't blame her—the show isn't even airing anymore). I wonder how aware they are of their facial expressions. The best semesters are when I have nodders, students who nod whenever I say anything even half true. "Poetry is still relevant," I say, and their heads go up and down like bobbleheads on a jostled shelf. In my Psych 101 class in university, I learned that if you're talking to someone but don't know what to say next, you should start nodding. This motivates your conversation partner to keep talking. Nodding can influence the nodder's own thoughts too, so even if I believed that poetry was entirely irrelevant—which I don't, but I'm just saying— if I nodded vigorously enough, I could convince myself otherwise.

I begin class by talking about the episode of *Pretty Little Liars* I streamed last night and how that show has way too many suspicious hunks. I say something trite about body image and the media, as an easy segue into talking about Jessica's poem. "Sooo, what did we like about this poem?" There's a set of identical twin girls who seem to be texting each other. I see one twin type on her phone and the other twin suppresses laughter, and then she types and the first twin smirks. If only they weren't laughing, I could pretend they were texting about what a great teacher I am.

"I like that this poem is relatable," says a boy in a Mooseheads jersey. I'd been calling him Mike the first

month of the semester because that's the name on my attendance sheet, but then he told me he prefers being called
Matt—except in the moment I can never remember which
name to use. So now I just make the *M* sound and muffle
the part after that.

"This poem flows really well," says Nose Ring. I like her,
despite her use of poorly defined verbs. She wears unassuming
hoodies and keeps the hood on throughout class. The hood
hides dark hair, which pairs unusually with her grey eyes. Her
appearance was already sort of bewitching, and then she
showed up mid-semester with a pierced nose. If she weren't
my student, I'm pretty sure we would be friends.

"Well, what's up with this rhyme scheme?" says my devil's
advocate student, and then I hear "I don't know if anorexia
is really worth writing about" from my controversial student.
The class erupts into a fantastic debate about whether some
topics are more worthy of a literary rendering.

"Just look at *Seinfeld*," says our one nodder. "It's a show
about nothing!"

"But that's not literature!" another student practically
shouts. I think he's on the debate team. I'm not even participat-
ing in the discussion, just sitting back and picturing this
moment as a scene from one of my favourite movies, *Dead Poets
Society* or *Mr. Holland's Opus* or *Dangerous Minds* or *Sister Act
2*. Excellent movies about excellent teachers, where all they have
to do is deliver some quotable quote—"Play the sunset," or
"Once a marine, always a marine," or "I'm not really a nun"—
for their classes to pass the standardized exam or win the
national choir competition. Twenty minutes pass and I conclude
the discussion by gently discouraging a suggestion from one of
the twins that the poem be written in the shape of an hourglass.

I give a brief lecture and then assign an in-class writing
exercise. Five minutes before class ends, I check to see if

they're still writing. Jessica is not writing. Her head is bent down, almost touching her paper, and her arms are stretched out in front of her, her pencil clenched in both hands. With their flexed tendons, her arms remind me of the braided cables that hold up a suspension bridge. It might be a yoga pose. Her hair, falling over her arms, is of such an indefinite brown that when it goes grey, probably no one will notice.

Two weeks later, I'm marking poems at my parents' house in the North End. My dad has returned from the hospital and taken a leave of absence from work. He has no plans to retire yet, though he keeps saying he will once his daughter's future is "settled." Now he spends his time discovering innovations from a decade ago. "I have registered on Twitter," he tells me. He's reading tweets on his laptop screen while another window streams *Slumdog Millionaire*. Lately, he's been really into Indians who have achieved Hollywood success. "Indians have come such a long way," he says, googling pictures of the actors. One features the ragamuffin children from the movie wearing tuxedos to the 2009 Oscars; another has them lined up at the Mumbai visa office. He turns the screen around to show my mom.

"We were just like them!" he tells her. "Many years back, of course."

"Speak for yourself," says my mother, chopping a large pile of vegetables.

My dad and I are at the kitchen table, and my mom is cooking dinner with ingredients I've never seen in our house—kale and flaxseed and avocados. I'm trying to imagine how she's going to combine it all, as I watch her pull out an egg carton from the fridge. I am certain my parents have never eaten eggs before, a suspicion that's confirmed when my mother cracks the egg by tapping on it with a spoon. She then breaks it over a bowl and attempts to separate the white by using the spoon to scoop out the yolk.

"The nutritionist suggested egg-white omelettes," my dad says.

"And salmon." My mother shakes her head.

"And she said to stop eating white rice," my dad adds. "Can you believe it? I've been eating white rice two meals a day since I was a small boy."

My father launches into a story about growing up in a house in rural Kerala. It sounds like the home of a cartoon gopher: clay walls, red dirt floors, root vegetables piled in a corner on a scrap of burlap. My father's sister still lives in that house, her back perpetually bent at a ninety-degree angle from years under low ceilings and doorways, and from carrying heavy things for long distances. My father claims that as children they took ten-kilometre walks with bags of rice hoisted up on the tops of their heads. This image clashes with the one I have of him yanking bags of rice from the trunk of his SUV.

"But one day," my dad continues, "there was no rice in the house." They went ten days without rice, eating curries made from gourds as they waited to harvest and sell their areca nuts so they could afford to go to the store in the nearest town. "For an Indian, rice is everything," he says, closing his eyes. I remember the time he made mushroom risotto from an Uncle Ben's packet, standing over the stove and stirring, tasting it with a surprised frown on his face, then stirring again, patiently, as though he could coax it into tasting better.

I don't know how to respond. How do you trade stories with people who have lived so much more life than you have? With people who have experienced real hunger?

Despite my hesitation, I root through my pile of poems, find Jessica's, and read it aloud.

"I don't know what to do with this," I say. "We discussed it in class, but it's like there's something missing from the discussion. Everyone loudly tiptoes around the fact that she's writing about herself. Of course, it'd be worse if they did acknowledge it . . ."

"How do you know the poem is true?" asks my mother. "Maybe she just watched some TV show and took the idea from there."

"Yeah, that's possible. But almost everything they write that's not science fiction is about themselves. Some will even admit it. And the writing just *feels* real. Like what you'd write in a diary. As her teacher, aren't I obligated to treat the piece as though it's true, even if it isn't?"

"In that case, don't you think you should inform someone?" asks my mother. "Her parents? Or the counselling office?" My mom has somehow burned the omelette. She reaches up to turn on the stove fan.

The guidance office in our school is a volleyball coach in a skirt suit. It's clear: a girl in my class is gradually destroying her body. But then, aren't the smokers out by the parking lot doing the same?

"The first time somebody turned in a poem like this, I handed it back with a note saying she could talk to me if there was a problem, or I could make her an appointment with the counsellor," I tell my parents. "She never came to me, but one of my student evaluations that year said I should 'mind my own goddamned business.'"

"Hmm." My mother scrapes burnt egg from the pan into the garbage disposal. She rinses the pan, gagging at the smell.

Perhaps it's mass hysteria: all the students in my Grade 10 class start writing about their bodies, too. We read one poem about

budding breasts that actually uses the word *budding*. There's
one about skin picking that I recommend the author submit
to the school arts magazine. There are only two boys in my
class, and Mike/Matt writes about the pressure to take ste-
roids, and the debater writes about being short. Jessica pro-
poses a class project: "Let's build a plaster woman." She
explains that we could each contribute a plaster body part,
even the boys, to symbolize a non-binary view of gender. Then
we will fasten the different pieces together with wire.

"We could write lines from our poems on it," suggests
the false-lashed eye-roller, and the nodding student begins to
nod, and soon everybody is nodding, and I agree, since really
you can do anything in an English class as long as you assign
a writing response afterwards.

The next day, they bring in rolls of plaster of Paris bandages and economy-size tubs of Vaseline. We fill empty yogurt
containers with water from the washrooms and space them
out on the desks. The devil's advocate, a girl with elfin ears
and a pixie haircut, plays music from her tablet, a mournful
playlist full of violin solos. It's not what I thought my students
listened to, and I wonder how well I know them, despite my
exposure to their thinly veiled autobiographical writing. The
humble notes of a bassoon form a soundtrack to nineteen
people covering themselves in plaster by dipping crumbly
sheets into cold water and moulding them around greased
upper arms and calves and necks and noses. The class resembles a plastic-surgery recovery room. The devil's advocate
carefully covers her chin, the waffle-weave bandages spreading upwards like wings.

The twins each volunteer a breast, and the controversial
student, who's on the rugby team and wore shorts today, says
she'll do her upper thighs. They build a privacy curtain by
draping jackets over chairs and backpacks stacked in a

mammoth pile. When Mike/Matt heads over to the pile to retrieve his backpack—"Gotta check my phone," he says—I point him back to the other side of the room.

"Can we use your stomach? You have such a flat stomach," one of the twins says to Nose Ring, who's sitting in a chair next to Jessica, so deeply buried inside her white hoodie that I think of ET on the bicycle.

"She's not interested," says Jessica, tersely, maybe a little jealous, even before the girl declines.

"I was going to do my hand," I tell Nose Ring. "Why don't you do yours instead?"

"Yeah, that sounds okay," she agrees, shrugging. She turns back to the twins and offers them her hand, palm facing up as though to accept spare change.

"Why would we want your hand?" the second twin asks.

Jessica says they can use her stomach, and instead of going behind the privacy screen, she lifts up her shirt and knots it high above her midriff. The twins rub Vaseline on her skin and begin applying the plaster, one sheet at a time, sculpting and smoothing the layers over her waist and ribcage until it takes on the shape and rigidity of a corset.

I excuse myself from the classroom, promising to return quickly, though honestly, I want to get away from all the bodies. As I approach the guidance office, I decide to pop in and talk to the school's one counsellor. Her door is open, and she's wearing sweatpants today.

"Hey Liz," I say. "Congrats on the Senior Girls' win last week."

"It was all them." She swivels her chair to face me. "They're a hardworking bunch of kids. Really put in the effort to improve." Volleyball trophies decorate her office shelves. "Can I help you with something?" she asks.

"Well, I have a quick question . . . I guess I just wanted a second opinion. Say one of your girls was showing signs of an eating disorder. Would you confront her about it, or . . . ?"

"That can get serious," Liz says. "We had a player at an away game once who vomited so violently it ruptured her esophagus. We had to take her to the ER in Moncton."

"Yikes . . . I guess you're right. I should maybe look into this further . . ." I'm thinking of the kids back in my class-room, all moving together towards a shared goal.

"Which student is it? What's her name?"

I hesitate. It strikes me that to give her name is to single her out—to separate her from the others. Exposing her in a way she hasn't asked for.

Over the weekend, I go with my parents to GoodLife because my dad has signed us all up for discount memberships he found on Kijiji. We walk purposefully into the lobby, where we are suddenly unsure of what to do with ourselves, never having been inside a fitness centre before. Until now, my exer-cising has consisted only of leisurely outdoor badminton games and brisk, anxious walks on the Halifax Waterfront. My mom signs up for a spin class, and later, disappointed, tells us that *spinning* is only another word for indoor cycling. My dad experiments with weight machines before a gym attendant hurries over and tells him to stop.

I escape to an elliptical machine, such an odd contrap-tion—it doesn't translate to real life the way a treadmill or exercise bike does. I'm worrying I might fall off and become tangled in the equipment's swivelling parts, when I see Jessica immediately ahead of me, climbing onto a treadmill in sporty spandex. There's an episode of *Full House* where eldest daughter D.J. is invited to a pool party and, with the goal of looking better in a bathing suit, she starts over-exercising.

She doesn't eat for three days. When offered cake, D.J. cringe-smiles, opts for a homemade water popsicle instead, and says, "Who needs cake when you can lick ice on a stick?" *Laugh track*. Later in the episode, she gets off a StairMaster and dizzily lurches to her knees, before her sister yells for help. Bob Saget, one of the show's many father figures, has a concerned talk with her. "Deej," he says, "I want you to promise me that you're going to eat healthy and exercise the right way." D.J. never skips a meal again. If only I could deliver concerned talks with Bob Saget's soft-spoken ease. If only sitcom writers would tell me what to say. I could cure every eating disorder in the school district.

I wonder if Liz has called Jessica to the office or telephoned her parents. Does she know it was me who reported her? On the treadmill next to her is Nose Ring, who has traded in her signature hoodie for a boxy T-shirt of the sort you'd be given at your dad's company picnic. I hadn't realized they were friends outside of class. The gym has a wall-to-wall mirror, and I imagine the girls spotting my reflection and glaring at me, raising their hands to give me two simultaneous middle fingers. I leave the elliptical under the pretence of buying a bottle of water. I imagine going to school on Monday and finding an empty, boycotted classroom, and scrawled on the white board: *Mind your own goddamned business*. I imagine a workshop mutiny, where every student disagrees with every single thing I say—all nineteen of them sitting at their desks, frowning and crossing their arms and keeping their heads statue-still, the twins texting each other to say that I am the worst teacher they've ever had.

The school lobby forms a T-shape with its intersecting hallways. At the top part of the T, inside a display case about nine feet long, is the plaster woman, wired together and suspended with string. It's a body cast without a body, displaying its hollow eggshell insides. They've installed it in a sidestroke swimming position, with one arm stretching forward and the other trailing back, bent realistically at the joints. Her outside is painted in streaky maroon and powder blue—the class couldn't agree on a colour. She shimmers garishly under two coats of varnish. Instead of clothing, she wears glitter that spells out lines from the students' poems in confrontational block letters and alluring italics. I have to lean in close to the glass to read them, and they are all about acceptance and hope and loving your body—lines from poems so sentimental that the students themselves, when forced to read their work aloud to the class, blush and stammer, and admit to having written them the morning they were due.

I go left, with the intention of heading to my classroom. It's early, so the hallway is empty except for one caretaker and one chair outside the guidance office, where Jessica is sitting, back straight, face so flushed it looks like she's been running.

I would really like to walk back in the direction I came, but I force myself to move forwards. Jessica turns towards the sound of my footsteps.

"Hey, Jessica. How are you this morning?" I ask gently.

Jessica blinks and stares wordlessly at me, processing. "How am I?" she says in a quiet voice, and then turns to face her lap. "I can't believe you did that . . . What were you thinking?"

I wait for a second before answering, wondering if there's any possibility she's referring to something else. But there isn't. They would have told her about the poem. How could she not put it together that it was me?

"I'm so sorry, Jessica. I just didn't have any other option." And this is true, isn't it? It's what I've been repeating in my head. I choose my words carefully, searching for something compassionate and real. "I'm worried about you."

"I *don't* have an eating disorder," she says, spitting out the word *don't*.

"It's okay," I begin, crouching down to meet her at face level and lowering my voice. I'm trying to project empathy, to show her that I'm not just a teacher but someone she can be honest with. It was, after all, *my* classroom where she felt comfortable enough to share a poem about being broken, ending in the line "I don't know what to do."

But she interrupts. "No. You're completely wrong," she says. Her eyebrows squeeze together incredulously, and she flings up her hands. "*Nur* is the one who has anorexia."

I stand abruptly and feel the slow rush of my blood awakening. A light-headedness. A clarity. In the hallway around the corner, behind protective glass, is Nose Ring—Nur's—hand, narrow and bony and now replicated in plaster. When confronted with this class project, she wasn't eager to coat her body in wet bandages. On my suggestion, she had pushed up the sleeve of her hoodie to unveil a hand so small it could only hold a single letter—the *d* in the word *steroid*. Not even a word that's meaningful to her situation. The rest of the letters spread down someone else's arm.

I feel nauseated. "I'm sorry," I say. I look down helplessly at Jessica. She is wiping her eyes. "I'll fix it. I'll tell them it was my mistake."

"It really doesn't matter at this point," Jessica says.

"Of course it does," I insist.

"You could have just stayed out of it. Now she hates me because the school told my mom and then she called Nur's parents. Now Nur is literally living at the hospital." Jessica is crying openly now, her words all jumbling together. "Something is wrong with her liver. But my parents think *I* have a problem. You know, you could have said something to *me* instead of going and telling the school. Why would you *do* that? We were figuring it out."

"I'm sorry," I say again, though I might as well have said nothing. "She'll be okay," I tell Jessica, hoping this is true, though it already feels like a lie. Because I know the way these things go.

At my parents' house, my father sits in front of his laptop, eating unsalted almonds from his cupped palm. "Mono-unsaturated," he tells me proudly. He pushes his weight back against his chair and crunches an almond. "Look here, Nina." He motions for me to lean forward to see the screen. It's playing a video of somebody's echocardiogram. Because it resembles a fetal ultrasound—black and white, blotchy and blurry, throbbing and glitching—I find myself searching for a human shape.

At what point of starvation does your heart start to weaken? Does it matter how small your arteries are when you are only a teenager? Or maybe it's more about chemicals—mineral deficiencies, electrolyte imbalances, things English teachers don't know about.

"That's neat, Dad," I say, but he can tell I'm not paying much attention. I told him what happened with the girls. He's already given me a lengthy, sitcom-quality concerned talk.

"Nina, we have no control over others' decisions," he says now, repeating what he said before.

"You could not have fixed her health issues . . .

"The girl would have gone to the hospital regardless . . .

"We have to let others choose their own path . . ."

There's an image in my mind of two girls, one dark-haired and one blonde, heads pressed together as they apply plaster, as they pack a bowl, as they sketch pentagrams onto their arms, as they share sheet music.

I'll later hear from Liz that Nur left the hospital using a walker, and that a month later she checked back in again. She'll lose muscle and bone mass. Jessica will organize a fundraiser to help Nur's family cover her hospital expenses. Nur's organs will fail one at a time: liver, kidneys, heart. Jessica will enroll in the nursing program at Dalhousie. By then I'll have left teaching for good, without telling anyone the reason: I don't want this kind of responsibility. It feels like a job for somebody both more and less human than I am.

The plaster woman will hang in the school hallway for years.

Everything You Need to Know

DOES EVERY TEACHER BEGIN a new semester longing for the students from the semester before? In January, I meet my new Grade 10 English class. They look identical to last semester's students, gangly and implausibly young. In my head, a dimpled Matthew McConaughey from *Dazed and Confused* drawls his yucky line about high school girls: *I get older. They stay the same age.*

The class is almost entirely female, some in sweatpants, some in full faces of makeup, some in both. It seems unfathomable that I will ever learn all their names, even though I have done so for every class I've taught for more than seven years. That's maybe 1,400 names learned and mostly forgotten. With every year, the learning gets harder and the forgetting gets easier. The students are watching me intently. Because I don't know their names yet, they're like a single entity, a cluster of amoebas that were short on resources, so they blobbed together into one multinucleate organism. The organism doesn't speak. It just stares.

Is it something about the room? There's this radiator that makes a noise at unpredictable intervals. The first time, I tell them it reminds me of a ghost rattling its chains, and we all chuckle at its horror-movie quality, but after that we never chuckle again. We have forgotten how. I distribute scrap paper for them to jot down answers to icebreaker questions (*What's your favourite TV show? If you could be any fictional character, who would you be and why?*). The radiator howls over me as I'm instructing them to write down their pronouns, and for the rest of the semester I will worry about whether I'm misgendering them. When I tell a joke, a girl wearing purple-red lipstick smiles, but I sense a lurking snideness. Usually a classroom is a good place to tell a joke: the audience is captive, and the bar for humour is incredibly low.

The radiator moans to life again. Each time I must decide whether to compete with the sound or wait awkwardly for it to finish. I pose an open-ended question about what everyone is reading, and nobody responds, though they seem to be listening. I answer the question myself. The radiator drowns me out, knocking and clanging, so persistent in its interruptions that I'm concerned about how much I'm repeating myself. What if I don't get through the lesson plan? This does not turn out to be a problem, because the students don't participate. In five minutes, we zip through material that was meant to take up twenty.

During the stretch break, nobody stretches. Nobody speaks. They scroll hypnotically down their phone screens until I tell them the break is over. Perhaps they are googling tips on how to make friends. I itch to check my own phone but resist, because I want to create an environment conducive to learning. Besides, my only notifications are for Old Navy marketing emails. I flip through my notes, underlining randomly, trying to appear busy and purposeful. On the attendance sheet, I draw an amoeba in black pen. I add a speech bubble next to it but leave the bubble empty.

Then the students are back to staring at me, waiting. I

know what they're thinking: *Teach us something. Teach us something we don't already know.*

To be fair, it's only that one class. My other classes chatter away and ask lots of questions: "Miss, do we need to bring our textbooks with us?" "Miss, how many words does the timed essay have to be?" "Miss, can I leave early to catch my bus?" Teaching Grade 10 English, though, is like the grinding of a rusted machine.

When I get home, I light up a joint before I even take my jacket off. Then I sit on my bed, hunched like a goblin over my laptop, peering at seven browser tabs and listening to audio clips to learn the correct pronunciation of *Goethe* and *Beaux Arts*. I search for energetic ways to frame the material, and for tactics that will force the Grade 10s to participate. I review the course schedule with dread: How will we ever get through the debate assignment?

I try small groups: "Okay, all of you wearing hats, over in that corner. Anyone who has been to the COWS ice cream factory in P.E.I., you can take that spot by the window." They drag themselves to their respective corners as though they're walking through the shallow end of a swimming pool. I assign them roles—a trick I learned from Toastmasters: Facilitator, Spokesperson, Note Taker, Info Gatherer. Occasionally I see an animated face, but it quickly settles back into impassivity. And when I have each group's Spokesperson talk, their ideas are delivered in monotone, using the minimum number of words.

"Very succinct response," I say, wishing for somebody to say more, to tell a joke or an anecdote. To fill up the space.

The rest of my time is taken up with professional development seminars, faculty meetings, supervision of extracurricular activities. I squeeze in Toastmasters meetings when I can, but even those are meant to improve my teaching. When people ask about my hobbies—which is a question that should be retired after middle school—I have to invent them. Geocaching, I say, though I don't know what that is. Crocheting, I say, though I find crocheting more difficult than math.

Eventually, when I'm exhausted from teaching prep, I give up and pull out the pink-and-gold cookie tin that contains my weed. After smoking, I lie on my side under two comforters and the electric throw, too tired to even google anything.

And then time collapses, and it's morning again and on to the next class.

In early February, I'm reading aloud to the Grade 10 English class from George Orwell's "Shooting an Elephant." I didn't have time to review it thoroughly in advance, and as I read, I realize how often he uses the phrase *yellow faces* to refer to the Burmese. *Yellow faces . . . yellow faces.* I'm not even absorbing the words in between. What are the students thinking as I read this? I avoid eye contact with Vicky and Ivy, the only Asian students in the class. I consider pausing midway to give more context about the vocabulary used during that time period, but their silence pushes me to continue. I can't stop. Can I get away with this because I'm Indian? A student in another class corrected me when I referred to myself this way. We had gotten off-topic and I was recommending the dosa place in Scotia Square Mall. "Miss, *South Asian* is the accepted term," he said, as I eyed his red hair, his freckles.

That night, I light a joint and examine the map of the world on my living room wall. The map is a stylized watercolour, more decorative than informative. South Asia seems to include Pakistan, India, Bangladesh . . . Sri Lanka hasn't made it onto this map. I suppose what we refer to as Asia is actually

East Asia? Is Russia basically Northern Asia? Continents suddenly seem so arbitrary.

A memory arises of a student from another class, who approached me to ask why the syllabus wasn't more inclusive. "When I registered for your course," she said, "I saw your name and I thought . . ."

And then, I'm flashing back to my Grade 10s. Their soft-jawed faces, features doughy and unsolidified beneath their unending gaze. *Yellow faces.* I try to focus on concrete, present objects: the wood grain of my coffee table, a green mug listing names of cities—London, Paris, New York, Halifax—resting on a coaster made out of Scrabble tiles. But my thoughts are paperclips and Grade 10 English is a super-magnet; I think of the stupid things I said and the smarter things I didn't say. At least twice today I lost my train of thought mid-sentence. Anxiety is thick in my chest now as I replay myself saying, "Orwell attended Eton College—you know, the private school where people like Prince William and Prince . . ." but I couldn't remember the other one's name. It was right there, hiding somewhere in the folds of my brain. The only reason I'd brought this up was to relate the essay to something they might care about. "Prince . . ." I hoped for the bell to ring. In a more talkative class, a student would have supplied the answer, but in Grade 10 English everybody just stared at me, expressionless, waiting. Again, I said, "Prince . . ." and the pause just kept going. Even the radiator was quiet now. I thought the clock behind me must have stopped clicking forward and that the bell would never ring and that we would stay there and ossify, books forever open on Orwell's essay.

I'm a *bad teacher*. And not like in that movie *Bad Teacher*. I'm the kind of teacher who promises more diversity on the syllabus, and while it's true that I don't have total control over the curriculum, I fully intended to deliver—only to spend the winter break considering other career options, trying not to think about teaching.

Nothing helps. I sit down on the rug. My thoughts are fragments, loud and rattling around, reminding me of the haunted radiator. Everything takes me back to that classroom.

Since I don't have time for a real relationship, I'm casually seeing this guy, Travis, who also smokes too much weed. He has the worst taste in . . . everything. The movies he likes feature implausible car racing. The sneakers he wears are too big. His jeans are too long for a grown man and bunch below his knees. In 2006 he got a tattoo on his arm in Mandarin (he does not speak Mandarin). He only wants to eat McDonald's burgers (I order the apple pie). He does not like podcasts or newspapers ("None of them?" I inquired), and when I asked what he thought of *Train to Busan*, he said, "It was okay, but it's Korean, and their storytelling isn't as good as ours." Travis is an unemployed engineer who grumbles that there are no jobs out there for a white male. I'm not sure why he's dating me. I'm only dating him because he has an orange-and-white beard that feels sublime when he kisses my neck and that reminds me of a cat I once knew.

We're at his place one evening after I've finished supervising the school arts magazine's weekly meeting. The only furniture he owns is a black leather sofa in front of a giant TV on a stand piled with a dozen video-game controllers. He's packing his bong with the weed I brought, and I'm complaining about my job—about the quiet class, not about the arts magazine kids, who are a bunch of sweethearts who love Studio Ghibli and wear giant glasses that hide their gorgeous eyes.

"They just don't say anything. And they're all staring at me, but I have no idea what's going on in their heads. It's unnerving," I tell him, not because he is the best confidant, but because it is my only available conversation topic. "You know, I think this might be it. I might be done with teaching." Earlier, I googled *I quit teaching* and found 93,300,000 search results. "I thought I'd gotten better at public speaking after Toastmasters, but still . . ."

"But your job isn't *public speaking*, per se," he says.

"What do you mean?"

"Well, most teachers spend hardly any time actually teaching. It's just like worksheets and stuff most of the time."

"That's not true. And who do you think makes the worksheets? And grades them? It's a lot of work."

"But can't they basically not fire you? You'd have to, like, molest a student." He laughs. "I'm, like, so jealous of you sometimes."

He has said this before. He said it one day after I left work early to go to a dentist's appointment, and another time when he was assuming my parents were rich ("Aren't you an only child?"). And again when I mentioned that somebody had left donuts in the staff room. I searched our text conversations for the word *jealous* and found more than a dozen results.

"Plus, you get the summers off. You barely work at all," he says now. "Must be nice." He gurgles loudly on his bong. I imagine grabbing it from him and smashing him over the head with it, like in a cartoon.

He turns on his movie and reaches for me with his tattooed arm—they're not-quite-black now, the squarish letters of the language he doesn't speak—and pulls me onto his lap to face him. Then he presses his mouth and beard into my neck. He is frustratingly good at sex, sensitive to my reactions in a way that seems totally out of sync with the rest of his personality. He throws our clothes off in all directions and I anticipate feeling sheepish later when I have to search for them. We slip around on his leather couch, with the car crashes lighting up noisily behind me.

"You like that, don't you?" he says, pinching both of my nipples and watching me, smiling smugly the whole time, and I don't know which one of us is using the other.

I start a list of potential future jobs:
- Massage therapist—but I don't like touching people.
- Librarian—but how many jobs are there? Would I have to move to Truro?
- X-ray technician—but how much radiation are you exposed to?
- Vet technician—but could I put an animal to sleep? Is it more tolerable to teach a class or to watch an animal die?

When I try to give up weed, I become an insomniac. I lie awake in bed, occasionally turning. After a couple of hours, I sit up and watch the opening credits of *Dawson's Creek* on YouTube, where they have the original Paula Cole theme song. Played from low-quality speakers in my dark bedroom, its loveliness is astonishing. I let YouTube auto-play through clips of those late-nineties kids growing up by the water with their small dramas and too-big feelings and ordinary dreams, and I'm dropped right into the past, nostalgic for those years when life felt momentous and full of new, important lessons.

All that remains from my high school experience is the palpable feeling of disillusionment. Not that it matters: now, everything you need to know you can learn on the internet.

How to whistle. How to write a sonnet. How to calculate the invisible forces of temperature, wind resistance, gravity. How to roll a joint. How to teach a class.

By March my bed is a sprawl of dog-eared essays and unfolded laundry; highlighters and mechanical pencils that later stab me in my sleep. My dreams are as restless as kids without recess. I dream that I'm standing at the front of my class but the students are all facing in the other direction, and instead of English I'm teaching organic chemistry, and instead of my notes I'm holding a tray of cheddar and pineapple. I dream that I have class in fifteen minutes, but instead of my apartment I'm at Travis's place, and I keep slipping back down onto that black couch, and then I slide in between the cushions like my childhood hamster that my dad accidentally sat on, and I hear Travis's voice calling from a distance, "You like that, don't you." In another dream I'm on the way to my classroom, but instead of the high school hallways, I'm navigating a market somewhere in Asia. I smell sandalwood. An elephant is stamping its way towards me. There's a rifle in my hands.

It's mere weeks until the end of the semester, and in my quiet class, we're discussing a student's response to a travel essay. It's styled like a brochure, with uncredited photos from the internet. In one of the photos, a woman in a bathing suit lounges on a beach, the sun falling across her body in a wide stripe. It isn't clear where the beach is. Brazil, maybe? Spain? I have barely been anywhere.

The second response we review is written as one long, unbroken paragraph, with no apostrophes at all. In the span of five hundred words, the student has written the phrase *I thought to myself* seven times.

"Our thoughts are always to ourselves," I tell them.

Maybe I'm sleep-deprived, but nothing seems as it should. I have this headache that feels like I'm wearing a child's-size headband. The radiator is radiating. One student is eating a Subway sandwich, though it's morning, and can you even get a Subway sandwich in the morning? The classroom smells like bread and vinegar. The window faces the sun, which is beating down directly on my face, too hot and too bright, though it's barely even spring.

The third personal response is too personal. An essay with a brief mention of divorce has sparked a tangent about the student's own parents' divorce. She describes sitting on the staircase and listening to her parents fighting, which is a cliché of course, but is it a cliché if it happened to you? I'm wrestling with the decision of whether to say something empathetic or stay professional and address technical issues. Her response contains no analysis of the selected reading, nor does it use any quotes, both of which are required according to the assignment guidelines.

The girl's name is Emily. She sits with her arms folded, holding herself. Her eyes are two moons, gleaming with expectation. I don't know anything about her, or how she might react. I don't know anything about any of them. Will sympathy embarrass her, especially after hearing the impersonal tone of everyone else's responses? Or is that what she is looking for? What if she begins to cry? What if she runs out of the room?

There is nothing unusual about this moment. It's nothing I haven't faced before. But suddenly I'm sure that whatever I say will be the wrong thing. And will have consequences. "This must have been hard to write," I say finally. My words sound canned, and have a weariness I'm unable to hide, though I mean them sincerely. It must have been hard to write.

Out the window now, I see a pair of girls standing under a maple tree at the edge of school property. The girl with torn jeans and pale hair cropped close to her scalp removes a cigarette from between her lips and passes it to her friend. The other girl, unsmiling in plaid, takes a drag, then drops the cigarette and grinds it under the heel of her Converse shoe. They blow smoke in the same direction, facing the road. There's no one around to tell them to get to class.

"I'm leaving," I say. "I bought an open-ended ticket to . . . Sri Lanka." I don't know if they noticed my pause. I don't know why I said Sri Lanka. I was thinking, maybe, of the market in that dream I had. Of how the country was missing from my map of the world, and so visiting it would be like disappearing entirely. Sri Lanka feels so far away from here, I might as well have said Middle Earth.

My class is alert now, for the first time all period. "You're leaving . . . our school?" asks one student. "Like, permanently?" Is the tone hopeful? I don't believe I've heard her speak before.

"Why?" asks another student. She took Grade 9 English with me the previous year, but back then she was a participant, constantly leaning forward in her chair, her arm raised in response. This semester, she's been part of the silence.

"Why not?" I reply, but this sounds too flippant. You need a good reason to quit a job. "It's time for a change," I try again, quoting a song lyric from somewhere.

The students talk over one another, animated and brimming with questions, forgetting their shyness. The Subway sandwich remains half-eaten.

"Do you think you'll come back?"

"Are you staying till the end of the school year?"

"What will you do in Sri Lanka?"

I lie and tell them I chose that as my starting destination.

"Was the ticket super expensive?" asks the writer of the travel brochure. She's right to question this; an open-ended ticket would be a stupidly expensive choice.

"I got a flight deal," I say. Another lie. I should have said Beijing. Or Frankfurt.

"Are you going to stay in a hostel?"

"Have you ever stayed in a hostel before? They sound so awesome." Everyone nods, agreeing that hostels sound awesome.

"I wish I could go somewhere," says Emily, wistfully.

"I have a friend there I might be able to stay with," I lie. And in response to their questions, I construct another dozen lies. It's like writing fan fiction about my own life.

Even before the day ends, the news that I'm leaving has spread around the school. The principal sends me an email to explain the proper procedures for resigning, politely suggesting I finish out the year to avoid complications.

Later, I phone my parents, and my dad answers. "Oh, hi there, El Niño. Haven't talked to you in ages," he says. We spoke yesterday.

I confess to him quickly, like a telemarketer trying to get to the closing pitch before the listener hangs up. There's a pause. I wait for the anecdote from his childhood and the paraphrasing of Deepak Chopra. The TV plays in the background—I hear an announcer's voice and a dinging bell.

"You left this job without having another position?"

"Yeah." I wait for him to tell me to beg for my job back.

"I see," he says.

Then I hear my mom's voice over the sound of the

television and my dad's silence. "Is that Nina?" she calls out. "Hi Nina! Haven't talked to you in ages!"

When I tell Travis the story of my quitting, he slides his hands under my shirt and says, "That's fucking pathological."

I book a ticket to Sri Lanka, to turn a lie into the truth. This costs $1,900, more than I've ever spent on anything. I text Jules, who offers to loan me her guidebook. Then she phones me up and tells me anecdotes from her own solo trip to Asia. I add all of her recommendations to a spreadsheet.

After the term is over, on my last day of teaching, Emily comes by my classroom to say thank you and goodbye. She unshoulders her backpack, then rests it on one of the student desks and opens it. "I have something for you." She hands me the unwrapped gift: it's a stuffed toy human. His face is serene, eyes forgiving below his high forehead. He sports purple velour, a frilly white collar, and glossy black boots. For a second, I wonder if it's supposed to be Prince.

"It's Shakespeare!" she says.

"Whoa, this is amazing! Thank you so much!" I pick up Shakespeare and give him a weird hug. "I'll display him prominently in my next classroom." I don't know why I said that. I might never have another classroom.

After I leave the school, I don't want to go home yet, so I take a walk, Shakespeare peering out from my handbag like a fancy woman's dog. I end up on Gottingen Street and wander into this artists' co-op store that sells old records and Lolita dresses and monkeys' paws. School is out, I think numbly, as I thumb through dusty game cartridges until I find *Super Mario Bros. 3*. I've never not been in school. I went straight from being in school to teaching at one. I sit myself down on the store's caved-in velvet couch, where they have set up an original Nintendo. For a good two hours, until some teen boys kick me off the couch, I'm absorbed by watching the pixelated figures hop and die onscreen, in a landscape that never existed. My hands cling to the controller in that familiar pose, moving with muscle memory. Holding this controller keeps me tethered to something. The tinny, comforting music speeds and slows. Mario runs and leaps and flies past 2-D clouds, as though it's he, and not I, who knows where the Warp Whistles are hidden.

There *are* markets and elephants in Sri Lanka, though neither is quite as I had pictured. The market has piles of bitter melon that resemble sleeping lizards. Fish are splayed cleanly on blue tarps, thin men folded over them. A man holds up a fish as I pass. "Best price," he says, opening its mouth to show me its teeth, he and the fish smiling in unison.

The trains brim with people. I hesitantly approach strangers to ask for directions. My voice is too quiet. They gesture for me to speak up. I muster up my Toastmasters persona, conscious of my aloneness. Because I haven't yet purchased a SIM card, I have no phone or internet access. It's raining, and my umbrella is already broken, and it's hotter than it ever gets in Halifax, and the sun sets earlier than I expected.

Before the trip I researched all the wrong things, and my overpacked itinerary is impossible to complete. Perhaps Sri Lanka was too ambitious for a first solo trip. I visit an elephant orphanage with a few Americans who are staying in the same guest house, but the elephants are smaller than I imagined and walk slowly, as if they know there is nowhere to go.

With the Americans, I try white water rafting, but afterwards I'm so shaken I don't want to do anything else. I just want to return to my room and watch *Gilmore Girls*, but I feel guilty watching Netflix when I should be having life-changing experiences. Anyway, the slow Wi-Fi makes streaming impractical. The Americans leave, and I'm alone again, once again wishing for companions.

From Sri Lanka I fly to Nepal; from there to India. I eat dosas that lack the crispness of the ones from Scotia Square Mall. I send my mother a photo of them on WhatsApp. She messages back: *Are you applying for jobs?*

Eventually, I take a flight back to Halifax. I retrieve my weed from the freezer, thaw it, and roll a joint while the flower is still damp. I go to my wall map, thinking I'll label the cities I've travelled to, before remembering that Sri Lanka is missing. I place dot stickers across India and Nepal, and then Canada and the U.S. There's so much empty map space. I change my mind and remove the stickers, but they don't come off easily; my fingernail leaves scratch marks on places I've already started to forget.

I practise writing breakup texts to Travis. There's a formula I find on the internet:

> Hey [so-and-so], I really enjoyed [doing such-and-such activities], but I don't feel [such-and-such feelings]. Thanks for [whatever date items he may have paid for or recommendations he may have provided]. Good luck on your search!

> *Hey Travis, I really enjoyed eating McDonald's and fooling around on your couch, but I don't feel like we're*

in love. Thanks for recommending I not experience
Korean narratives. Good luck on your search!

In the end, I don't text Travis and he doesn't text me.

I run into the high school principal at Pete's Frootique, a city grocery that sells charming things you can't get at Superstore, like Montreal bagels and chocolate-covered potato chips. I end up at Pete's three or four days a week, a reward after my long city walks, though I can no longer afford to shop there. The principal is reading the back of a package of Cadbury jaffa cakes. There's a whole section for British snacks.

He sees me before I can pretend I didn't see him. "Nina, you're back from your trip!" He hastily re-shelves the jaffa cakes. "How was it?"

I say something about elephants. "How's your summer going? Have you had any time to relax?"

He vaguely references a trip to the cottage. We both know he will never relax. He's the kind of principal who spends the summer developing motivational seminars on introducing iPads to the classroom. It's possible he has a Pinterest board devoted to it. I realize now how much time his planning must take.

"I didn't have a chance to give you your teaching evaluations from the last semester," he says.

"Oh, that's okay . . ."

"Aren't you curious?" he asks, softly but frowning. "Anyway, I've left them in an envelope for you in the office. No pressure to pick them up." He tugs on the neck of his T-shirt and I'm startled by how old his skin looks, how exposed. "Nina . . . you were a good teacher." He coughs into the side of his fist, then tells me to enjoy the rest of the summer vacation—it must be automatic, since he knows I'm not coming back.

Of course, I pick up the evaluations immediately. The alternative is to leave an envelope full of anonymous critiques of me out there in the world. The hallways are busier than I expect, the building under loud construction, students loitering in tentative summer-school cliques.

At home, I prepare myself. I make a jug of iced tea with tea I picked up in Sri Lanka. I float a lemon slice in my glass. I use a straw, though I vowed to stop using straws to save the environment one straw at a time. I spread the evaluations out on my kitchen table, careful not to let condensation from the glass get on them. Some comments are written in all caps, as though shouting. Some are written in tight black script, others in round purple ballpoint letters. In a few cases, I recognize the handwriting.

Thank you so much for your kindness this year.

I may have been quiet, but I was listening.

She told us she divides her classes into 15-minute segments to keep us from getting bored. What a great idea!

Her passion comes through in every class she teaches.

Her jokes are hilarious.

She's so patient when explaining things.

I bring up facts I learned in her class in conversations all the time.

It's because of your class that I decided to become an English teacher.

She cares.

There are some classes where you spend the whole time laughing. Where you say something and somebody else responds and then somebody else, and nobody raises their hands and you just talk—as if you're having a brunch conversation with old friends, as though a waitress is coming around shortly to refill your mimosas. On the last day of those classes, students applaud and shake your hand on their way out. Or did I imagine this? Did this ever really happen? If it did, I know it wasn't me who made it happen. It's chemistry, the crackle of personalities in the room. It's luck, pure luck.

Once in a while, in those classes, I'd start talking and find myself more articulate than I ever was in real life. I would forget that there was anybody or anything outside that classroom at all. Here was a spider in my mouth spinning music, and here was the crescendo like a pouring of silk, the delirious feeling of epiphany.

Facsimile

I'M ORIGINALLY FROM HALIFAX, I type, and then delete. *Halifax born and raised*, I type, and then delete. *I used to be a high school teacher*, I type, and then delete.

It's 3:30 p.m. at Uncommon Grounds, my favourite coffee shop in Halifax because of how big the scones are. My laptop is open in front of me—a Dell Inspiron I just ordered on sale. With one hand I'm crumbling my cheddar-chive scone, while with the other I work on my dating profile. I wipe crumbs on a napkin before opening a photo in Photoshop. It's one of the few pictures I have of myself, because usually I'm the one holding the camera. In this photo, I'm standing on the Halifax Waterfront, smiling blandly. A tall ship casts a shadow over me, its spars decorated with festive, multicoloured pennant garlands. I search online for an image of a shark, extract it from its background, and paste it onto my photo. Then I clone-stamp and blur and filter until the shark looks like it's really there, eager-jawed in daylight, leaping over my head towards the ship. This will be my profile picture. My hopes are that it will make people laugh and that it will start conversations, so that I don't have to.

I get up, toss my napkin in the compost, put my empty plate in the bin for used dishes, and head to the washroom. When I return to my table, my laptop is gone.

As a Haligonian, I trust other Haligonians. Maybe not every Haligonian, but Haligonians as a group. Halifax is a city where everybody's on a first-name basis with Glen the busker, who plays the accordion from his electric wheelchair on a corner of Spring Garden Road. Where folks wave back at the Harbour Hopper, the amphibious tourist vehicle full of Americans on a cruise-ship excursion. Where a city bus driver strums a ukulele to entertain passengers at long red lights. Where Global News featured a story about masked men wandering the city performing random acts of kindness. I always thought Haligonians would watch my stuff when I went to the washroom.

There's a student sitting a few seats over. "Did you see somebody take my laptop off that table?" I ask him, pointing and trying to hold back panic.

He pulls out one earbud and says, "Wha?"

I repeat my question, but he shakes his head and claims he didn't see anything, then puts his earbud back in and is no help at all. I go back to the table and inspect it thoroughly, as though this will make the laptop rematerialize. Bizarre that my handbag is still there—did the thief just miss it, hanging off the back of the chair, beneath my sweater? Perhaps they assumed correctly from the quality of the bag itself that there was nothing in it worth taking. Perhaps they didn't have enough time.

I catch the bus to my parents' house, and it stops by a high school. A big group of students gets on. It's been a couple of months since I've been in such close proximity to so many teenagers. Everyone has a backpack on. Standing directly in front of my sideways-facing seat are two girls in high-cut soccer shorts that expose their splotchy thighs. To their left stand a boy and girl in mid-conversation. I can't see their faces and don't want to be caught turning to look, but the girl's backpack is in my periphery. It dangles a pair of anime charms—a squat pink bird with black pupils; a doll with an aggressive countenance and blue painted-on hair. I wonder at what age she will decide to retire these to the back of a desk drawer.

"So, what would you say are the flaws in my personality?" asks the girl.

"Flaws?" the boy repeats.

"Yeah, I want to know what you think."

"Well . . ." He thinks for a second. "You're not confident in yourself. And that makes you awkward around other people. It shows that you're not confident."

"Right, right, confident," she responds, her voice trailing off.

"Okay, so what about me? What's wrong with me?"

"Nothing," the girl says. "There's nothing wrong with your personality."

"You recently bought that computer, no?" my mom says when I tell her about the laptop, shortly after arriving at their house for dinner.

"Yeah," I admit. "I can't believe somebody just took it."

"But you'll need that though, no? To find a job?"

"And to watch Netflix," I joke.

She shakes her head.

We're in the kitchen, and she's unfolding a sari she ordered on eBay, draping its raw silk weight over her forearm. UPS delivered it with unexpected duty charges that were more than double what she already paid the seller, defeating the whole purpose of buying a sari on the internet.

My dad limps into the room, clutching the piriformis muscle that's been bothering him lately. "Oh ho ho! That must be Nina's wedding sari!"

"Ayyo, such a cheap sari? No way man," says my mom. "And you must be dreaming." She drops her chin and peers at me over her bifocals. "This one is never going to get married."

"Hey, don't say that. Knock on wood." My dad raps his knuckles on the kitchen table before giving my shoulder two squeezes. He sits in the dining chair across from me, grabs a handful of crispy chickpeas from a bowl on the table, and starts crunching. "How is the 'online' dating going? Do you have anyone on the line yet?" He mimes a laugh.

The reason I'm online dating is that I'm in my mid-thirties and have never been in a serious, long-term relationship. This is cause for concern, given that I have Indian parents, who exist to bear children who get married and bear children who get married and bear children, and so on until nuclear war renders us barren. "How can your dad be happy when his only daughter isn't settled?" my mother asks me, on a semi-weekly basis. Every once in a while, I get a call from an unknown number and it's an Indian man she has urged to phone me up.

"The dating would be going well, except that my laptop was stolen so I never finished my profile."

"What, really? Oh, gee whiz. Criminals lurking everywhere these days," says my dad.

"You know, your parents have a computer," my mom chimes in. "Parents are also very good at managing dating profiles."

"Very true," says my dad. "We are natural experts at such things."

"Ah, thanks but no thanks."

"Did you tell the police?" my dad asks.

"Police won't do anything," says my mom, refolding the sari and tucking it back into its brown paper. "Nirmala Aunty's bicycle was stolen and police were useless. Now she walks to the office."

"If you need, you can borrow one of our computers," says my dad. "We have too many of them."

After dinner, he brings me down to the basement where he keeps all his electronics. He has a joyous passion for owning devices but lacks an equal fervour for making them work. Also, he throws nothing away. If a computer contracts a virus, it's banished to the basement. Against an unfinished concrete wall, he has a row of off-brand Billy bookcases (he's boycotting IKEA because he disapproves of the store's labyrinthine layout). The shelves are a thicket of wires: unused USB cables wind around abandoned laptops. Chargers and adapters are jammed in among nearly every defunct generation of BlackBerry, a brand he continues to buy out of loyalty to Canadian enterprise. A VHS player reigns from the top shelf, next to a stack of 5¼-inch floppy disks. There's also a disassembled Christmas tree on the shelf for no good reason.

My dad digs until he finds a laptop. We spend another few minutes searching for a power cord to match. "Here, try if this works," he says, handing the cord to me. He hovers nearby while I plug it into the wall and sit cross-legged on the carpet, waiting for the laptop to boot up.

"So, how are things going otherwise?" he asks.

"Oh, you know, same old." I face the screen and type in the internet password.

"Finances and all are okay? Without the job?"

"You don't need to keep asking." I pause, attempting to flatten the ripple of irritation I'm feeling. "I'm looking for a job. I really am. It's just not that easy in Halifax."

"Test the sound. I think it has some problem," he says.

I open up YouTube and play the first video that comes up—a clip from *America's Got Talent*. A girl sings soundlessly onstage with such obvious sincerity it makes me cringe. My dad is right—the sound doesn't work, but the computer can access the internet, and that's all I really need.

"I know you are trying, Nina. Don't take it that way. I am only saying, if you need money, we can help you. If you are having difficulties paying rent, there is always a place for you back at home." His voice frays at the edges. "Why did I work so many years, if not to help my only daughter?"

I know I should be grateful and thank him for this generosity, but the idea of moving back home is like being pulled under a wave. It's wholly unbearable. On the laptop screen, the four judges sit waiting, each above a giant, slightly squashed letter *X* that will light up either in red or blinding white, depending on whether she wins their approval or not. I nod, and keep nodding for a while, until my dad wipes his eyes and goes back upstairs.

Though my profile consists only of a photo where I'm about to be eaten by a shark, when I check my inbox there are seven messages.

hey there beautiful
how's it going?
great smile, let's chat over a coffee . . .

Only one has commented on the shark: *Nice photoshop skills. :)*

I delete all the messages except the last. I scan the guy's details: he's 6'1", of mixed European descent, has a job (though he doesn't say what it is), and likes baseball, Indian food, and snorkelling. In one of his photos, he's standing on land while wearing a snorkel, which I'm hoping is code for having a sense of humour. The photo is captioned *I look below the surface.*

I respond: *Thanks! Have you seen anything interesting in Halifax waters?* My online messaging style is falsely jovial.

I exit his profile and check boxes to select my search filters: single, monogamous, looking for a relationship, employed, speaks English, age thirty to forty. That seems like the bare minimum. What comes up is a catalogue that's unsettlingly infinite—I click through pages of results with no indication of how many pages of results there are. You could scroll on forever. Results appear in a different order if you refresh the page. Do the results repeat? The site's unintuitive interface includes a section that works like Tinder—their biggest competitor—for those who'd rather just swipe through photos. I swipe left on three and then instantly regret it. Those people are gone. Released into cyberspace. Perhaps they no longer exist at all.

A week later, I'm back at Uncommon Grounds to meet the Snorkeller. I arrive early to avoid the awkward shuffle of bill-paying. Instead of my usual scone or coffee, I'm drinking a cup of genmaicha to seem like somebody cultured and hydrated with perpetually fresh breath. I had a job interview here a few weeks ago, and this feels like déjà vu—rehearsing questions and answers in my head, reminding myself to sit up straight, make eye contact, and to smile, but not too much. I choose my usual table far back, near the window, which was shattered and repaired so recently there's still a small pile of crushed glass swept into one corner.

I have a full view of the café so I'll be able to see when the guy enters. We've only exchanged a handful of messages, mostly about ideal snorkelling locations. This is a topic in

which I have neither knowledge nor interest. He suggested we
meet, and I said yes, because it seemed rude to say I'd prefer
to chat longer and about a greater variety of subjects first. I
watch the door. A man comes in and I look questioningly at
him and he returns the look, before turning to hold the door
open for his wife, who's pushing a stroller. A short while later,
another man enters, and I try to picture him in a snorkel
mask to figure out if it's the right guy, but then a group of
his friends waves him over. A third man enters. He checks
the right side of the café, where there are displays of fancy
chocolate bars, packaged rum cake, and sweatshirts screen-
printed with Halifax word collages. When he turns to his
left, he catches my eye and smiles. When I stand to greet him,
I realize that 6'1" is much taller than I thought, or maybe it
just seems that way because he's so skinny. I imagine him
crouching in a shallow bay, wearing a wetsuit and spitting
water. We're a complete physical mismatch—he's about half
as wide and twice as tall as me. The way he takes a quick
up-and-down glance and then retreats into blankness makes
me think he knows it, too. Unless I'm "mind misreading,"
a phenomenon my therapist told me about where you incorrectly assume people are judging you, when they're just
thinking about baseball stats or the rare variety of trout they
spotted yesterday.

"Hey!" I say.

"Hey." His eyes wander around as though I couldn't possibly be his date, and then he squints at my face like maybe
he expected a clearer complexion. "You got your own drink?"
he asks, pointing at my tea.

"I was just early, so . . ."

"I would've gotten your drink, but okay." He seems a bit
offended. "What's good here? You want anything else?"

"Oh no, I'm okay. The scones are massive. Also, the granola bars use marshmallows as the glue—you know, to bind the granola together?"

"That sounds fattening." He gestures towards the coffee counter. "I'm going to grab something."

"Oh, sure, go for it."

He returns with peppermint tea. "Those scones are far too large. Can you eat a whole one of those? I bet you can't, you're so tiny. Like a bird!" He reaches out and grasps my wrist between his thumb and index finger.

"Oh, no, I usually just eat three bites and save the rest of it," I lie. I'm not so much tiny as average-sized, but I can tell he likes the idea of a woman with bird bones, someone delicate enough to tuck into a napkin and pocket like leftover pastry. "I'm more of a tea drinker," I add. Eighty per cent of what I've said so far is a lie. How do I fall in love with somebody who prefers hot toothpaste water to marshmallows? Maybe he's a vegan. Maybe he's an empath who believes he can feel the pain of butchered animals. Maybe I will give up butter for him. "Are you a vegan?"

"No, I just don't eat garbage," he says, laughing. He removes the teabag so it doesn't over-steep and places the used bag on his napkin, where it leaks onto the table's dark wood grain.

"Have you been here before?" I ask.

"Yep." He sips his tea, either bored by my question, or lost in thoughts of baseball and trout.

"I come here a lot. I like to work here 'cause I just can't seem to get anything done at home . . . too many distractions . . . You know, like I'll just watch *The Bachelor* when I'm supposed to be working . . ." I'm saying nothing in a lot of words.

He sips his tea.

"Actually, this is crazy, but I was here like a week ago, and my laptop got stolen from this very same table."

"That sucks." There's a long pause. We both contemplate the walls as though they are of great interest. They're painted to resemble vintage signs, weathered text in once-bold colours. "Oh, so that shark photo."

"Yeah?"

"How long ago was that taken?"

"Um, like a month or two, I think?" I know exactly when it was. It was taken at the very end of June, two and a half months ago, on my last day of teaching. After I left the school, I'd gone for a long walk, meandering down the waterfront on my way to Gottingen Street, and on an impulse, I'd asked a stranger to take my photo. I liked the idea of an ordinary photo taken on a pivotal day. Only I would know the story behind it. The summer crowds hadn't yet formed, but I could smell fish and chips and fried dough. While the stranger toyed with the zoom, I had a momentary flash of sheer freedom, a realization that I could spend whole days on the waterfront if I wanted to, doing nothing at all. But there were teeth at the edges of that freedom. And by the time the stranger had finally taken the photo, the feeling, along with my smile, had faltered.

"It doesn't look like you."

I don't know what to say to this, because the photo does look like me, or at least, what I think I look like. But who knows how accurate that is?

"Also, why did you add a shark to the photo?"

Because it's hilarious, dumbass. "It's a metaphor," I say. "And shouldn't every photo have a shark in it?"

He sips his tea. "And the smile—it doesn't look natural."

"Wait, you mean the shark's smile?" I ask.

"No, yours. It's unnatural. You're just smiling for the camera."

"Isn't that what you're supposed to do?"

We talk briefly about snorkelling and Indian food. He explains that it's unlikely a shark would appear in the Halifax harbour. He tells me where to find the best Indian food in Halifax. In my head I recast this as an anecdote to work into a Toastmasters speech: *Fellow Toastmasters, raise your hands if you've ever tried online dating!* He finishes his tea. We don't hug or mention meeting again. Date over.

I buy a scone and pull out my borrowed laptop, grateful that my automatic backup saved all my documents to the cloud. I download what I need, but as I'm searching through the folders, I notice a file I don't recognize: *me.bmp*. Curious, I download that, too. It opens in Microsoft Paint and shows a photo of a girl around thirteen years old. She's dark-haired, brown-skinned, and fish-cheeked like a model, but from her eyes you can tell she's hamming it up for the camera. She's utterly confident, mid-strut in an orange-toned living room. Perhaps a friend the same age took the photo, in that limbo time between school and dinner. Around the image, she's used the paintbrush tool to draw sloppy stars in white and red.

Once I'm home, I change into sweatpants and the "Eat More Butter" T-shirt I got at Two If By Sea, a Dartmouth café where the croissants are the size of a healthy baby. I sit on my bed, smoking a bowl and watching an old episode of *The Bachelor* with no sound and eating discount birthday cake with my hands, wishing aliens would abduct me so I wouldn't have to worry about unromantic things like online dating.

As the Bachelor does damage control during a group date, one of the women frowns and then quickly smooths it into a close-mouthed smile, and I wonder what toxic thing he's just said to her. I open another window to browse through the dating website while reflecting on its competing interests: 1) to help people find partners on the site, gaining positive word-of-mouth and promotional Success Stories; and 2) to prolong the search and thereby keep collecting membership fees. I had opted for this website over the apps because the longer self-descriptions in each profile made the process seem less gamified, less like flipping through a deck of cards—each card showing a potential vision of the future.

But either way, we'll develop carpal tunnel and tennis elbow, clicking touchpad buttons or scrolling down phone screens for the perfect match. We'll corrode our organs with bottomless cups of coffee and pints of Rickard's Red on endless first and second dates. Online dating is an embarrassing punishment for a mediocre crime: not finding love in the pre-internet world.

The Bachelor cuts to commercial. The screen turns black, reflecting my face. I'm a contestant. I smile with the fakest smile I can muster. Blue frosting in my teeth.

My stolen laptop backs up twice a week, so I start checking the files on Mondays and Thursdays. On Monday, there's another photo—likely taken with the laptop, of the same girl but now with a shimmery face and eyelashes so long and so false they make the photo look 3-D. *Makeover!* is scrawled shakily across the photo with the Microsoft paintbrush. I want to teach her how to use Photoshop. I want to Photoshop a shark into the background with a speech bubble and send it to her. *Give me my laptop, or else.* The next week, there's a crudely assembled meme—a Shiba Inu with a knowing side eye. His doggy face has been cropped and pasted on to a loaf of bread, the photo topped with broken English phrases in Comic Sans: *wow. so hip. much happy.* That Thursday, there's a pair of tanned, thigh-gapped legs on a beach, though it might only be a pair of glistening hot dogs set next to each other to resemble legs. It's another meme—hot dog legs. The following Monday, there's Grumpy Cat, grumping about Mondays.

Is this girl, this lover of old memes, the laptop thief? Did she lurk behind the comfy chairs in Uncommon Grounds, waiting for a trusting dimwit to leave all her valuables behind when she went to use the washroom? Or did the girl merely buy the laptop from an amateur thief who didn't know how to reformat a computer?

There is no name on the photos, no identifying detail. But if I'm patient, I figure she'll eventually upload a homework assignment with a name on it, and then I'll call the police. Unless she's the type of student who always forgets to include her name.

On Date #2—set up not through the website but by my mother—I tell the guy I used to be a teacher. He says: "Teaching is a good job for a woman." And: "Just so we're clear, if this works out, you'll move to my house in Moncton and get a job within a practical driving distance."

When my mom calls to see how the date went, I tell her what the guy said, and she says, "Teaching *is* a good job for a woman." She reminds me that Moncton is a city with the highest tides in the world and the lowest housing prices in Canada, as well as dinner theatre and a tourist attraction where your car rolls uphill in an optical illusion. "Give him a chance. How can your dad be happy when his only daughter is unsettled?"

If this were a horror movie, every Monday and Thursday I'd check my online backup and find something more terrifying than before: An animated GIF of a screaming mouth. A suicide note with no signature. A JPEG of the inside of my apartment, with a shark pasted onto it.

Instead, today there's only a video of the same preteen girl in a pale yellow leotard and a grey hoodie, dancing with bare feet on shag carpet. I drag and drop a screenshot of her into Google Images, to do a reverse image search. I find only pictures of other girls in yellow leotards, who otherwise look nothing like her. I go back to the video. She's in a basement, I think, judging from the small window high up near the ceiling that leaks golden light into the otherwise dark room. She wheels her arms, touches her toes, eyes closed the whole time. The leotard creases at her flat waist. Once again, because of the laptop's missing sound card, I can't hear the music. Watching her stirs in me a bodily resonance, an unlikely mix of bliss and urgency. I imagine the soft tick of hi-hat. I feel the song's beat through each snap of movement, each flex of a limb.

Date #3 is with a doctor. We go for a glass of wine at Obladee, a local wine bar, since coffee dates might as well be job interviews—except if you get the job, you must marry the interviewer and have sex with him for the rest of your life. The doctor has red hair and sunburned arms. Shouldn't doctors know about sunscreen?

"Another glass?" he asks after I've savoured my Nova 7— tart, coral pink, and delicately sparkling. I sample it every week at the Seaport Market, pretending I've never had it before. I consider a second glass, but I haven't eaten, so I suggest a walk instead. He doesn't like this. "Or how about mini-golf?" he asks. His smile looks like he's pretending.

"I didn't know we had mini-golf in downtown Halifax," I say.

"Oh, it's just outside of town. I have my car, so we can drive there." He smiles again, exposing his pointy incisors, which seems like an obvious sign that I should not get into his car.

"Could we do that next time, maybe? I'd still be up for a walk, though. Like, just around the waterfront? We could get ice cream at COWS . . ."

He extends his arm smoothly across the table for the cheque, paying for both of us while I'm still reaching uncertainly for my wallet. We go for the shortest walk ever from Barrington Street to the waterfront, his legs long and moving fast, with me like a squirrel scrambling to keep up. Then he selects a bench under some trees, facing the water, and he sits very close to me, legs touching. He puts a broad hand on my knee, and my stomach cramps with repulsion. How to uninvite this uninvited hand? I shouldn't have let him get the cheque. An unleashed dog approaches—a black lab holding a stick between its teeth. With some relief, I see its friendly owner wave from way down the boardwalk. I scratch the dog's ears and his tail wags.

The dog points his nose at the doctor, and I wonder what it is he's sniffed out.

"Nice doggie," says the doctor. He doesn't touch the dog. "What do you want, doggie?" His voice is as flat as Saskatchewan.

Obviously, the dog wants somebody to throw the stick, so I throw the stick. The dog bounds away. I wish I was a flea buried in his fur, so I could run away, too.

"Well, how about I give you a ride home?" says the doctor.

"Oh, that's okay, I live really close." Not true.

"It's late, though. You'll be cold."

"No, no, I need the exercise. I have a sweater."

"My car is parked right over there." He points to an expensive black vehicle in an empty lot.

"I'm literally five minutes from here."

"All right then," he says, tersely.

We stand up. He holds his arms out for a hug, so we hug. He clutches my shoulders and his hands feel like talons. He kisses me on the mouth, off-centre, hard-lipped, unwelcome.

The next day I get a text. *I'm barbecuing, want to come over? I could come pick you up?*

I send him a simplified version of my polite breakup text formula: *Hey, it was really great chatting with you yesterday. I don't think we're quite a match, but I wish you luck on your search!*

No response. He didn't say what kind of doctor he was, and now I will never know. Pathologist? For weeks after, I search *The Coast* for news of murders.

I log into my dating profile one morning and my shark photo is gone. In its place is a photo of a young white woman straight out of an L.L. Bean catalogue, standing in a field and wearing a gingham shirt, her long chestnut hair falling in beachy waves. There are new likes, new messages—so many it's as if I've taken a deep sip of a strong drink. My dopamine surges. Hope.

But then I realize these likes and messages aren't for me. They're from older men in New Brunswick, rural Nova Scotia, P.E.I., even as far away as Maine. I open up the messages and see that someone has already responded to them. *Hi, I'm Carly . . .* say the responses. When I check the People You Like section, it shows that someone has logged into my profile, expanded the age range and distance radius in my search criteria to the maximum, then swiped right on dozens of these men.

Someone has hijacked my profile, but for what purpose? Catfishing? General meanness? I'm sure whoever did this isn't the girl who took my laptop. Because why would she care about any of this? It's the kind of prank that might be funny if it were brought up hypothetically in conversation. The kind of prank a boy might post as a brag on an internet forum: *I hacked into the dating profile of some lady in her thirties and matched her with a bunch of seventy-year-olds!* How hilarious.

The poor internet security on my dad's old laptop is likely to blame. I change my password, unlink my PayPal account, and message customer service. I feel stupid and vulnerable. I think about deleting the account, but without it, the days ahead are empty. So I spend hours installing antivirus software, setting up a password manager, restoring my profile. I spend hours more blocking dozens of men who remind me of someone else's grandfather, who have sent messages to the stock-photo woman, telling her how pretty she is.

On Date #4 I'm asked: "Why are you still single?" It's not the first time I've been asked this question. *How has nobody snatched you up?*

"I'm selective," I say.

There might be some truth to this. At university, I dumped a guy after two months because he wouldn't watch an Alfred Hitchcock movie—not because he was afraid, but because it was in black and white. "You'll regret this," he said. "I've dated girls way hotter than you."

Another guy had a running gag about building the perfect girlfriend. "If I could build the perfect girlfriend . . ." he'd say, and then list the qualities of mine he wanted to change—the length of my hair, the courses I'd signed up for, the amount of time I spent talking about baked goods.

Another, while walking me back to my dorm room late at night after a party, pointed at a bush and said, "That would be a good place to rape a girl."

Another I dumped because he always rubbed his thumb against his fingertips when talking about money, as though he couldn't contain the itch of wanting to have it. And later, when he shoved his fingers inside me, it seemed so greedy; I knew he would take whatever he could.

Four weeks after my laptop is stolen, the girl uploads a close-up selfie with a name signed at the bottom: *Teena*. I type the name into Twitter, Facebook, then Instagram, and I find her—Teena Mitchell, the only Teena in Halifax. She's posted the same selfie to her Instagram account, which also has a photo of her standing on the modest lawn out front of a row house, hand on a thrust-out hip.

I call the police on their non-emergency number. "I don't know where the house is exactly, but I know she's in the metro area, I have her name, and I have a photo of her," I say.

"Who is this, Nancy Drew?" asks the man on the phone. He laughs and laughs.

But a couple of days later I get a phone call from a police officer who says he's downstairs and has my laptop. I buzz him up. "Here it is!" He hands it to me. "Great detective work."

"How did you find the house?" I ask.

"Oh, we recognized it right away. It's part of an affordable housing project down on Gottingen. I went over there, and the kid just started crying, 'It wasn't me! I'm innocent!'" He says the last part in a high-pitched imitation of a child's voice, slapping his thigh.

In my hands, the laptop feels heavy and unfamiliar. I turn it around. There's a neon sticker over the Dell logo, that says *Just dance dance dance.*

||||||||||||

I meet Date #5 at Uncommon Grounds. It's safer here: It's walking distance from my apartment. There's no alcohol except in the rum cake. The only thieves are little girls.

He buys a bar of dark chocolate with bits of pistachio and dried apricot, and unwraps it delicately, like he's Charlie searching for a golden ticket. He places the chocolate on top of the wrapper, on the table between us, and motions for me to have some. "I like this place. Good food and sweatshirt options."

"It's a great place," I agree. "The scones are massive."

"Massive scones—amazing!"

We're quiet for a moment, and I feel a tenuous kind of peace. A square of chocolate melts against my palate, and I can see that he's mulling over what to say next.

"So, you said on your profile that you *used to* be a teacher. Can I ask why you don't teach anymore? If it's not too personal . . ."

"Oh no, that's okay. I guess I just wasn't prepared for . . . You have so much influence as a teacher. Over children's lives, I mean. And in the classroom, you have to be teaching, of course, and doing teacherly tasks like handing out photocopies and telling people to stop talking, but you also have to be constantly aware of how fragile your students are. Sometimes it's almost a high, and then other times it's like being an air traffic controller—just . . . too much." I've surprised myself by being honest. Usually if the topic comes up, I say the marking and lesson prep were cutting into my me-time.

I tell him about this activity the principal had us do at a faculty meeting once. It began with him briefly discussing the Hippocratic Oath. He handed out copies and had us underline parts that might relate to teaching.

"We didn't know what to do with the parts about fever charts and cancerous growths. But there was stuff in there that really resonated."

"First, do no harm," says Date #5.

At the meeting, we came up with our own list of promises, working initially in pairs and then calling them out for the principal to write in marker on sheets of chart paper. We rewrote it as an oath for teachers:

> I will remember that there is art to teaching, and that warmth, sympathy, and understanding may outweigh the teacher's pen or the school's report card.
> I will not be ashamed to say, "I know not."
> I will respect the privacy of my students, for their problems are not disclosed to me that the world may know.
> Most especially must I tread with care in matters of life and death. If it is given me to save a life, all thanks. But it may also be within my power to take a life; this awesome responsibility must be faced with great humbleness and awareness of my own frailty.

We left that last statement the way it was.

At the next faculty meeting, the principal brought a typed and printed copy. The tone in the room was oddly solemn, almost ceremonial, as we passed the document around, along with a ballpoint so everyone could add their signatures to it. I kept hearing the pen's wobbly click.

"I know this is really earnest and nerdy, but I saved the copy of the oath and taped it to the inside of my teacher's desk. Even when it was covered in paperclips, I could still see it there, underneath. Maybe after all that, quitting makes me sound like a coward."

"Not at all," he says. "I get that. No judgement, I spend most of my day hiding behind a screen."

"Speaking of screens, my laptop was stolen here just over a month ago."

"Oh shit, not your laptop! You must be a loyal customer, though, to keep coming here."

"I did manage to get the laptop back." I tell him what happened. I tell it like it's a funny story. "The police called me Nancy Drew."

"But wait, what happened to the girl?"

"I don't know," I say. I don't tell him that what will happen to her is what happens to every girl. That her experiences will empty her. That there's a point when a girl becomes a meme, a facsimile transmitted, a carbon copy folded and passed along. That she'll end up a weak and staticky version of the original. I don't tell him that I can't stop thinking about her, or that they never asked me about pressing charges—is that only an option you're given on TV? I don't know what the consequences were.

I tell him about the table we're sitting at—my usual table by the repaired window. I was here when the window broke. A deer came crashing through the glass, then thrashed around for five minutes, leaping onto tables, trying to get out. Customers held up chairs as shields, protecting themselves and one another. We huddled by the washroom hallway. We clutched each other for safety, exhaling a shared cloud of coffee breath. They found the deer later, confused and injured, with deep lacerations on its back and belly. In the CBC article about the incident, there was a quote from a witness: "I don't know how it didn't get its blood on us."

I go on four more dates with this guy. He's the kindest person I've ever met. He responds thoughtfully to all of my anecdotes.

He wants to lock it down. "We should go to the food truck festival," he says, even though the food truck festival is two months away, and we have committed nothing to each other. He holds my hand and tells me he wants me to meet his friends. He asks permission before he kisses me. He tells me he's deactivated his dating account. When I sign in, his photo has been replaced by a faint grey outline of a man. "I'm not interested in meeting anybody else," he says.

I deactivate my account, too. I picture marrying him under strands of twinkle lights and white mayflowers on the roof of the Seaport Market. I know my parents would like him. But I put off answering his latest message. It goes unanswered, and so does the next. I ghost him. I'm a ghost.

The next time I check, Teena's Instagram account is gone.

What I imagine is this: She's walking home from a summer job babysitting for a family in the South End. Headphones on, she's shimmying slightly as she walks, thinking about dancing, about the shape and positioning of her feet—heel, arch, toe. She wants to record herself, so she can play it back and perfect her movements, but she doesn't own a recording device. It's a long distance from here to Gottingen, so she stops at Uncommon Grounds for a $3 treat—hot chocolate, or a granola bar made with marshmallows. She sees an unguarded laptop on a table, slides her headphones down and glances around quickly, then slips it into her backpack and walks away without looking behind her. Her heart is beating fast. She'll never come to this café again. Ahead of her are the laptop's limitless possibilities—and the future, opening up like a mouth.

Broken Telephone

WHEN I TELL Jules about the blog I've started, she says I should have done this in 2004. "That was the heyday of blogging. Nobody has a blog anymore. Maybe you could try Twitter instead?"

But I'm not concise enough for Twitter.

If I had a time machine, I type into the blogger window, *I'd go back to a time when blogs were cool.* I click Publish.

Jules and I are at Uncommon Grounds, where we meet once a week to work on our respective projects—she's writing a Toastmasters speech, and I'm trying to figure out how to monetize my blog with ads. The name of my blog is "The Time Machine." I've customized a WordPress template and designed this whole H.G. Wells–inspired header with ink-drawn Morlocks. In each post I describe a hypothetical time-travel scenario. I keep it small-scale, so no preventing the Holocaust, no building a bombproof dome around Damascus, no restructuring the Catholic Church to keep a priest from ever touching a child.

Yesterday, I blogged about going back to the nineties to keep my mom from getting rid of our original Nintendo. She says she doesn't remember throwing it out, that she would never do such a thing. But if not, where is it? I've searched my parents' basement and garage; their walk-in closet that resembles an above-ground recreation of the Little Mermaid's underwater hoard. When I was ten, I had the arrows from the game controller imprinted into my left thumb. I still play *Mario Bros.* once every six months or so at the co-op store, though usually the space is occupied by others who, like me, are pulled there by nostalgia. Video games now are too complicated for me— even the Super Nintendo has fourteen controller buttons, requiring the dexterity of a bomb squad. I blog about the life of the missing NES, likely still intact and functional, waiting in a trash pile, never to biodegrade.

I'm taking a break to eat my marshmallow granola bar when I hear a notification ding. There's a comment on my blog—the first one ever. "Jules, did you comment on my blog?"

"Nope," she says, and goes back to chewing on her pen.

I click to open the comment. In italicized Garamond, the anonymous comment reads: *Blogs were never cool.*

The next day, I blog about going back in time to avert the moment when I froze onstage at a music school recital, only four out-of-tune notes into an oboe sonata, a moment immortalized through the lenses of a dozen video cameras. Up next was the three-year-old piano prodigy who further humiliated me with Rachmaninoff.

Another anonymous comment: *Who cares.*

Over the course of the week, I blog about going back in time to be nicer to my parents, to keep myself from quitting music lessons so that I'd now be an oboe virtuoso, to spend less money at Starbucks, and to erase the thousand sad hours I spent watching all twenty-three seasons of *The Bachelor.*

A blog of regrets, writes the anonymous commenter.

"Well, he's kind of right, isn't he?" says Jules. "You're writing about going back to fix things. Trivial things, but still."

"I guess I did just rewatch *Being Erica*."

I add the show—about a woman with a ho-hum life who travels to the past to prevent her mistakes—to the widget on my blog that lists links to TV shows involving time travel. It's funny that my two readers both think my blog is about regret. I have only one regret worth mentioning, and I wouldn't mention it on the internet for any stranger to see.

I decide to write a new post where I travel to the future. But what is there to do in the future except witness all the ways we've ruined the world? In my post, I go to the year 2200 and the Earth is an inhospitable stone, former cities drowned under swollen seas. Humans are potatoes, simmered to death inside their skins. The faces of people I used to know are fossils peering out from igneous rock, to be studied by alien scientists. I embed a video clip of the *Twilight Zone* episode where the Earth has been shaken out of its orbit and moves gradually closer to the sun. A woman sweats profusely in her New York City apartment, painting canvases filled with images of a burning skyline. "Paint something cold," her neighbour begs. A wall thermometer shows the temperature as it passes 110 degrees and keeps rising. The paintings begin to melt.

Climate change is a hoax, writes Anonymous. *And you've forgotten to mention the episode's twist ending. Also, you watch too much TV.*

"How do I respond to these?" I ask Jules. "Help me come up with something clever."

"Ignore him," she says. "Don't feed the trolls."

The real reason I started the blog is to produce some writing samples for my application to write TV show recaps for a website. The troll is correct: I do watch too much TV. Not long ago, Jules was showing me this photo of a cat wearing sunglasses, and I said he looked exactly like Caldicott C. Cat from *Puttnam's Prairie Emporium*. Jules replied, "I have no idea what you're talking about." So I told her *Puttnam's* was a children's show filmed in Saskatchewan in the late eighties. Set in a general store, it featured Caldicott the wisecracking puppet jazz cat who, despite a lack of opposable thumbs, was a phenomenal saxophone player. Mounted on the store wall was the head of a puppet beefalo who spoke in a "duh, who me?" voice. I always wondered if that beefalo could remember being hunted. Rounding out the show's ensemble cast were human actors playing a charming Canadian family. The store was magic. It literally sold happiness in a can. And in the store's closet was a time machine that was always on the fritz.

"Only you would watch this show," said Jules.

"Yeah, I know," I said. And I thought about how true this was, and how everything reminded me of something I'd seen on television. Perhaps that was a little bit sad. But it was also an opportunity.

While I've done some freelance writing recently, it involved condensing classic literature into as-brief-as-possible web summaries to save students from reading actual books. (James Joyce stories boiled down to bullet-point statements: *Man stands in doorway and has epiphany.*) My only other paid writing experience was crafting messages for ecards where you can paste a photo of your friend's head onto the animated body of a dancing frog. Neither was exactly representative of my voice. Side benefits to my blog are seeing how much I can make from Google Ads, and occupying a few hours of my vast unstructured time. There's so much of it—time— when you're a freelancer who's not great at self-motivation. My calendar is just rows upon rows of white squares. Looking at it gives me vertigo, as though I'm an astronaut untethered in blank, limitless space.

There's also this: right before I started the blog, I received a Facebook invitation to the memorial page for my best friend from high school. According to the page's About section, she died of a drug overdose, which seems like too much detail to include. *Celebrating Amy Cormier's Life*, it says in the default font, with a picture of Amy front and centre, as if this were any other Facebook event—a live music show, or a lecture on sustainability. What would Marshall McLuhan say? If Amy's name wasn't at the top of the page, I might not have recognized her. Eyes joyless and unfocused, deep lines down her cheeks. In the days since her death, friends have flooded the page with comments:

I can't believe it's true. Amy, I miss you so much . . .
I will always remember the beautiful times we had . . .
Words heartfelt and generic.

To be honest, I'm too far removed from Amy now to feel actual grief. This person who was once the most vivid part of my daily life is now just a social media afterthought. The punchline to a dark joke whose opening I can't recall.

When I pass by teenage girls at the Halifax Shopping Centre, they're so clearly of a different generation, if not a different species—they are more sophisticated, more knowing than we ever were. And yet I still feel like I could step into one of their bodies, like it could be me and Amy browsing through cheap earrings or eating endless packets of New York Fries as though we had nothing but time.

Amy's personal Facebook page hasn't been deleted. The two most recent posts of hers are a dog meme and a selfie where she must have been wrecked out of her mind. Why hasn't anybody taken these down? And what lasting words and images of mine would remain on the internet, if I were to die right this second? So I publish the blog and upload myself to the cloud—another kind of afterlife.

I blog about my daydreams of going back to witness history: to pinch a feather off the back of a dinosaur (*Not if he eats you first*, says the troll); to walk upright next to the first humanoid to do so (*I prefer a sexy simian slouch*, says the troll); to visit my ancestors in precolonial India (*Barbarians*, says the troll, *before the British beat you into shape and taught you how to play cricket*). I blog about walking down fresh roads before the automobile crushed its first human victim—Bridget Driscoll, U.K., 1896 (*See you in hell, Bridget!* says the troll). Before the ozone ever needed to repair itself. Before the first smokestacks blew plumes above our houses (*Let's see you manage without petroleum products*, says the troll).

I respond: *But oh, to breathe the air of a pre-industrialized world, before anybody ever coined the word "pollution."*

The troll copies and pastes from somewhere:

Pollution: mid-14c., "discharge of semen other than during sex," later, "desecration, defilement" (late 14c.), from Late Latin pollutionem (*nominative* pollutio) "defilement," noun of action from past participle stem of Latin polluere "to soil, defile, contaminate," from por- "before" + -luere "smear," from PIE root leu-"dirt; make dirty."

I blog about travelling a hundred years into the past to bring a stranger back with me to present day (blog post title: "Back to the Present"). The stranger marvels over my cellphone. "This is a telephone? Why, how incredible!" He's shocked when I press a button and the screen lights up, alarmed when I play a David Bowie video on YouTube, since, in his era, TVs haven't yet caught on. "What's 'Ground Control'?" he asks. I feel undeservedly proud, as though I invented this technology myself. When I play *Jurassic Park*, he screams and hides behind the sofa. "It's just CGI," I reassure him. I invite my new old-time friend to my parents' house, and my dad enthusiastically takes the guy into the backyard to show off the drone he got for his birthday. Next time, I'll blog about introducing mass-market paperbacks to somebody from the fifteenth century, when the printing press was a mere glint in Gutenberg's eye. Or about bringing a woman back with me and amazing her with equality.

Bring the woman to me, I'll amaze her, too, says the troll. I delete the comment.

I'll amaze her till her body doesn't work anymore, says the troll.

I delete this comment too, but not before I picture a woman folded into thirds, bones cracking.

Delete all you want, says the troll. *I'm still here.*

And another comment: *By the way, I know you. From a long time ago.*

When I was six, my family took a trip to Seattle and we saw the Fremont Troll. Three decades later I have a much greater appreciation for public art, but at the time I couldn't understand why people were crawling up on the troll's gargantuan claw to have their pictures taken. This wasn't what I had visualized when my teacher told us stories about trolls, who spoke in riddles and pocketed coins, elbows popped jauntily outwards. In the photo of me, I stare up terrified at this hulking monster two hundred times my size, a car crushed in his fist, his stone-sculpted head holding up the Fremont Bridge like

it's made of Styrofoam. He lurks in the debris and sludge.
Mortar crumbles around him. His beard drips into his chest,
and his body is the colour of mud. His single chrome eye has
a cataract-like abrasion; it appears to see nothing at all.

"Do you think he actually knows you?" asks Jules. "He's a
troll, after all. You can't exactly take him at his word."

"But why would he say that otherwise? Plus, he's a Halifax
troll. That's like, troll-lite. Until those last couple of comments, he just seemed kind of playful."

"Wait, you don't have your real name on this thing, do you?"

"Umm."

"Nina! Don't respond to him," says Jules. "And get some
other people to comment, so the troll gets diluted."

But how can I not respond? I check Google Analytics and
narrow down his location to either Halifax or Zimbabwe. I
read articles with titles like "Trolls Are Winning the Internet,
Technologists Say," "How Brands Stay Classy in an Age of
Internet Trolls," and "Are Online Comment Trolls Actually
'Psychopathic Sadists'?"

I start a new post and write: *If I had a time machine, I'd
go back in time and make it so the troll who comments on this
blog was never born.* I hit Publish.

What's this? says the troll, minutes later. *Am I the troll?
Who's trolling who now?*

Yup, that's you. You're the troll, I type in the comments
box. *Do you really know me? Where do you know me from? How
do I know you're not lying?*

*How do you know what I know? How do I know you don't
know what you say you don't know?*

I think you're lying, I type. *You're just some guy who stumbled across my blog.*

His reply contains a link. I hesitate for a second, wondering if it will lead to tedious spyware, but of course I click on it anyway. It's an image file: an old photo of my high school class. Students clumped together wearing cargo pants and really big shirts, and the teachers smiling at the back. I'd forgotten this photo was ever taken. In it, I'm circled in digital red pen.

I imagine the troll at his computer, sitting in an unlit basement, a black silhouette like an anonymous documentary subject. In my mind, the silhouette takes on a particular shape. There are only so many people this could be. What the hell, I figure. *In that case*, I type, *I'd like to interview you for my blog.* I need to know who this is. I expect him to decline, but I guess his ego wins out.

Fame! he replies. . . . *Fortune?*

I mean, it's not like I'm going to pay you. When are you free to meet?

Meet? Ha. Ha. Ha. Just post the questions here.

Nope, I respond.

A minute passes, then ten. I wander away from the computer, assuming he won't respond. When I return with a cup of coffee, he's written a new comment: *Obladee. 8pm tomorrow.*

Because I've been on dates at Obladee, I keep trying to shake the uncomfortable sense that I'm here for a date now. The place is lit with hanging amber bulbs. There's a wall of white scalloped tile, and dark wooden shelves holding a collection of wine bottles; a chalkboard with a handwritten list of cheeses. I arrive early and secure a two-person table near the washroom so we don't have to sit at the communal table with all the young professionals.

The man who walks in the wood-and-glass door is

hunched over, angular and underfed, and has an outsized beard; he looks like Kafka, but with the facial hair of Dostoevsky. Does this make him Kafkaesque? He stands out in his T-shirt, too casual for the location. When he makes eye contact and heads towards me, I suppress an overwhelming urge to tell him, "No, just go away." But I also feel relief, even as my body sags with a strange disappointment. He isn't who I both hoped and worried he might be.

As the man sits down in front of me, the interaction seems pointless, the moment deflated.

"You're buying, correct?" he asks, in a voice low and crackling. It's impossible to tell how old he is.

"One drink." I'm here now, so I might as well talk to him.

He glances up and to the side, at the chalkboard on the wall, combing his beard with his fingers. "And a cheese plate."

"All right." I half laugh in disbelief. "And a cheese plate."

The waiter comes by and is excessively friendly. I try to match his friendliness as I order two glasses of Sauvignon Blanc and some cheese for the troll, who watches me with his lips pressed together smugly. "Scratch that, make mine a flight of wine." He waits to see if I'll challenge him, then selects a flight off the menu. I shrug.

After the waiter leaves, the troll leans back in his chair, crosses his arms and his grasshopper legs. "Eager to please, eh?"

I ignore him and reach into my bag for my phone. "Can I get a photo of you?"

"Absolutely not." He blocks his face with his hands as though I'm a paparazzo.

"How about an artistically fuzzy image with, say, only your hands in focus?"

"Okay, but no face. No identifying features."

I take a photo of his hands, one laid over the other. I keep wanting to laugh at how seriously he's taking himself. The

photo looks like a free stock image, except that he has the
slouch of a ten-year-old boy. I'm pretending to know what
I'm doing, but I've never interviewed anybody before. Out
on the table comes my notepad of questions, just as the waiter
sets our wine in front of us. Suddenly this all seems very funny.

"So, when did you start trolling?"

"That's your opening question? Why does that matter?
Sooo fascinating. Here, take this Pulitzer." He makes as if to
hand me a glass of wine, then downs it. I assume this is meant
as a power move.

Next, the waiter brings three different cheeses arranged
artfully on a slate board, with slices of baguette, seed crackers,
and olives. "Enjoy!" says the waiter.

"Thank you," says the troll, politely.

Don't laugh, I tell myself. If I laugh, he will certainly
leave. Or spend more of my money on wine. I muster up my
teacher persona. "Okay. Let's get to a tougher question, then:
Why do you do it? What do you get out of posting annoying
comments on people's websites?"

He wrings his hands in a mock plea. "Why do you do it?!"

I ask a few more questions. He gives circular non-answers,
piling crumbly chèvre onto hunks of baguette and taking
moist, audible bites, as though he has just discovered cheese
for the first time and finds it scrumptious. I think about
plucking a bit of Avonlea Clothbound Cheddar off his plate,
just to see how he would react.

"To be honest," I tell him, "I only started thinking of you
as a troll because that's what my friend called you after she saw
your comments. You seem more like a leprechaun than a troll."

He pauses with a wine glass in one hand and a spreading
knife in the other. "You don't know what you're talking
about." There are crumbs on his thin lips as he clenches his
jaw under his raggedy beard.

"At worst a goblin," I add, smiling at him, and setting down my notepad and pen to sip my own wine.

He leans forward, his face illuminated by the tea light flickering in a glass between us. "You don't know about goblins, do you? They live on human teeth."

The waiter interrupts. "How are we doing here?"

"Everything is delicious," the troll tells him. When the waiter leaves, he turns back to me. "Gobble, gobble. Isn't that what goblins say?"

"I'm pretty sure that's what turkeys say." I laugh, finally. I can't help it.

He narrows his eyes, then deliberately swipes his hand sideways, catlike, knocking his empty glass over the edge of the table. Without thinking, I reach out and catch it before it hits the ground. I feel like I've just caught a pop fly. "Whoa," I say, as he blinks. "No need to break the stemware." I place the glass carefully back on the table. "You're trying really hard to be interesting, aren't you? What's your name, anyway?" I ask, but he shakes his head and doesn't answer.

I check my list of questions. Jules and I had brainstormed them together, and then I arranged them into an order of increasing intensity. There's one near the bottom of the list that draws my attention: *Is there anything you regret posting?* I don't ask this question. I know he'll just say no. The last question on the list is *What's the worst thing you've ever said or done?* It's juicy. It's the question you ask at a slumber party to show how edgy you are. But I hold off and decide I've been over-directing. I'm going to treat him the way I would a classroom full of lively students and just let the conversation flow in its own direction. "Why don't you just tell me about some of the ways you've trolled people? Your proudest moments."

It seems to work. He's thoughtful for a second, still

drinking and munching but alert now, with the luminous eyes of a real fairy-tale monster. "Well, let's see, I've hacked into the odd dating profile, changed a woman's search settings, that sort of thing," he says, smirking. His pupils don't quite line up. I check behind me to see what he might be looking at, but there's nothing there. "I like to be creative, but sometimes I just call everybody a cunt. Oh, one time I wrote a lot of dead baby jokes in the comments section of an article about a mother convicted of drowning her own baby. Any time someone commented, I'd post a new joke as a reply. By the way, how do you make a dead baby float?" he asks.

"I don't need to hear the punchline," I say.

"Take your foot off its head. Ha! Hmm, but let me think . . . Oh, you'll appreciate this one: I posted on a city planning forum that Halifax should have two sidewalks, one for whites and one for everyone else."

"Are you actually a racist, or do you just say that stuff to get a rise out of people?" It strikes me that I'm indifferent to hearing his answer.

"Does it matter? I trolled a rape victim once."

"I'd rather not hear about that."

"This girl from my university who everybody knew—"

"I told you I don't want to hear about it."

"You asked, though. Didn't you?"

What am I doing here? I'm quite literally feeding the troll. I'd been anticipating wit, but he's just a gross man with off-putting manners who harasses people. And whatever the worst thing he's said or done is, I don't want to know. Why would any reasonable person want to know the answer to these questions? "Okay, this isn't really working," I say, pushing back my chair and trying to catch the waiter's eye. "Thanks for your time, but I see now an interview with you wouldn't fit in with what my blog's about anyway."

"You want to know how I know you?" He pulls out his phone. Swipes and presses the cracked screen. When he glances back up at me there's a peculiar look on his face—the uncanny knowledge of somebody who has been to the future and back. There's something familiar about him now, but I still can't place him. He holds the phone up close to my face, but the screen is too bright in the dim bar. As I pull my head back and my eyes adjust, I recognize Amy's Facebook memorial page. The main photo has been changed. It's the same class photo he posted on my blog, but I'm uncircled. Instead, there's Amy in the front row, sitting cross-legged in the grass, wearing a grey sweatshirt with *Sir William Alexander High School* written in forest green. She's smiling, the Amy I used to know. Each of her eyes is crossed out with a crimson *X*. At the bottom of the photo, someone has added text in the same dark red shade: *Drugged-up sluts deserve to die.*

The troll sits back, watching for my reaction. When I say nothing, he says, "You knew Amy. Cormier. She was a real bitch in high school."

"Her family probably saw that," I tell him quietly, though I know he doesn't care.

"Maybe." He shrugs. "Who do you think made the page, though?" He swipes and presses the screen again and shows it to me. Points at the name of one of the page administrators. "That's this guy." He aims the thumb of his free hand at himself. "Funny, how people send private messages to the dead. Do you plan to monitor your Facebook messages when you're a corpse?"

I taste tannins and acid. The back of my throat goes dry, and I can't get any words out.

Around us there are regular people having regular con- versations. At a nearby table, the waiter chuckles and says, "You didn't enjoy that at all, did you?" as he takes away an empty plate. Out the window the evening has turned indigo. A woman walks by, pulling her collar up against the fall air.

"I sent that message to her private page," I tell the troll.

"And how hard do you think that was to hack into? Just look up *how to hack into a Facebook account*. A zillion nosy parents have travelled that road before me."

The waiter approaches, and says, "And are you folks still doing okay over here?" I ask him to please leave us alone. The troll finishes another glass of wine.

"How did you get that photo?" I ask, trying to change the subject.

"Are you kidding me?" he asks, eyes full of scorn. He points to a kid in the back row, skinny and wearing an ecstatic grin. *Sam.* My memory of him is a blip. A tiny crease in the timeline: A boy who talked to himself. A boy onstage at an assembly, karate-chopping the air. Amy's fluke of a boyfriend for what, a few months? And then we never spoke of him again.

After I first saw Amy's memorial page, fluorescent white and Facebook blue, with bland comments written all over it—now I wonder if they were even written by real people—I sent her a private message, the most honest thing I've ever written. I was in my childhood bedroom, at my parents' house, where I'm staying temporarily to save money until work picks up. It's the same old room. Nobody has gotten around to repainting it, so the walls are still a startling black. In the moment, time felt fluid, changing shape to fit the container. The world had rushed forward, but I was still here. In my message, I told her everything I couldn't tell her when we were kids.

My biggest regret is a thing I push way down and don't let myself remember. And yet details surface in my thoughts at unexpected times, like Ogopogo stretching his neck up from Okanagan Lake before sinking back, a blurred shape in the water. When I was fourteen, I had sex with a grown man. Or rather, he had sex with me. It happened only once, and I can't even picture what he looks like anymore, though I can still feel his face, rough and urgent under my hands.

Mr. Mackenzie. My Grade 9 English teacher, who stands at the back of that high school class photo in a blue button-down, sleeves rolled to his elbows, projecting such ease.

I've searched for him over the years—in the phone book, on Netscape, eventually on Google. After he left my high school, he taught in Dartmouth for a while, but then he disappeared. Where has he been since then? I wonder if he's done internet searches for me, if he's read my blog or found me on Facebook, if he's examined my photo to see how much I've changed.

I'd half thought the troll might be him. Though why would he be commenting so glibly and obscenely on my blog? I had brushed this question aside. It wasn't like I'd expected an apology, or even that I wanted to confront him. I had just wanted to know if he was still in this world somewhere or if he had walked off its edge; if he was still married, if he was still a teacher, if he'd aged; if he'd become a grizzled, twisted old troll. If he had taken on his true form. But most likely he is the same as he was, only older, living mundanely, reading a book in a cozy living room chair, somewhere not too far from here.

On my laptop I've bookmarked an interview with Samantha Geimer, the woman Roman Polanski raped when she was thirteen. *Thirteen.* When I was thirteen, I still had my collection of Polly Pockets displayed on a shelf in my bedroom. In the same interview, Geimer quotes her mother as saying, "You were never the same person after that."

The only person I ever told about Mr. Mackenzie was a therapist I saw in my late twenties, who said, "But it was consensual, right?" He recommended mindfulness exercises and said I should try to live in the present.

I remember leaving the therapist's office and wandering around Halifax, tweeting photos and tagging them with #100HappyThings. It was trending at the time. I posted photos of COWS ice cream in a waffle cone, a cornflower blue house at the west end of Quinpool Road, the large bum of a Newfie dog lumbering down the waterfront. Recently I saw a popular Twitter thread where people posted photos of themselves from the worst times in their lives. In the photos, they're grinning at sporting events, beaming on beaches. The captions say things like *This was right before I tried to commit suicide.*

The troll drinks his wine and eats his cheese. Behind him, the young professionals in pressed black clothing clink their glasses to celebrate an ordinary day. The troll taps on my notepad with one finger. He is saying something, but I can't quite put together what.

I should storm out of the bar, assert myself. *Storm* is the kind of word I used to love examining with my students. It can be a noun or a verb. You can see a storm or be a storm or be caught in one or carry one inside you like an extra lung. I don't storm out, because I have to get the check. This reasoning will seem silly later, but right now it is an anchor. If I don't pay, the troll probably won't either, and the busy, affable waiter will have served us for nothing.

"Blog . . . interview . . . Hey, are you listening to me?" says the troll. He snaps his fingers in front of my face, and it's as though I can watch the sound of the snap glide away, past the clinking glasses, and out the door to where the evening has grown fully dark. I haven't brought a warm-enough jacket. The troll finishes eating and drinking, shoves back his chair, and leaves.

I wonder if he got what he came for.

When the waiter brings the cheque and finds just me, his face is gently surprised and sympathetic. He hands me the machine and I tap my card.

"Cheer up! Plenty of fish out there," he says, with a wink.

I'm back in my old room and I can hear my parents downstairs, eating a late dinner. Sitting on my bed, under the light of a single lamp, I search the internet for that *Twilight Zone* episode, "The Midnight Sun." The episode opens: Outside a woman's window, the sun is a white diamond. A close-up shot of the woman's face, a sheen of sweat across her troubled forehead. A thermometer where the mercury can't go any higher.

How accurate is my memory of high school? Here is the gritty floor under one palm as I sit in the hallway alcove during lunch. The hallways narrowing at one end like a bottleneck, pushing everyone uncomfortably close. The almond scent of Amy's hair—or did it smell like chemicals? The brassy, triumphant sound of the school band, exquisite and enveloping, not a single note or person out of place. The high school as alive and complicated as a world. If I travelled back to those years, how familiar would they look? I read once that memories are altered through remembering. Every memory you have is only a memory of the last time you remembered it. Our pasts are just broken telephone messages we transmit to ourselves. Could I spot the differences between a drawing of the actual past and the past that's been mutating in my memory for all this time? On which side of the building had our mothers dropped us off? Did the school assemblies really have that level of fanfare? For how many weeks had we worn those goth clothes? How would Amy have described that place, or me, or our friendship, or any of it, if I had asked?

Tomorrow, I will delete the blog and it will exist only as an internet ghost that drifts through servers somewhere. Even so, in my head I compose a new blog entry about travelling back to when I was fourteen and living my whole life over, knowing what I know now, curating my life to resemble most Facebook timelines: a gallery of only good things. Or maybe I'll bring a past version of myself to the present—to the future, even—and show her how everything turns out. A crazy thing happens to you when you're fourteen, I'll tell her, but you live a normal life. It's just something that happened a long time ago, though it's there permanently in your brain chemistry— a wrinkle in grey matter, a flaw in a synapse. It's almost as if it happened to someone else.

Sam was right about that *Twilight Zone* episode. I had forgotten the ending. Rod Serling's matter-of-fact narration: "All of man's little devices to stir up the air are now no longer luxuries. They happen to be pitiful and panicky keys to survival." The twist is a classic. It was all a dream. The Earth isn't headed towards the sun but away from it. The final scene, in grainy black and white: a woman wakes up shivering, in a world that is impossibly cold.

Acknowledgements

Thank you to my editor, Anita Chong, for her care with every sentence, and for always knowing what questions to ask. To everyone at McClelland & Stewart, for the hard work and magic of turning a Word document into a book. To my agent, Stephanie Sinclair, for opening the doors, and for believing in this story when it was only a draft. To the editors at *The Dalhousie Review*, *The Fiddlehead*, *The Malahat Review*, *The New Quarterly*, PRISM *international*, *The Puritan*, *Best Canadian Stories*, and *The Journey Prize Stories* for publishing new, unproven writing. To the Writers' Trust of Canada, for their generous support. To the Banff Centre for Arts and Creativity, for time and space.

To my friends, especially Jacqui Simmons, the only person who reads all of my stories. And to the friends who sat and wrote with me in busy cafés and empty classrooms, with our Pomodoro timer running.

To Halifax, for its utter charm, and for forgiving my inaccuracies.

To Mom and Dad and Jay, for their big hearts and open minds.

Thank you to the exceptional teachers I've had, especially Professor Lydia Fakundiny, who taught me to read aloud, and who told me that writing wouldn't be a pipe dream.

||||||||||||

I have taken some creative liberties in adjusting timelines and real-world details to fit the story. These include descriptions of locations, high school grade levels and curricula, and dates related to book publication, TV broadcasts, exhibitions, and other events.

||||||||||||

The epigraph by Sophocles appears in *The Oxford Dictionary of Proverbs* (fifth edition), edited by John Simpson and Jennifer Speake (Oxford University Press, 2008).

The epigraph by Jim Henson appears in *It's Not Easy Being Green: And Other Things to Consider* by Jim Henson, the Muppets, and friends, edited by Cheryl Henson (Hyperion Books, 2005).

p.6: The episode of *Dateline* described is from season 13, episode 3, Bethpage, Long Island. Aired November 11, 2004.

pp.58–60 and 72: The quotations from *The Edge of Evil*, including from Geraldo Rivera's foreword, appear in *The Edge of Evil: The Rise of Satanism in North America* by Jerry Johnston (Word Publishing, 1989).

pp.96–97: The Nabokov story described and quoted is "A Bad Day," from *The Stories of Vladimir Nabokov* by Vladimir Nabokov (Alfred A. Knopf, 1995).

p.96: The episode of *Fraggle Rock* quoted is episode 104, "You Can't Do That Without a Hat." Aired January 31, 1983.

p.105: The episode of *The Wire* quoted is from season 1, episode 12, "Cleaning Up." Aired September 1, 2002.

pp.141–142: The list of proactive measures for teachers being bullied is paraphrased from the Study.com article "What You Can Do as a Teacher Who Is Bullied by Your Students" by Michele Vrouvas, posted December 2019, https://study.com /blog/what-you-can-do-as-a-teacher-who-is-bullied-by-your -students.html.

pp.153–172: The Toastmasters' roles, Table Topics, speech stages and objectives, and the "Four Ps" are taken from www.toast masters.org as well as various Toastmasters newsletters.

p.172: The quotation from Aristotle is from *Physics*, translated by W. D. Ross, in *The Complete Works of Aristotle*, edited by J. Barnes. (Princeton University Press, 1984).

pp.186–187: The episode of *Full House* described is from season 4, episode 8, "Shape Up." Aired November 9, 1990.

p.231: The CBC article about the deer incident at Uncommon Grounds is "Deer smashes through Halifax café," CBC.ca, June 20, 2011.

pp.235 and 251: *The Twilight Zone* episode described and quoted is from season 3, episode 10, "The Midnight Sun." Aired November 17, 1961.

p.238: The definition of *pollution* is taken from the *Online Etymology Dictionary*, https://www.etymonline.com/word /pollution.

p.248: The interview with Samantha Geimer quoted is "Samantha Geimer on Roman Polanski," by Emma Brockes, *The Guardian*, September 18, 2013.